Praise for Brenda Novak

"Novak perfectly captures the feel of small-town life,
and her powerful story of two lonely, fragile people who
find another chance at love is a sweetly satisfying and richly
rewarding romance."
—*Booklist* on *Stranger in Town*

"This story should appeal to readers who
like their romances with a sophisticated touch."
—*Library Journal* on *Snow Baby*

"A one-sitting read! Kudos to Brenda Novak
for an insightful and emotional story
that tore at my heartstrings."
—*The Best Reviews* on *A Baby of Her Own*

"Once again, Brenda Novak delivers
a stunningly magical performance."
—*Wordweaving* on *A Family of Her Own*

"Novak's story is richly dramatic,
with a stark setting that distinguishes it nicely
from the lusher world of other romances."
—*Publishers Weekly* on *Taking the Heat*

"Readers will be quickly drawn in
to this well-written, multi-faceted story that is an engrossing,
compelling read."
—*Library Journal* on *Taking the Heat*

"*Cold Feet* left me breathless. Any book by
Brenda Novak is a must-buy for me."
—*Read.......... .....Reviews*

"Bren........ ....gling story with imagery
............eathless."
.... Christine Feehan
............QN Books)

Dear Reader,

Little did I know when I set out to write this story that I was
plunging myself into such a complex situation. But then,
I must like getting in over my head. Those of you who've
read my other stories can probably attest to the fact that
they occasionally stretch the boundaries of series romance.
Anyway, poor Reenie has her hands full in this book—but
don't worry, I manage to make it up to her in the end. Not
everyone deserves a guy like Isaac.

Of all the books I've written, I have to admit that I'm
probably most curious about reader response to this one.
I wonder what people will think of Keith—crucify him or
forgive him? And Elizabeth—does she deserve her own
happily ever after? Then there's the old conflict between
Gabe and the half sister he never knew....

I always enjoy returning to Dundee. I hope this has become
a comfortable place for you, too...a bit like returning home.

If you have access to a computer, don't forget to visit my
Web site at www.brendanovak.com and enter my Contest
Bonanza, where you can win one of several fabulous prizes,
including autographed books, See's Candies, Waldenbooks
gift certificates, dinners at Chili's Bar & Grill—and a $500
shopping spree at the store of winner's choice! Also, I love to
hear from readers, so feel free to e-mail me from my Web site
or write to me at P.O. Box 3781, Citrus Heights,
CA 95611.

Until next time,

Brenda Novak

BIG GIRLS DON'T CRY
Brenda Novak

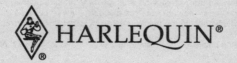

TORONTO • NEW YORK • LONDON
AMSTERDAM • PARIS • SYDNEY • HAMBURG
STOCKHOLM • ATHENS • TOKYO • MILAN • MADRID
PRAGUE • WARSAW • BUDAPEST • AUCKLAND

ISBN 0-373-71296-0

BIG GIRLS DON'T CRY

Books by Brenda Novak

HARLEQUIN SUPERROMANCE

HARLEQUIN SINGLE TITLE

HQN BOOKS

To my editor, Paula Eykelhof, who has been instrumental in making the Harlequin Superromance line what it is today. I'm sure I speak for all the authors you've worked with over the years when I thank you for your willingness to take a few calculated risks, for your commitment to good quality writing and meaningful stories, and for being such a pleasure to know. On a more personal note, I can't tell you how much I appreciate the confidence you've had in me and the support you've given me. We've already done nineteen books together, but I'm looking forward to at least twenty more!

CHAPTER ONE

Los Angeles, California

KEITH O'CONNELL WAS LYING. Isaac Russell could tell.

Surprised, he slowly lowered his fork while studying his brother-in-law's face. Keith wouldn't meet Isaac's eyes. He wouldn't look at Elizabeth, either. And there were other signs. The way he hunched his shoulders and kept fidgeting with his hands, constantly moving through the stack of mail near the telephone as if he hadn't gone through it twice already. The slowness of his responses. Even the irritation in Keith's bearing bothered Isaac, because it indicated that he didn't like being questioned.

And yet the subject was so innocuous....

"From the sound of it, the accident was horrendous." Elizabeth seemed oblivious to her husband's discomfort as she added another pancake to Isaac's plate. "I was surprised that you didn't mention it."

Isaac was too full to eat any more, but he said nothing. He waited for Keith's answer, hoping that he was somehow misinterpreting his brother-in-law's body language.

"What?" Keith finally glanced up as though he'd lost track of the conversation in his preoccupation with the mail. But it was obvious—at least to Isaac—that every word had registered.

"That forty-five-car pileup in Sacramento," Elizabeth responded. "You never said a word about it."

"Oh...well, they had it mostly cleared away by the time I came through," he said, his voice low and noncommittal.

Isaac saw the confusion in Elizabeth's hazel eyes. Carrying her own plate to the table, she scowled at her husband. "But the paper said it took the better part of a day before they could open the freeway. How did you get through? Traffic was stopped for miles. I saw a picture."

Another strained silence, then he muttered, "It must've happened before I got there, honey."

Isaac was tempted to look away to avoid what he was seeing. If his sister was having problems in her marriage, he didn't want to know. He wanted to continue to believe she'd met the man of her dreams and would live happily ever after.

But he couldn't ignore the warning signs. Elizabeth was his only sibling. He'd taken care of her through the dark years after their mother had died, when he was fourteen and she was eleven. They'd gone to live with their father and Luanna, the woman he'd married, and Luanna's son, Marty, who was younger and far more spoiled than they'd been. Isaac was the one who'd hurt for Elizabeth when the other girls made fun of her long, spindly legs and uncoordinated movements. He was the one who'd bought her tampons when she started her period and tried to explain how to use them. He was the one who'd gotten her a date for her sophomore homecoming dance. The following year, once she turned sixteen and lost that coltish look, he didn't have to worry about twisting anyone's arm to generate male interest. The boys were standing in line by then. But that only meant he'd had to watch out for her in a whole new way.

He'd always tried to protect her because of the fragility engendered by their childhood.

"According to the article I read, it happened just before your plane landed," Elizabeth said. "You must've driven right into it. It's a miracle *you* weren't hurt."

Keith dropped the letters he'd been holding, but he kept his eyes averted while he pulled on his overcoat and closed his briefcase. "I guess I was too preoccupied to pay any attention," he told her. "You know how much stress I've been under."

Keith's response made Isaac even more uneasy. He liked his brother-in-law, who was a hardworking, sincere, honest guy. So what was going on with Keith today?

"The fog was so thick no one could see a thing, Keith," Elizabeth said. "*Eighteen people died.* How is it that you—"

"I'm telling you it was the stress," he interrupted. "And speaking of stress, I've got to go or I'll miss my plane."

He came forward to kiss her temple. She hesitated as though she was going to stand up and give him a proper send-off, but he didn't allow her the chance. He was working his way around the table, saying goodbye to the children.

"Do you really have to leave so soon?" eight-year-old Mica asked.

"Every two weeks, babe. You know that."

The misery that entered her brown eyes seemed magnified by her glasses. "But the spelling bee is next Wednesday. I wanted you to come watch."

Finally showing a response that felt authentic to Isaac, Keith mussed her hair, which was the same dark blond as his own. "I saw you beat your whole class, didn't I?"

"It's not over yet. Now I'm going up against the rest of the school."

"I'm proud of you, honey. But you know how demanding my job is."

"I hate your job," she grumbled.

"Daddy's job is what puts food on this table, young lady," Elizabeth said. Obviously, she was trying to teach Mica to give her father the proper respect—but Liz didn't look any happier about Keith's leaving than the children did. Isaac knew her husband's long absences were hard on her.

"Mom will tape your spelling bee for me," Keith told his daughter. "We'll watch it together when I get back."

Mica frowned over what was left of her breakfast and didn't answer. But she allowed him to give her a quick squeeze. Then he moved on to his five-year-old son, who had golden hair and wide hazel eyes like his mother.

"What about my soccer game?" Christopher asked.

"I'll catch the next one, buddy," Keith said. "And then we'll go get ice cream again, okay?"

Chris brightened considerably. "Okay!"

"You took him out for ice cream?" Mica gasped. "What about me?"

"You were at your friend's house."

"You could've brought me a cone."

He winked at her. "You can come with us next time."

The natural affection between Keith and his children made Isaac wonder if he'd jumped to the wrong conclusion a few minutes earlier. Keith wasn't the type to do anything that would hurt his family. So what would he have to lie about?

By the time his brother-in-law came around to shake his hand, Isaac had convinced himself he'd been imagining things. This was the man he'd been so happy to see his sister marry—as opposed to, say, Matt Dugan, the guy she *used* to date.

"I guess you'll be gone when I get back, huh?" Keith said.

Isaac nodded. "I've been here a week already. I need to get home and organize my notes."

"On the forest elephants?"

"Exactly."

Keith grinned and shook his head. "I don't know how you Tarzan types do it, man. I'd go nuts camping out in the jungle for so long."

"You wouldn't if you loved it as much as I do."

"Maybe not. You certainly make it look easy."

"I'm single. I have only myself to worry about." Isaac liked it that way. After taking care of Liz for so long, he enjoyed having the chance to focus solely on his work.

"Well, come and see us again before you head back to Africa, okay?"

"I'll try. A lot depends on whether or not I get the grant money."

"It'll come through eventually. It always does."

Isaac had been lucky so far. "We'll see."

Scooping his keys off the counter, Keith headed to the living room. The front door banged shut. Then silence fell over the table—except for the sudden chime of the clock.

"I hate it when he has to go," Mica complained.

"Me, too," Christopher said.

Isaac checked Liz's reaction and found her staring into her coffee cup.

"What's up?" he asked.

Her sudden smile appeared forced. "Nothing. Why?"

"Are you still thinking about that accident in Sacramento?"

"Not really."

"Where's Keith off to this time?"

"Phoenix. He goes there a lot. He's training personnel on how to use the new software he's developed."

"He must like what he does."

She sighed. "So much he won't put in for a change."

"Is everything—" because Mica was watching, Isaac purposefully veered toward the generic, using only his tone to convey that he meant something deeper "—okay, Elizabeth?"

His sister's delicately arched eyebrows lifted. "Between me and Keith?" she asked in a low voice. "Of course."

"You're sure?"

"Positive." She waved a hand in a dismissive gesture. "The constant traveling gets to me occasionally, that's all. It's hard to maintain a normal family life when he's away half the time."

"Would you like me to stay here with the kids this week so you can fly to Phoenix and be alone with your husband?" Isaac was really anxious to get back to the university. Classes would be starting soon. He had to get his syllabus prepared for microbiology, which he'd be teaching in the spring semester, if the grant money didn't come through before then.

But this was Elizabeth. He and his sister had grown up with the understanding that no matter what the world threw at them, they'd always have each other.

He thought she might need him now.

She tucked her long blond hair behind her ears, then took a sip of coffee. "No," she said, her cup clinking against the saucer. "That's sweet but, to be honest, I don't think he'd want me there. He doesn't like me to bother him while he's working. We rarely hear from him when he's out of town." She rubbed her temples as if battling a headache. "His company demands so much from him. But he enjoys his work, so…what can I do?"

Isaac rubbed his knuckles against his jaw. "Are you sure he wouldn't like you to join him? He's been traveling for years. All that work has got to get old after a while."

"Like your trips to the Congo get old for you?" she teased, her perfect teeth glinting at him as she smiled.

Isaac returned her smile, then sobered and reached out to touch her arm. "Liz?"

She took another sip of coffee before answering. "Hmm?"

"How do you think he missed that big accident in Sacramento?"

Her forehead wrinkled as she considered the question. "I don't know." Although her plate was still nearly full, she pushed it away. "It's possible I have the dates mixed up. He comes and goes so often."

Despite her attempt to sound casual, her response didn't ring any truer than Keith's answers had earlier.

"Do you really think so?" Isaac asked, afraid he was missing something important.

Another flicker of a smile—and an almost imperceptible glance at the children. "I do."

Dundee, Idaho

IT WAS STILL AWKWARD. Even after nearly two years.

Taking advantage of a moment when Lucky Hill was studying the menu, Reenie O'Connell made a face at her brother to let him know she expected a more valiant effort from him. Then she curved her lips into a bright smile as the half sister they hadn't known about—until their father spilled the secret after Lucky had returned to town as a grown woman of twenty-four—looked up.

Unfortunately, admonishing Gabe did little good. He was too stubborn. His granitelike expression didn't soften, and Reenie could tell he was making Lucky uncomfortable. Every few seconds, her eyes darted his way as if she was looking for some small sign of acceptance.

"So…should we rent something in Boise?" Reenie asked, trying to keep Lucky distracted by pressing forward with plans for their father's sixtieth birthday party.

"I don't think so," she replied. "Boise's over an hour away and too impersonal."

"But Dad's been in the state senate for…what? Twenty years? He's got a lot of acquaintances and professional associates. We need someplace big."

Lucky tossed her curly, strawberry-blond hair over her shoulder. "Who says we have to invite all his professional associates? I vote we include only those people who are closest to him. Then we could have the party right here in Dundee."

When there was still no response from Gabe, Reenie jumped in. "You have a point," she mused. "We don't want to turn this into another tedious political engagement. Lord knows Dad's suffered through enough of those."

"Exactly," Lucky said, and her gray-blue eyes darted Gabe's way once again.

Reenie added another spoonful of sugar to her coffee, even though it was already too sweet. She needed something to do with her hands. "In that case, I guess our best option would be to have it at the Running Y Resort."

Lucky's reaction held a little *too* much enthusiasm. "That's perfect. Don't you think, Gabe?"

"Fine by me," he muttered, but it was hardly the warm endorsement Reenie knew Lucky had been hoping for. Their half sister seemed to crave Gabe's approval. She asked about him all the time. Whether or not things were going well for him and Hannah, his new wife. Whether or not he'd be at the family dinner on Sunday. (If Lucky was planning to attend, the answer was always no.) Whether or not he might come to dinner at her place if she were to invite him....

The smell of coffee filled the air as the waitress stopped by with a steaming pot. Lucky leaned back to allow her to reach across the table. Then, when the waitress walked away, she asked Gabe if he'd like more cream.

When he barely answered, Reenie wanted to kick him under the table. She would have, except she knew it wouldn't achieve anything. He wouldn't feel it. The car accident that had ended his professional football career almost four years ago had left him paralyzed from the waist down. He'd been in a wheelchair ever since.

Nothing to do but plunge ahead. She'd hoped planning Garth's birthday would draw them together. Lucky had even left Sabrina, her one-year-old daughter, with her in-laws this morning so the three of them could meet without any added distractions. But considering Gabe's smoldering resentment, Reenie's expectations were falling fast. At this point, she only hoped they could survive this little get-together without Lucky heading home in tears.

"So how many should we invite?" Reenie asked.

"Gabe?" Lucky asked, immediately deferring to him.

He shrugged. "I don't know. A hundred?"

Lucky cleared her throat. "A hundred is still quite a lot," she said, obviously trying hard to be tactful. "What about thirty or forty? We want it to be comfortable, not too crowded. I think it'll be more meaningful to Dad that way."

Reenie knew Lucky had been so focused on trying to state her preferences politely, she probably hadn't even noticed a muscle flexing in Gabe's cheek when she referred to Garth as Dad.

God, this was miserable. Reenie understood that Gabe was trying, or he wouldn't have come today. She also understood that he was still struggling with the changes that had been forced on him in recent years. But what had happened between their father and the most notorious prostitute in town wasn't Lucky's fault. "I think thirty or forty is the way to go," she said.

This time Lucky ignored her. "Gabe?"

Reenie watched her brother's deep blue eyes, eyes that were almost a mirror image of her own, meet and clash with Lucky's. She curled her fingernails into her palms. "Never mind my…er…*our* surly brother," she said quickly. Gabe's eyebrows shot up at the "brother" part, but Reenie continued anyway. "It's already two out of three, right?" She plastered another smile on her face.

"I'd like him to have some input," Lucky said, her voice steady. Instead of glancing away, like before, she glared at him.

Gabe clenched his jaw again, and the gap in the conversation stretched, filled only with the sound of clattering dishes coming from the kitchen and the murmur of voices around them. Reenie would have piped up with something, but she knew it was unlikely either of her companions would respond. They were in their own little world now. Lucky's demeanor indicated she'd finally given up trying to change Gabe's attitude.

"What is it you want from me?" Gabe asked at last.

"I'd like to know what you hold against me," Lucky said. "What I've done to make you dislike me so much."

Reenie swallowed hard, expecting the situation to blow up in her face, and was surprised when Gabe backed off.

He jiggled the ice in his water glass. "Do whatever you want," he said gruffly. "As far as I'm concerned, the two of you can plan the whole thing. I—"

"Forget the party," Lucky interrupted, holding her chin at a challenging angle. "Just answer my question."

His scowl darkened. "I don't want to talk about this."

He started to wheel himself away, but Lucky stood and intercepted him, boldly placing a hand on his well-muscled arm. "No, I'll leave. You stay and keep on pouting about the fact that your father slept with my mother twenty-six years ago, since you can't seem to get over it," she said. "But I want you to know I've finally realized something." She grabbed her purse before turning her attention to him once again. "I was a fool for wanting you to like me. I was a fool for trying as hard as I have to convince you I might make a good friend." She gave him a bitter smile. "Go to hell, Gabe. I don't care if my husband loves you like a brother, if the father I've grown to respect worships the ground beneath your feet, if Reenie insists that you aren't the ogre you seem to be. The moment I come into the picture, you're not the man everyone thinks you are, and I don't want to be part of your life anymore," she said. Then, head held high, she strode proudly to the exit.

Reenie heard the bell jingle over the door as Lucky left, but it was several seconds before she could let go of her breath. "Happy now?" she muttered.

Gabe was still staring after their half sister, looking stunned. Finally he blinked and focused on Reenie. "I didn't do anything to her. I've never done anything to her."

"That's not true, Gabe. All she wants is your acceptance. But you've turned your back on every overture she's made." Reenie slid around the vinyl seat. "As far as I'm concerned, you got what you deserve."

"Where are you going?" he asked, obviously surprised that she'd desert him, too.

"Keith will be home today," she said. "The girls and I have things to do."

CHAPTER TWO

Los Angeles, California

ISAAC COULDN'T HELP puzzling over Keith's behavior. He vacillated between believing he must have misconstrued the situation, and wondering what his brother-in-law was hiding. A forty-five-car pileup was no small thing. A traveler would definitely notice something like that. And Isaac didn't believe for a moment that Elizabeth had mixed up the dates. She wouldn't have pressed her husband as hard as she had if there was any possibility of that.

Maybe Keith had spotted the congested traffic and exited the freeway before realizing the extent of what had happened. And maybe, somehow, he had missed all the news reports of the accident the rest of the day.

Isaac didn't know a whole lot about Sacramento, but he'd been there once, years ago, to meet up with an old girlfriend who'd long since passed out of his life. If he remembered right, the airport was pretty far out of town, connected to the city by only one street, a major freeway. But that could've changed....

Hoping that he'd arrived at a logical explanation, Isaac stared at a map of Sacramento on the computer in Keith's home office. It looked as if there were a few exits off Interstate 5 that Keith could've taken. But the airport still sat amid large tracts of farmland. Would someone not very familiar with the area, someone sitting in fog thick enough to cause that big a pileup, know how to get around a traffic jam when there were so few options available?

It didn't seem entirely plausible, but there was always the possibility that Keith knew Sacramento better than Isaac thought. He certainly traveled enough.

"Isaac?" Elizabeth called from the kitchen.

"What?" he replied, still studying the map.

"Telephone."

Isaac blinked in surprise. He'd been so absorbed in what he was doing he hadn't even heard the phone ring.

Leaning to the right of the computer, he breathed in the scent of furniture polish as he reached for the handset.

"Hello?"

"Isaac?"

A strong British accent immediately identified the caller as Reginald Woolston, Isaac's Department Head at Chicago University. "What's up, Reggie?"

"Good news. I just received a call from the Research Grants Program of the Center for Tropical Forest Science."

Isaac sat taller. "And?"

"They're forwarding your application to the interview committee. They'd like to meet you."

With Reginald's help, Isaac had submitted his application months ago, before he'd left the Congo. It was about time CTFS finally reached the interview process. "When?"

"That's the bad news. Your appointment is scheduled for tomorrow. Can you make it?"

Isaac scowled at the iridescent glow of the computer monitor. "I'm in California!"

"I'm well aware of that."

"Can't we schedule an appointment for next week so I can have a chance to get home?"

"I'm afraid not," his boss replied. "The committee meets only once a month. If you miss tomorrow's meeting, it will push your application back thirty days."

Isaac didn't want to delay his chances. Not when he was so

eager to return to his research. "No, I'll…" The black line that was Interstate 5 was all that stood out on the Sacramento map as he leaned back. "I'll catch a flight out right away."

"Good for you. I was hoping you'd say that."

Isaac could hear Elizabeth telling Christopher to get his backpack. She worked from nine until three each day managing a large dental office, but she'd taken the week off to spend with him and had kept Christopher out of day care, too. Now she was getting ready to drive him to his kindergarten class, which started at noon. "Did they sound interested?" he asked Reggie.

"You know the committee type. They rarely give anything away. 'We've had numerous applications,' and all that rot."

Isaac chuckled at Reginald's British colloquialism. When he talked to Reg, he nearly found himself saying, "I say, old man," or "jolly good, then."

"You've made the first cut, as we expected," Reg continued. "But I've heard Harold Munoz is also applying, and he's done some great work in the past. The competition will be fierce, so let's make the most of the opportunity, shall we?"

Harold Munoz was more interested in making a name for himself than he was in saving Africa's population of forest elephants. Isaac didn't like him. But, with any luck, Isaac would be the one going back to the place that had captured his imagination like no other. "If I get the grant, how long will it be before the money comes through? Did they give you any indication?"

"Judging from experience, it could be three months, or it could be two years, right? You've been through this before."

He had been through the process, but Isaac wished Reg would show some excitement. After all, Reginald shared Isaac's passion for Africa and all the animals to be studied there. He used to lead teams to the Republic of the Congo himself, before he accepted the corner office at the university and officially hung up his "field" clothes for a monotonous series of tweed jackets. "Just making conversation," Isaac said.

"I see. Well, it's too early to tell."

And, as usual, Reg was too conservative to speculate. "Right. I'll see you later, then."

"Do you need a ride home from the airport?" his boss asked before Isaac could hang up.

Isaac considered his options. He'd returned from the Republic of the Congo almost a month ago, but as soon as he'd settled into his small condo and caught up on what he'd missed at the university, he'd come to California to see his sister, niece and nephew. He didn't really want to contact some friend or other he hadn't spoken to in over a year and suddenly ask a favor, which meant he'd have to take a cab. He figured he might as well spend the time talking to Reg, rather than ride alone. "Sure, if you don't mind."

"I don't mind. Leave a message on my voice mail with your time of arrival. I'm heading into a faculty meeting right now."

Isaac agreed and disconnected, then retrieved the phone book so he could arrange his flight. Fifteen minutes later, he was eager to pack so he wouldn't miss his plane.

Quickly collecting his day planner, he stood and started out of the room. But then his eye caught the computer screen once again.

Keith must have taken the exit called Power Line Road and avoided the whole pileup, he decided. Elizabeth admitted that when he was out of town she rarely heard from him. He was probably as absorbed by his work as Isaac was and had forgotten about the detour in Sacramento by the time he returned home.

In any case, what Isaac had sensed in his brother-in-law this morning wasn't anything to worry about. Elizabeth was going to be fine.

With a click of the mouse, he closed the map.

Dundee, Idaho

REENIE SLOWED as she passed the small farm for sale a few miles from her home.

"Mommy, why are you stopping?" six-year-old Isabella demanded from the back seat of the old minivan.

Reenie had just picked up her three daughters from school. It was raining and had been for most of the afternoon. She could smell the crushed autumn leaves on her children's boots, the cool wet of the outdoors on their raincoats and umbrellas, the musty scent of their damp hair. "So I can dream," she said.

Angela, older than Isabella by two years, was sitting in the back, too. "Mom loves that farm, silly," she said. "Since it went up for sale, she stops here almost every time we pass by."

Reenie smiled at Angela's don't-you-know-anything attitude and pulled onto the shoulder so she wouldn't cause an accident.

"Are you sure Daddy won't move here?" Jennifer asked. The oldest at ten, she always tried to claim the passenger seat. But for safety's sake, Reenie made her ride in back with her sister.

The wipers continued to beat across the windshield. "I'm sure," Reenie said, watching as great gusts of wind turned the rusty weather vane on the old barn.

"Can't you talk him into it?" The snaps of Jennifer's raincoat made a popping noise as she removed it.

"No." Suppressing a sigh, Reenie turned down the heater. She'd tried to convince Keith that the Higley farm would be a wonderful place to raise their girls. She'd spoken to him about it again and again, but he wanted no part of such a big project. He wasn't the type to remodel or farm, he told her. He traveled too much.

But she'd thought the farm might eventually provide a way for him to settle down and stay in one place. They could raise and sell a certain breed of dog or horse or pig. They could stable horses or plant crops or lease out the extra land. Reenie knew how to ride. She could even give lessons to the kids in town who rarely had the chance to sit in a saddle. Maybe she and Keith wouldn't make a mint with their little farm, but he wasn't earning all that much right now. The company he worked for made plenty of grandiose promises for later, but "later" never came. At least with the farm they'd be together. If finances became a problem, she could always go back to teaching. The life she had now was nice, comfortable. She took care of her girls, helped her mother with various charities and volunteered at the elementary school. But it wasn't enough. What she really wanted was a good challenge. And for Keith to stay in Dundee.

"He won't move here *ever?*" Jennifer pressed.

"Maybe in a few years." All his traveling had to be taxing, but Keith never complained. He loved his job, and she loved him. It was that simple. She'd known there wasn't anyone else for her the day they'd first met. He'd walked into the Homecoming Dance, the new kid everyone had been talking about, and Reenie's heart had dropped to her knees. She couldn't remember ever having that kind of reaction to another man. It wasn't because Keith was so handsome, although his rugged, angular face, dark blond hair and brown eyes certainly appealed to her. His confidence was what drew her, his strength. He was one of the few boys she couldn't intimidate with the force of her own personality.

"What time's Daddy coming home?" Angela asked.

Reminded of Keith's call, which she'd received at her mother's house earlier, Reenie frowned and put the transmission into Drive. "Not for a while."

"But you said he'd be here for dinner!" Jennifer complained.

The heater whirred softly as Reenie leaned forward to glance up at a darkening sky. "He would've been, if not for this storm." She threw them a rueful smile. Jennifer and Angela looked almost exactly like Keith, especially Angela, who insisted on wearing her blond hair short. Blue-eyed Isabella, however, had hair so dark it was nearly black, like Reenie's.

"There's always some reason he can't be here," Jennifer muttered.

Ignoring the pique in her daughter's voice, Reenie checked over her shoulder before pulling onto the road. "I guess the weather's even worse in Boise."

"Is he stuck up in the sky, circling around and around, like that one time when it was snowing and he couldn't land?" Angela asked, sounding a bit frightened.

"No. The plane hasn't even taken off yet. They're holding it in Los Angeles until the weather clears up."

"He'll be home tonight, though, won't he?" Isabella said.

Lightning flashed across the sky and thunder boomed in the distance. Then the patter of the rain grew deeper, sounding like tiny pebbles bombarding the windshield. "I hope so," Reenie replied. She missed Keith when he was gone, missed his warmth in her bed, his support with the girls, the smile he reserved for her alone. She felt as if half her life was locked in cold storage. But when Keith came home, he made the wait worthwhile.

She felt decidedly warmer remembering the last time they'd made love. They'd been as eager for each other as if they'd been newlyweds, despite the fact they'd been married for eleven years. Maybe the absences did that for them. Maybe the traveling, much as she hated it, wasn't *all* bad.

She had to believe that, didn't she? Or she wouldn't be able to tolerate his job any longer.

Their small wooden house came up on the right, a few miles after the cozier neighbourhoods of Dundee gave way to ranchettes. As soon as Reenie pulled into the driveway, Jennifer released her seat belt and pounded the back of Reenie's seat in excitement. "Hey, you're selling Dad's Jeep!"

Reenie gazed at the vehicle parked beneath the tarp Keith had attached to the side of the garage. She'd just put the For Sale sign up this morning. "I'm trying."

"After it sells, will we have the money to buy a horse?" Jennifer asked.

The engine sputtered as Reenie turned off the ignition. "I doubt it, honey. We don't have anywhere to stable a horse."

"We have a big yard. The Oakleys down the street have horses."

"We'd have to build stables in back or pay the Oakleys for board. And I'm sure your dad won't go for either option. He's planning to buy a motorcycle with the money."

"Maybe we'll get enough for both." Angela tugged her back-pack onto her shoulder. "Has anyone wanted to buy it yet?"

"Not that I know of." Reenie selected the key that opened the house so she'd be ready for the dash across the wet yard. "Some-one might've called, but I've been gone all day."

"Let's go see!" Isabella said.

Reenie grimaced at the sky, hoping for a letup that didn't ap-pear to be coming. "There won't be many people out looking at cars in this weather."

"It'll sell," Jennifer said confidently. "Everyone loves the Jeep."

"I hope you're right." Reenie wanted part of the money, too—for Christmas.

"Hey," Isabella said, her voice so loud it nearly made Reenie's ears ring. "Uncle Gabe brought our swing!"

Since the accident, Gabe had started making the most beau-tiful armoires, rocking chairs, beds, tables—even clocks and, ev-idently, tree swings. But after the way he'd handled their meeting with Lucky this morning, Reenie didn't want to think about him or his peace offering. She didn't want to forgive her brother too fast. She'd tried calling Lucky twice since breakfast and hadn't been able to reach her.

"Remember to take off your boots in the mudroom," she said as she stepped out of the car. "I just had the carpets cleaned."

They all ran for the back door and piled into the little ante-chamber that led to the kitchen. Old Bailey, their bassett hound, greeted them by wagging his whole hindquarters as they tossed their boots in a corner and hung their raincoats on hooks.

Reenie finished first because she wasn't wearing a hat or a sweater under her coat and passed into the kitchen to find the light blinking on her answering machine. Pressing the button that would deliver her messages, she leaned on the counter, hoping to receive some word from her husband.

Sure enough, Keith's voice came into the room, as warm and steady as always. "Hi honey. I'm still in L.A. It looks like it'll be a few more hours, so I'm going down the street for a real meal. Don't wait up for me. I love you," he said. "I'll get home as soon as I can."

The machine beeped and Reenie stood. Yet another night alone with the girls.

"His job'll be the death of me," she muttered.

Los Angeles, California

ISAAC HELD TIGHT to his boarding pass as he strode briskly through the airport, weaving in and out of the small clusters of people who were toting more luggage than he was or had stopped for one reason or another. His plane was leaving in forty-five minutes, which meant they'd be boarding in fifteen. Seven hours after that, he'd reach Chicago, where Reg would pick him up and take him home. He'd get in late, but the thought that he wouldn't have any trouble making his meeting tomorrow morning filled him with relief.

Hiking the bag that contained his laptop computer higher on his shoulder, he left the ticketing area. But when he reached the security checkpoint, he felt a flicker of concern. The line was longer than he'd expected, and it wasn't moving very fast.

"Come on, come on," he muttered impatiently, tapping his boarding pass against the palm of one hand as they inched slowly forward.

A moment later, the line stopped altogether.

What was the holdup? Leaning to the left, he tried to see around the people in front of him. An old lady was arguing with security personnel about having to remove her shoes, as if she hadn't watched everyone else do the same thing for the past thirty minutes. A couple of college boys were taking their computers out of their bags and putting them in gray bins.

God, at this rate—

Suddenly Isaac caught sight of someone familiar. The man had his back to him, so it was difficult to be sure, but he looked exactly like Keith.

He had to be wrong, of course. His brother-in-law had called Elizabeth just an hour or so ago to tell her he'd arrived safely in Phoenix. If he was in Phoenix, he certainly couldn't be here.

But that guy…

Moving to the other side of the line, Isaac tried to get a better look. At first someone inadvertently blocked his view, but then the line spread apart and Isaac finally caught the profile of the man he'd been trying to see.

It was crazy! He looked exactly like Keith. He was even wearing the same camel-colored overcoat.

The strange feeling he'd had earlier that morning, the sense that something was terribly wrong, swept over Isaac again. He didn't care what Elizabeth had said about Keith reaching Phoenix, this man *was* her husband. The longer Isaac watched, the more certain he became.

Taking his cell phone from his bag, he dialed Elizabeth's number. "Hey, Liz," he said when she answered.

She sounded surprised to hear from him, probably because she'd only dropped him off a few minutes ago. "Did you miss your plane?" she asked.

"No, I'm going through security right now."

"Then…did you forget something?"

"I don't think so. I was hoping…" He cleared his throat. "Keith made it safely to Phoenix, right? I mean, he called you before we left the house, didn't he?"

"Yeah. He called around two."

"Did he say what the weather was like?"

"Nearly eighty degrees. In November. Can you believe it?"

"No." He couldn't believe it. He couldn't believe that Keith was even in Phoenix, because Isaac was standing right here, staring at him. "You don't think he forgot anything, do you?"

"No, why?"

"Just wondering."

"Isaac, you're acting strange."

A woman's voice came over the intercom. "This is a security announcement…"

Isaac bowed his head so he could hear above the noise.

"What do you care about the weather in Phoenix?" Elizabeth was asking him. "And what do all these questions mean?"

Isaac couldn't say what was going on. But he was determined to find out. "Nothing. I'm…" His mind groped for an explanation.

"You're what?" she said when he didn't finish.

Reeling… "Passing the time," he finished lamely. "Keith and I didn't get much of a chance to talk, and I was curious about his schedule. When do you expect him back?"

"In two weeks or so."

"Is he always gone two weeks?"

"Give or take a day here and there. If the kids have something special, he'll occasionally come home early. Sometimes work demands that he make allowances on the other end." She paused. "Why?"

"No reason," he said, feeling numb as he imagined Keith on the phone to Elizabeth. *I'm here in Phoenix…the weather's beautiful…nearly eighty degrees…*

"Isaac, what's the matter with you?" she asked.

She didn't suspect Keith's deception, he realized. His baby sister, who'd already been through so much, probably had a nasty surprise in store for her, and he was going to have to be the one to break the news to her.

But not now. Not until he knew exactly what was going on. "Nothing."

"Something's wrong. You never act like this."

He swallowed a sigh. "I'm fine. I've gotta go, okay? I don't want to miss my plane," he said, and hung up.

Fortunately, the line was now moving faster. Ahead of him, Keith went through the metal detector, then started putting on his expensive Italian loafers.

In a few seconds he'd be fully dressed, recover his belongings and head to his gate, Isaac realized. But which gate would that be? Isaac had to know.

Letting the stress he felt show in his face, he turned to the person in front of him. "I'm terribly sorry, but I'm about to miss my plane. If you can afford the time, would you mind letting me go in front of you?"

It was a woman and her daughter. They politely stepped aside and let him through, and several more people did the same. He was nearly to the metal detector when Keith slung his carry-on over his shoulder and walked off.

Isaac cleared security and collected his things, hesitating briefly when he realized that Keith had moved in the opposite direction to the one Isaac needed to go. If he followed his brother-in-law, he'd miss his plane. Which meant he'd miss his interview.

Picturing his sister at the breakfast table this morning, so trusting and gullible and, along with her two kids, disappointed to see her husband go, he cursed softly. Then he gazed down the long corridor, managed to pick his brother-in-law's tall figure out of the crowd far ahead and started to follow.

CHAPTER THREE

ALONE ON THE TENNIS COURT, Elizabeth lowered her racquet to glance at the new diamond-studded watch Keith had given her for their eighth wedding anniversary a few weeks ago. It was just after six. Renate, who helped them out for a couple of hours each afternoon, would've picked up Mica and Christopher from their various after-school activities by now. They were probably already on their way home.

Elizabeth wanted to be with them. Usually she enjoyed going to the country club, especially when Keith was home. They played doubles as often as possible. But she wasn't in the mood to be here right now. It wasn't easy having Keith and Isaac leave on the same day. Their departures allowed the loneliness that sometimes plagued her to move closer.

Holding her racquet between her legs, she adjusted the ribbon that gathered her thick blond hair into a ponytail and attempted to shrug off her melancholy mood by telling herself the exercise would be good for her. Keith had given her these lessons for her thirtieth birthday two months ago and expected her to take them. She could do that much. He loved that she could beat almost any woman she played, even most men, and didn't want her to lose any of her ability.

He didn't want her to lose her figure, either. Which was probably why he insisted that they were finished having children, even though Liz would have liked one more.

She winced at the memory of the comment he'd made when

they were making love the other night. "Wow, babe, what are you eating when I'm gone? Feels like you're putting on a few pounds."

He was right, of course. She was comfort eating, trying to help pass the long evenings when he was away. But it wasn't as though she'd turned into a blimp.

Throwing the ball into the air, she smacked it hard and watched it rocket to the other side of the court. It landed right in the corner, almost on the line. A perfect serve.

"Looking good."

Dave Shapiro, the club pro, had finally deigned to show up for her lesson. But, from the way he was watching her, she couldn't tell if he was referring to her serve or her legs.

"You're late," she said.

As usual, her attempt to redirect his interest did little good.

"I'm worth the wait."

She adjusted her visor as he swaggered over—and stiffened when he stood behind her, lifting her arm in the motion of her serve.

"You were holding your wrist like this, see?" He made a point of having her look up. "That's exactly the way I want you to hold it. Every time."

He was a little too close. Liz could feel his body's heat, despite the cool November air, and remembered some of the suggestive things he'd said to her in the past. She knew, if she gave him any encouragement, he'd flirt even more.

But she'd never get seriously involved with him. No matter how handsome he was. No matter how badly she needed to feel desirable. After going through some of the most difficult years of her life without a mother, she wouldn't do anything to jeopardize her own small family.

"You're a beautiful woman, you know that?" he said.

"And you're about seven years too young for me," she replied, smiling because he was so obvious.

He shrugged. "That isn't the reason you're not interested."

Maybe Dave was cocky, but she appreciated how honest and direct he could be. "Not exclusively, no."

He hesitated for a moment, his attention roving over her short skirt. "Your husband's a lucky man."

"Commitment's an important part of loving someone, don't you think?" she said, and served again. Too long.

When his eyes finally met hers, his grin spread up one side, making him appear even more boyish than usual. "*I* think your husband's gone too often. It isn't wise to leave a wife alone so much."

"He trusts me," she said simply.

Dave cocked an eyebrow at her. "Do you trust him?"

"Of course."

"You don't think he's ever visited a bar or a strip club and wound up in someone else's bed?"

To be honest, she had considered that possibility. Her husband retrieved his voice mail and his e-mails when he was away, and responded if she needed him. But he never answered his cell phone during those long absences and rarely bothered to call her. She often wondered what he did when he had some spare time. Especially on holidays. At least once a year, he missed a major holiday because a network went down somewhere in the company. Did some of the other guys ever take him out for a drink? Or to a party?

She couldn't picture it. He said most of the guys at work were jerks and he refused to socialize with them. He wouldn't even attend the annual Christmas party. When she asked him how he spent his evening hours, he denied having any fun at all. "I try to get as much done as possible while I'm gone so I can be more available to you and the kids when I'm home," he said. And he made it easy for her to believe him. Although he worked while he was home—quite a bit, actually—he was completely devoted to her and the kids. She'd never seen him so much as look at another woman.

So rather than become an insecure nag, she'd chosen to trust him.

"He's a workaholic, which keeps him pretty busy," she said. "And he loves our kids as much as I do."

Dave reached down to retrieve a stray ball. "Maybe you're as lucky as he is. But if I were a gambler, I wouldn't bet on it."

"You barely know him!" she said.

"He's a man, isn't he?"

"That's pretty cynical, not to mention sexist," she accused, slugging him halfheartedly in the arm. "Anyway, you're wrong."

"How do you know?" he asked.

She claimed the ball and served again. "Because I know my husband."

AT THE AIRPORT, Isaac sat in a row of chairs one gate away from Keith. Other passengers crowded into the space between them, occasionally obstructing his view, but Isaac didn't move any closer. He didn't want his brother-in-law to know he was being watched, even though, from what Isaac could tell, he didn't appear to be particularly concerned about those around him. He didn't seem to be doing much of anything unusual—except going to the wrong city. According to the sign behind the desk, he was waiting for a flight that had been scheduled to leave for Boise, Idaho, this morning but had been delayed because of bad weather.

Boise. Why in the world would Keith be going there? Isaac might have guessed that Softscape, Inc., the company Keith worked for, had decided to send him somewhere else at the last minute. But that call saying he'd arrived safely and was already enjoying the sunshine made no sense. A man didn't play such an elaborate charade without a reason.

What was Keith's reason?

Isaac glanced at his watch. He'd missed his own flight to Chicago more than thirty minutes ago, so that decision had already been made. He knew he might regret his actions—certainly Reginald hadn't been happy to hear the news—but Isaac felt strongly about getting to the bottom of his brother-in-law's mysterious behavior.

In order to do that, he needed to follow Keith to Idaho. But if he took the same flight, he risked being seen.

He considered making arrangements through another airline, but decided it would be too difficult to coordinate his arrival with Keith's. He was afraid if he let Keith out of his sight for very long he'd lose him.

Isaac contemplated several different scenarios before deciding that his best bet was to buy a first-class ticket on Keith's flight. He'd board before all the other passengers, sit in the last row of coach and bury his nose in a newspaper. Unless the flight was packed, which he could already tell it wasn't, he doubted anyone would even sit next to him. His brother-in-law would get on and most likely take a seat much farther toward the front. Then Isaac would follow him off the plane when it landed.

The woman behind the counter was telling folks it'd be at least another hour before Keith's flight could take off. Isaac had heard her say it half-a-dozen times, so he wasn't concerned about being able to purchase a ticket. There were a lot of people milling around, but most seemed to be waiting to go to Portland.

When a group of businessmen passed between him and his brother-in-law, he finally stood and started toward the escalators. Keith had settled in to work on his computer. He wasn't going anywhere, at least not until they boarded the plane.

Then Isaac would be going with him.

Dundee, Idaho

REENIE COULDN'T HELP waiting up. She knew it was crazy to lose sleep when she had to get the girls off to school in the morning. But she still felt that old rush of anticipation when she knew her husband was coming home.

She sat in the living room, the filmy black lingerie she'd bought in Boise last week hidden beneath the heavy fabric of her robe, sipping a glass of white wine and playing with Old Bailey's silky ears. Her dog had been acting a little sluggish lately, but he was eleven years old and suffered from arthritis, so that was to be expected. "You're okay, aren't you Bailey?" she asked.

He licked his snout and gave her a short whine, and she sighed, hoping she'd been imagining his lack of appetite and increased lethargy.

Taking another sip of wine, she listened to the wind buffet the trees against the house. A steady drip fell from the rain gutter at the side of the house, but the worst of the storm had blown over. Conditions must have improved in Boise, too, because Keith had called at nine-thirty to say he was boarding his plane. Surely, he wouldn't be much longer.

The ring of the telephone startled her. She wasn't used to receiving calls so late. Her husband rarely called when he was gone. If he hadn't been delayed, she doubted she would have heard from him at all today. He would have simply appeared, luggage in tow, as he always did.

Pulling her gaze away from the silver sheen of wet pavement that lay beyond her big, sloping front lawn, she extricated herself from Bailey, who padded after her as she answered the phone in the kitchen. She hoped Keith wasn't calling to say his plane had been forced to land elsewhere.

"Hello?"

"Reenie?"

It wasn't Keith; it was Gabe. She knew her brother well enough to guess he was feeling badly about this morning. That was why he'd brought the girls a tree swing. But she'd already promised herself she wasn't going to forgive him too easily.

"Hope I didn't wake you."

"No. Keith's getting in soon."

"You haven't talked him into quitting that lousy job yet?"

"It pays the bills."

"It makes you miserable."

She raked her fingers through her hair. "He's afraid he won't be able to replace his paycheck. And he says he's used to the traveling, that I should be used to it by now, too."

"Are you?"

"Mostly I'm tired of having him gone. But I'm not sure it's fair of me to demand he give up what he feels successful at, what he loves. Besides, what if he's right and he can't find anything better?"

"He'd be fine. It's time he started thinking of you and the girls."

"He's good to us."

"When he's around." Gabe fell silent for a long moment, then drew an audible breath. "I'm sorry about this morning," he said, offering the apology he'd probably been working on all day.

Because the words sounded as though he'd had to drag them out of some place very deep, they melted Reenie's heart almost immediately. So much for not forgiving him too easily.

Oh well. Maybe they argued often. They were both passionate people. Stubborn. Opinionated. But their arguments never lasted long. Regardless of their ups and downs, Reenie knew Gabe would do anything for her, and she felt the same way about him. "I know you're still having a hard time with what Dad did," she said. "But it happened so long ago, Gabe. And Lucky really is—"

"A nice person," he interrupted. "I know. You've told me that before. I keep thinking I'm over whatever it is that makes me dislike her. But then I see her and…" His sentence trailed off.

Bailey, tired of waiting for Reenie to return to their cozy spot in the living room, lay across her feet.

"She's your best friend's *wife*," Reenie said, trying to approach the situation from another angle.

"Which only complicates the situation," Gabe replied. "Dad. You. Mike. I'm cornered."

"Sometimes it's better to accept what we can't change."

"You think I don't know that?"

Considering the accident that had stolen so much from him, she guessed it was more a matter of her poor brother reaching his "tough luck" threshold before they'd even learned about their father's affair with the infamous Red.

"Hannah thinks I should give her a call in the morning," he said.

Hannah. Gabe's wife was so immovable in her love for him. If not for the strength of the relationship that had developed between them, and Hannah's two boys, he'd probably still be closeting himself away in the remote cabin where he'd lived for two years after the accident. Instead, he'd bought a house in town and was coaching football at the high school.

Reenie wondered if she was expecting too much of him. Her brother *was* making progress. But it didn't hurt to encourage him. "I'm sure Lucky would be glad to hear from you," she said.

The sound of a car in the driveway brought Reenie's head up. Bailey, who was hardly an excitable animal, lumbered to the door and gave a rare "woof!"

Finally. Her husband was home. She was going to talk to Keith about the Higley farm. Again. She knew having him around more often would be good for the family. Not only were his long absences driving her crazy, but she had this…this terrible sense that his traveling threatened her and their children in some way.

She knew he'd laugh at her the moment she admitted it to him. Until recently, she wouldn't even admit it to herself. But she could no longer ignore what she felt. She wasn't being insecure or overly possessive. Keith was becoming increasingly distant. Sometimes she'd be talking to him, possibly speculating on what their lives could be like if he did something else for a living, and his mind would just drift off. She needed his attention again. She needed him to concentrate more on her and the kids and less on work.

Hearing Keith's key in the lock, she told Gabe she'd call him tomorrow. Now that she and Keith would be face-to-face, and alone, she was going to sit down with him and tell him exactly how she felt. His job—or his marriage. He'd have to choose.

But as soon as her husband walked through the door, she found herself in his arms and knew she wouldn't bring up the subject tonight. She didn't want to argue. He was whispering how much he loved her, how much he'd missed her, and his hands were slipping beneath her robe, seeking the places on her body that craved his touch.

She'd already put up with his traveling for nearly eleven years. She supposed her ultimatum could wait one more night.

ISAAC SAT in the back seat of the taxi he'd hired at the airport and stared across a narrow country road at the house Keith had entered only a few minutes earlier. A quick glance at the clock on the dash next to the meter in front told him it was 11:58 p.m.— a little late for Keith to be visiting a friend.

Frowning, he let his eyes rove over the house. Made of wood and painted white, it had been built some years ago but, like the yard, it was well kept. He could see the top of a swing set over the back fence. A tricycle with pink tassels dangling from the handlebars waited near the front door. A detached garage took up a large section of the right-hand side of the property, but it didn't look as though it was being used to house vehicles. There was a Jeep, parked beneath a tarp and sporting a For Sale sign. A minivan sat in the driveway next to the blue SUV Keith had driven.

"You gettin' out?" the cabby asked when Isaac made no move to open the door.

"No."

"You want I should take you somewhere else?"

"No."

The license plate of the minivan said, 1 I LUV. Keith's license plate was pretty conspicuous, too. It read, MY3GRLS, which had made him quite easy to follow.

Isaac lightly rubbed his lip. He'd risked his grant to follow Keith across two states, but he still wasn't sure what his brother-in-law was up to. He only knew it didn't look good. Especially when two figures, a man and a woman, appeared in the window. The glaring porch light made it difficult to see much detail, but a softer light coming from another room in the house threw both their bodies into relief.

They were kissing. The man was Keith. No question. The woman he didn't recognize. He couldn't discern any specific features, not even the color of her hair.

"Meter's running," the cabby reminded him.

When Isaac made no response, the driver rolled down his window and lit a cigarette while Isaac watched Keith shove the woman's robe off her shoulders. When Keith bent his head to kiss his partner's neck, Isaac looked away. He felt sick. Elizabeth was going to be devastated. This would hurt Mica and Christopher, too.

What should he do? Dropping his head in his hand, he pinched the bridge of his nose, trying to think.

"That's not *your* wife, is it?" the cab driver asked, smoke curling from his nose as he spoke.

Again, Isaac didn't respond. He was too busy searching for an answer. But no answer presented itself.

When he glanced up again, the figures in the window were gone. No doubt they'd moved to the bedroom.

Imagining his brother-in-law making love to another woman caused rage to cut through Isaac's terrible disappointment. He had to do something; he had to stop what was happening. For Elizabeth's sake.

"Wait here," he said, and got out. Wrinkling his nose against the cabby's cigarette smoke and the car's exhaust, he pulled his coat close and strode briskly across the street. He'd teach Keith a lesson. Break his nose. Something!

Isaac's mind told him a fistfight wouldn't solve anything—he hadn't been in a fight since he was seventeen—but his heart pumped eagerly in his chest as he cleared the driveway. He wouldn't allow his brother-in-law to have sex with this woman!

Anticipating the satisfying impact of his first blow to Keith's face, Isaac barely heard the rumbling motor of the waiting taxi as he slipped inside the chain-link fence that surrounded the front yard. He passed the trike with the pink tassels, stepped over a small pair of rubber boots lying near the steps and opened the screen door so he could bang on the wooden panel behind it. But then he hesitated. There was a crayon drawing taped to the door.

He blinked, his hand poised in the air. The drawing depicted several stick figures. One was obviously larger than the rest and, judging by the hair, was a man. The other figures were as crudely drawn but they were much smaller and seemed to be gathered around the man. At the bottom, a child had written, "Welcome Home, Daddy. We missed you. Jennifer, Angela and…" He couldn't read the last name. Whoever had signed the drawing had attempted to write in cursive, which he or she obviously didn't know how to do.

Welcome home, Daddy….

Chills rolled down Isaac's spine as he slowly lowered his hand to his side. Was this woman also married? Was her husband away on business? Could Keith have been driving her husband's car?

Isaac wanted to knock and demand the truth. But the tricycle with the pink tassels, the little boots and the childish note stopped him. There were children inside….

God, what was going on? How many lives would Keith's affair destroy?

Taking a bolstering breath, Isaac glanced back at the waiting taxi just as the cab driver finished his cigarette and tossed the butt carelessly away.

He had to think, gain some perspective.

Suddenly the porch light winked off, leaving Isaac in the dark. He froze where he stood on the front step, waiting to see if whoever had turned off the light had heard his approach or spotted the green-and-white taxi parked in front.

But the next several seconds ticked by and nothing happened. Keith and the woman were probably too involved with each other to notice anything less than a sizable earthquake.

The rain began to fall more heavily, but Isaac couldn't move. Most of his life, he'd done his best to protect his little sister. She'd had no one else.

But, heaven help him, there wasn't anything he could do to protect her from this.

CHAPTER FOUR

RELUCTANTLY, ISAAC LEFT Dundee behind and had the cabdriver drop him at a motel next to the Boise airport. He would've liked more time in the small town where Keith had spent the night. But he couldn't haunt Dundee while his brother-in-law was around. He didn't want Keith to know he suspected the affair. Not until he had a better sense of what was happening. Besides, his luggage had gone on to Chicago when he missed his plane and he wouldn't have had any transportation in Dundee. The town wasn't large enough to offer car rentals or bus service.

He had to go home. But what he'd witnessed didn't make it easy to leave. At least a hundred questions crowded to the forefront of his mind as he lay in the double bed, staring down the alarm clock on the nightstand beside him. Did folks in the area know Keith? How often did he appear and how long did he stay? Who was the woman he'd taken in his arms? Where had he met her—and how? What plans did he have for the future? Surely Liz's husband didn't feel he could continue lying to her indefinitely.

Or did he?

He'd come back later, when Keith was in L.A., he decided. Then Isaac wouldn't have to be so discreet. He could poke around, ask whatever he wanted.

Now he needed to sleep, so he could get up early and fly out. He couldn't make his interview, but he was anxious to be home.

Problem was sleep wouldn't come. Traffic rambled by; the

television in the room next door blared too loudly. He was still getting used to such noise after spending more than a year cocooned in the deep jungle.

The ice machine not far from his door clattered, and he swore softly under his breath. But it was the memories that really bothered him—the memories he hadn't let himself think about for years. Elizabeth repeatedly waking in a cold sweat, shaking from some terrible nightmare. Luanna, their stepmother, who was the cause of those nightmares, constantly belittling her. *Can't you do anything right?...You clumsy idiot...My hell, if you had half a brain you'd be dangerous...Look at the way you did these dishes. You're not worth a damn, you know that?*

For some reason, Luanna had been kinder to Isaac. He'd grown up feeling guilty for getting away with the little things Elizabeth would be punished for doing. Things like leaving his clothes on the floor, or forgetting to put his plate in the dishwasher. Maybe it was because he didn't need Luanna as much as Liz did, because he didn't really care whether she liked him or not. There was a certain amount of safety in indifference.

But Liz had been younger and much lonelier. She'd desperately craved the love they'd lost when their mother died, and it seemed to be that neediness that made Luanna so harsh. At any rate, Liz's vulnerability gave Luanna her power. The more Luanna punished Elizabeth, the more insecure and forgetful the girl became. The more insecure and forgetful she became, the more Luanna found reason to punish her. It grew into a never-ending cycle, one which Isaac could not stop. Whenever he tried to defend Elizabeth, Luanna would turn on him, and he'd run away from home. A day or two later, he'd go back because he couldn't leave Liz there alone.

He'd built up a deep resentment of his father for not putting an end to the petty meanness. To this day, they weren't speaking.

Fortunately, Elizabeth had slowly gained the strength she'd needed to stand up to their stepmother. When she was seventeen, she'd run away herself and refused to go back. She'd graduated from high school while living with a girlfriend and spending most weekends sleeping on the floor of Isaac's dorm room. Once he'd obtained his degree, he'd tried to help her get through college, but she'd left school to become a stewardess, which she seemed to really enjoy. That was when she met Keith. They'd married, had two children, and Liz had been happier than Isaac had ever seen her.

Which was all about to change.

Isaac shifted to his back and fixed his gaze on the ceiling. Who was the poor schmuck Keith's new lover was cheating on? Did he have any idea what his wife was doing?

Sleep, he ordered himself and tried to stop thinking. But it was no use.

Finally he snatched the phone from its cradle and leaned back against the headboard to dial. A call this late would probably wake Liz. But he had to talk to her, if only to remind himself that she was older and stronger than she'd been before, that somehow she'd be okay.

"Hello?" Her sleep-filled voice seemed to reach across the line and grab him by the throat.

"Hello?" she repeated when he didn't answer right away.

"It's me."

"Oh good, you got my message." Her last word thickened with what sounded like a yawn.

"Your message?"

"On your answering machine. I wanted to make sure you got in safely."

"I'm fine." Isaac hated lying to her. She thought her husband was in Phoenix. She thought her brother was in Chicago. Yet they were both in Idaho, of all places. But, guilt or no guilt, he wasn't about to admit the truth yet. First, he needed to understand more about what was going on, figure out a way to soften the blow. "Have you heard from Keith?"

Isaac knew she had to wonder at his sudden preoccupation

with her husband. Other than the usual felicitations, they didn't talk about Keith a whole lot. But Isaac couldn't help asking. He wanted to know who Keith really was. Obviously, his brother-in-law wasn't the man Isaac thought he knew. Hell, he wasn't even the man Liz thought she knew—and she'd been living with him for eight years!

"Unless there's a problem with the kids and I leave a message that I need him to call me, I usually don't hear from him till he gets home, remember?"

She'd already told him that, but she didn't sound impatient.

Isaac watched the lights from passing cars flicker behind the drapes, thinking that Keith's calling habits seemed pretty damned convenient. "Where do you leave a message?"

"On his voice mail."

"Could you give me that number?"

"You want to talk to Keith?"

It wasn't going to help anything at this point to further rouse her suspicions, so he tried to defuse her surprise. "I have a friend who's planning a visit to Phoenix. I thought maybe Keith could tell him a little about the area."

"He should be able to tell him plenty. He goes there often enough. You got a pen?"

Isaac turned on the lamp, then squinted against the sudden brightness. "Go ahead," he said when his vision cleared and he'd located the pad and pen provided by the motel.

She rattled off the number, then yawned again. "I'm beat. I'll let you go."

"Liz?"

"Hmm?"

"Do you ever think about Luanna?"

His sister sounded more awake and slightly wary when she answered. "I try not to. Why?"

"Just wondering."

A pause. "Has Dad tried to call you or something?" she asked.

"Not recently. Have *you* heard from the asshole?"

"Don't call him that, Isaac. He wasn't the best father, but... we're not kids anymore."

"You've forgiven him?"

"I don't see the point in holding a grudge. I'm older now. I have Keith, the kids. All's well that ends well, right?"

Isaac wished she'd become a *little* jaded so he wouldn't have to worry about her as much. *All's well that ends well....* It hadn't ended yet.

"I mailed Dad a picture of the kids for Christmas," she was saying.

"How'd he respond?"

"He sent them each twenty bucks."

"Generous of him."

"It's an acknowledgment," she replied defensively.

Isaac dropped the sarcasm. "I guess." Another pause. "What about Luanna? She have anything to say?"

"She wasn't part of the exchange. Dad's note was brief. A simple 'Merry Christmas,' and the money."

"Well, she's got her own precious child to worry about, right?"

Some rustling came through the line before she spoke again. "I bumped into Joe Stearns a few weeks ago."

"Marty's best friend?"

"Yeah. He said our stepbrother's getting divorced."

"Couldn't happen to a nicer person."

"We haven't talked to Marty for eight years. Maybe he's not so bad anymore."

Isaac doubted that. It'd take someone like Marty forever and a day to change enough to become tolerable, but he didn't want to get into an argument with Liz. Better to change the subject. "Tell me something."

"What?"

"What would you do if things suddenly...went wrong in your life?"

"In what way?"

"I don't know. Say…you and Keith split up."

"Where is this coming from?"

"Don't you ever imagine worst-case scenarios? What you might do if you faced a sudden reversal?"

"No, Isaac, I don't. I'm trying to bury the old fear. To trust. To believe in good things. I've had enough nightmares."

Isaac covered his eyes with his free hand. "Right. Well, it's late. I'd better let you go," he said. *Before I really upset you.*

"Are you okay?" she asked, obviously worried.

"I'm fine. Everything's fine," he said. Then he hung up and dialed Keith's cell phone. He couldn't leave things *exactly* as they were. The devil in him wanted to see his brother-in-law sweat.

As expected, his call went straight to voice mail. Not surprisingly, Keith didn't pick up when he was with "the other woman."

"You've reached Keith O'Connell at Softscape, Inc. Please leave your name and number, and I'll get back to you as soon as possible."

Bastard. "Hey, Keith. A friend of mine has business in Phoenix and has invited me to come along and do a little golfing. I told him you were there already and might be able to show us around," he said, expanding the lie he'd given Liz. "We arrive—" he thought quickly for a date that would be soon yet plausible: it was already Thursday "—on Monday. Give me a call, okay?"

He left his number and disconnected, wondering how long it'd take for Keith to respond—and what excuse his brother-in-law would offer.

"SO WHAT DO YOU SAY?" Reenie leaned up on her elbows and grinned at her husband, who'd awakened her by kissing her neck a few moments earlier. She loved it when his hair was ruffled from sleep and his whiskers created a dark shadow on his jaw.

He looked younger then, less like the corporate type he'd become and more like the boy she'd fallen for at the Homecoming Dance.

"Reenie, please," he said, throwing an arm over his eyes. "I just got home. Don't start in on me already."

Her hopes fell a little. "But the traveling is *killing* me."

He peeked at her. "*You're* not traveling. *I* am. If I don't mind, I don't see why you should."

"Are you kidding?" she said. "I'm tired of having you gone. Of spending half the night waiting up for you. Of worrying about plane crashes and terrorist attacks."

"I have more of a chance of getting killed in a car accident than a plane wreck. And I telecommute when I'm home, so I rarely leave the house. You probably see more of me than most wives see of their husbands."

Frustration caused Reenie to clench her jaw. They'd had this argument so many times she was beginning to feel as though they were on some kind of merry-go-round. She missed him, he came home, they made love, they argued, he left. And then it started all over again.

She needed to stop the cycle.

"That's not true," she said. "You might stay home, but you're still working when you're here. I don't get any more of your attention than if you worked outside the house those two weeks. And you're missing a lot of important events with the kids when you're gone."

He'd closed his eyes again, but she knew by the deep vee between his eyebrows that he was far from relaxed. "Like what?"

"Like Jennifer's school play last week."

"You videotaped it for me, didn't you?"

"Of course. But she played Tinkerbell, which was a big part. Going to those things without you just isn't the same."

He opened his eyes, but his scowl didn't ease. "I'm doing the best I can," he said. "Anyway, I'm home for two whole weeks. Why not enjoy our morning together instead of trying to make my life miserable?" As he sat up, the blankets fell to his waist, revealing the flat stomach and muscular chest Reenie admired so much. After sleeping with him for eleven years, she knew every inch of his body. She knew his moods, too, and recognized the irritation in his expression.

"*When* do you want to talk about it?" she challenged. "When you're home you say, 'Don't ruin the time we have together.' When you're gone you're too busy to call, or you say, 'We'll talk about it when I get home.' What do I have to do? Make an appointment with you to air my grievances?"

"You shouldn't have any grievances," he said. "You've got the house, the kids, your folks, the town you grew up in. What more can a woman ask for?"

Despite her desperation to change the situation, Reenie couldn't help wondering if she was being as selfish as he implied. The possibility that she had no right to ask him to quit Softscape, Inc., always undermined her resolve. But she'd put up with his job for eleven *years*. Wasn't that enough?

"I want to buy the Higley farm," she said. "Myrtle has lowered the price by twenty thousand. At this point, it's a *steal*. And I know we can make it work. I'm ready for a new challenge, for something we can do together."

He chuckled softly, as if she was Isabella, asking for her own reindeer for Christmas. "It's a broken-down old farm. And you don't know the first thing about running it."

She tried not to let his patronizing tone get to her. "My parents gave me riding lessons when I was growing up. I know how to care for horses."

"That isn't farming."

"Horses are part of the experience I'm looking for, and I could learn the rest. I realize it'd require a sacrifice on your part. But I've been sacrificing for your job since we got married. When is it my turn? Why is what you want always so much more important than what I want?"

God, that *did* sound selfish, Reenie realized. Was it? Should she simply continue to kiss her husband goodbye every two weeks and quit dreaming of a time when she wouldn't have to do so? Or did she have the right to call the shots once in a while?

"I'm the one who's supporting the family." Shoving the blankets aside, he got up and strode naked into the bathroom. "I'm good at developing business software, and I know I can pay the mortgage with the job I have right now," he called out through the open door. "I don't think we'd even be able to make the electric bill if I decided to become a farmer. I don't know the first thing about it."

"You wouldn't be doing it alone. I'll be there to help. We can make it work, Keith. I know we can."

The toilet flushed and the tap in the sink went on. "What's up with you, Reenie?"

"I don't know what you mean."

"Since when did you become so…clingy?"

Reenie's jaw dropped. She was clingy? Because she wanted him home at night like a regular husband? "You don't want to be with me all the time?" she asked.

When he came out of the bathroom, he was pinching his neck as if the tightness in his muscles was giving him a headache. "That's not it. You're…driving me insane with all of this—" he made an impatient motion with his hand "—badgering."

"If I'm making your life so miserable, maybe we need to split up and go our separate ways."

She'd never suggested such a drastic measure before. Even *she* was shocked to hear the words spoken aloud. And she could tell it had an effect on him, because the color drained from his face.

Crossing to the bed, he gathered her in his arms. "Hey, don't talk like that. We're going to be together forever, remember?"

They'd made that promise to each other, but… She leaned her forehead on his shoulder. "I want you home at night instead of flying all over the country."

The tension in his arms slackened, and he pulled away. "I'll think about it," he said, drawing on his boxers. But Reenie knew "I'll think about it" was just another ploy to get her to back off. "I'll think about it" was Keith's Plan B. If "Why are you starting a fight when we could be having fun together?" didn't work, he'd say something noncommittal yet pacifying.

"That's not good enough, Keith," she said. "You've told me you'll think about it before, but you never do. Left to you, the subject would never come up."

He shoved his legs into a pair of jeans. "How do you know that? You don't ever give me a chance. You start hounding me the moment I walk through the door."

"That's not true."

"God, Reenie! Can you just…quit?"

She got up on her knees. "I have a right to express my wants and desires," she said stubbornly.

"So do I."

"You've had your way for eleven years!"

"Give it a break," he snapped.

Would he ever face the issue squarely? "Quit trying to dodge this conversation and *talk* to me."

"We're not talking, we're shouting. And you won't be satisfied until I tell you what you want to hear. But I can't quit my job!"

"Why not?"

He turned away and started going through his drawers. "Because we need the money," he grumbled.

"There are other ways to make money."

"I love what I do."

Reenie's heart felt as if it were turning to lead. "Do you love it more than you love me?" she asked softly, clutching the sheet to her chest.

When he glanced back at her, something flickered in his eyes, something warm and solid, something she'd been depending on their entire marriage. "Of course not," he said. "How can you even ask me that?"

"I'm miserable, Keith. Why won't you make a change?"

He came to the bed and took her hands. "I will," he said. "But give me another year. Okay, babe? One more year. Please?"

Reenie stared at him. The warmth of his hands surrounded hers, but that warmth didn't seem to course through her like it used to. Another year. She didn't know if she could tolerate six more months. But a small knock sounded at their door and, as soon as Keith opened it, Isabella burst into the room. Watching her squeal as her daddy threw her into the air, Reenie knew she wasn't really willing to break up their little family.

TWO HOURS LATER, Keith sat at the desk of his home office, staring blankly at his computer screen. He had so much to do, but he couldn't concentrate. He'd just received word from Softscape that they were running into a glitch on the new inventory control program he'd created for large merchandisers and needed him to return to L.A. right away. After spending nearly twelve hours at the airport yesterday and barely getting to see Reenie and the girls, he hated the thought of going back so soon. But he knew better than to put the company off. When Softscape first moved their offices from Boise to L.A. nine years ago, everyone had been grateful that he was willing to commute. He'd been with them almost since the company first started. But management had changed since then, and his new boss wasn't particularly pleased with the amount of time he spent out of state. Charlie was looking for any excuse to insist he move to L.A. and appear at the office five days a week like everyone else; Charlie acted like Softscape owned Keith.

Because he was earning almost as much as Charlie, the company basically did own him, Keith thought with a frown. There was little chance he could support two families working anywhere else.

We need you here by Monday. The words of the e-mail he'd just read seemed to grow and then shrink. It was Friday now. That gave him only two days in Dundee. What was he going to say to Reenie come Sunday?

He could hear his wife talking to Old Bailey in the kitchen as she fed him the table scraps from breakfast. After getting the girls off to school, she'd made Keith some pancakes, eggs and sausage, and brought him coffee. But the food was growing cold at his elbow. He had to figure out a way to tell her he was leaving again, a way that wouldn't upset her too much. This morning she'd actually mentioned splitting up.

The panic he'd felt in that moment rose inside him again. He couldn't let that happen. He couldn't lose her or his girls.

"How's it goin' in here?"

Swiveling in his seat, he found Reenie standing at the door wearing only the see-through lingerie he'd removed—far too quickly—last night. With her long, shiny dark hair, deep blue eyes and small, compact body, she was certainly striking. Every bit as pretty as Elizabeth. Only in a completely different way. Reenie was a nature lover—earthy, real, demonstrative. She felt every emotion to the extreme, argued passionately and made love the same way.

Liz, on the other hand, behaved like the typical upper-class city girl she aspired to be—reserved, refined, elegant. She was a generous lover, but there was some small part of her she held in reserve. Sometimes he found himself saying things to her, hurtful things, just to see if he could pierce that protective shroud, get as close to her as he felt to Reenie. But Liz avoided emotional extremes as much as Reenie embraced them.

Eventually, he had to figure out a way to let Liz down easy, to tell her that he'd made a dreadful mistake, that he already had a family in Dundee. He knew he couldn't live the way he'd been living forever. But he couldn't even begin to imagine how Liz— or Reenie, for that matter—would react.

Feeling the onset of the panic that overwhelmed him so often of late, he took a deep breath. He'd fix everything next year, he decided. Or the year after that. It would be a lot easier when Christopher and Mica were older.

"Wanna take a shower with me?" Reenie asked, her voice sultry, her grin suggestive.

Keith let his eyes lower over her soft round breasts, her small waist, the flare of her hips—and felt his body react. He really should've taken more time to admire her in that sexy lingerie last night. But he was always too eager when he first came home. He had to feel her beneath him right away. Her warm response reassured him that she still believed in him, that she was still in love with him. Once he knew that, he could relax and slow down when they made love again.

She came toward him, and he quickly stood to block her view of the computer. He'd tell her about his summons to L.A. later. After they made love. Or tomorrow. He didn't see any reason to ruin the little time they had left. What she'd said this morning had really frightened him.

Bending his head, he kissed her exactly the way she liked. He needed to give her something she couldn't get anywhere else. "You wouldn't really leave me, would you?" he asked when they finally made their way into the bedroom. "You've never even slept with anyone else."

"I know."

"Tell me you love me," he said.

"I do."

"We're a family, right?"

She threw her head back as he kissed her breasts, touched her elsewhere. "Right."

"And families stick together," he murmured against the skin of her throat.

"For better or for worse," she repeated as she wrapped her arms around him. But when he pulled back to look in her face, he saw the sad little smile those words engendered, and the fear returned.

CHAPTER FIVE

Chicago, Illinois

KEITH'S CALL CAME on Saturday, catching Isaac in his car on the way to the university.

"Hey, why are you coming to Phoenix?" his brother-in-law asked, as engaging as ever. "I thought you had work to do at home."

Isaac marveled at the fact that Keith sounded perfectly normal. Was it only the night before last that he'd seen him with another woman? "I figure another week off work won't matter. I haven't been golfing since before I went to Africa. And the weather in Phoenix is pretty good, isn't it? This time of year, it's got to beat Chicago."

"It's beautiful here," Keith said without hesitation. "Not a cloud in sight."

God, he was a good liar. Isaac wondered if it was still raining in Idaho. "So what do you say? Can you do it?"

Would Keith squirm? Make up some excuse?

"I'd love to, man, I really would," he said. "But I won't be here. I have to head back to L.A. tomorrow."

"So soon?" Isaac struggled not to sound suspicious.

"My company's having trouble with a new piece of software I developed. They need me there to work out the bugs." Keith sounded sincerely disappointed.

"Do they call you home early very often?"

"Not often, but occasionally. L.A. is our base."

Isaac pictured the blurry shape of the female he'd seen through the window of the modest white house—the house with the childish note that had acted like a talisman against his intrusion. "What about the, um—" he cleared his throat "—people you were supposed to train in Phoenix? They won't mind letting you go?"

Keith's laugh sounded rather uncomfortable. "They won't be happy about it, but…I don't really have a choice."

Maybe the woman's husband had returned. "Does Liz know you're coming home?"

"I'm just about to call her."

Keith had to be telling the truth. He knew it was likely that Isaac would be speaking to his sister in the next few days. "I'm sure she'll be glad to hear the news."

"Now I can watch Mica in the spelling bee."

Isaac slowed as he approached the exit that would take him to the university. "Mica's a great kid."

"She is. So smart. But Chris is, too."

Were the children the only reason Keith kept coming back to Liz?

Isaac's call-waiting beeped. Glancing at the screen, he realized it was Reginald and knew he had to take it. "I've got to run, Keith. I'll talk to you later, okay?"

He switched over but couldn't quite erase the vision in his mind of Keith kissing his lover. "What's up, Reg?"

"Isaac, where are you?"

"Nearly in the parking lot. I'll be up in a minute."

"Please tell me you're wearing a tie."

"Of course I'm not wearing a tie. It's Saturday. No one at the university wears a tie on Saturday."

"Then I'm afraid you'll have to turn around. You're going to need one."

"For what?"

"The committee has agreed to interview you this afternoon."

"*Today?*"

"It was the only option. Mr. Zacamoto, the chair, leaves for Detroit on Monday."

"I thought I had to wait until next month. Why would they be so accommodating?"

"Because of your recent and very extensive experience in the Congo. They're trying to expedite your application."

That meant he was probably the center's favorite contender for the grant. "Great," Isaac said, allowing himself a huge sigh of relief. He couldn't wait to fly back to Africa and continue his research. But now that he knew Keith was heading to L.A., Isaac needed to finish up a little business in Dundee first.

"MOMMY, THERE'S A stranger here!"

At the sound of Angela's voice, Reenie pulled her head out of the refrigerator, which she'd been cleaning, and tossed her rag in the sink. A stranger? Reenie had grown up in this small community. There was hardly a stranger in all of Dundee.

Quickly wiping her hands on a towel, she tucked the wisps of hair that had fallen from her ponytail behind her ears and hurried to the front door.

On the porch stood a tall man, maybe an inch or so taller than her husband. He wore his thick dark hair, which had significant curl at the ends, longer than she liked, but the golden cast to his eyes made them intriguing.

"Hello." He was a stranger, all right. Reenie would've remembered the unusual color of his eyes, if not the long, dark lashes that framed them. Only the thick eyebrows that encroached ever so slightly on the space above the bridge of his nose kept those startling eyes from looking too feminine.

He turned the smile he'd just given Angela on her. "I'm Isaac Russell." He seemed to hesitate briefly, as if he expected some reaction to his name. But she was fairly certain she'd never heard of him before.

"Rena O'Connell," she replied, and extended her hand.

He'd already moved to shake with her, but froze. "Did you say *O'Connell*?"

Reenie hesitated. "Yes. Does that come as some sort of surprise to you?"

"No." He briefly gripped her hand in a firm, warm shake, then let go. "Nothing like that. I—" he cleared his throat. "I wanted to be sure I had your name right, that's all."

"Sounds like you've got it." It struck her that there was something odd about his reaction. "What can I do for you?"

He cleared his throat again and tipped his head toward the driveway. "I'm, um, here about the Jeep. Is it still available?"

She hadn't received a single call on the Jeep since putting it up for sale a week ago. Trying to bury her dissatisfaction with her husband's hurried departure, she'd thrown herself into a cleaning frenzy and had forgotten all about it. "Yes, it is."

"Jennifer!" Angela called. "Someone's here about the Jeep!"

Reenie's oldest, who'd been doing homework in her room since school let out, appeared with Bailey at her heels. The dog preferred her to almost anyone else, probably because she was a gentle soul, quiet and studious. She never tied bells around his neck, or forced him to give the neighbor's cat a ride, or insisted he wear a Santa hat at Christmas, as Isabella and Angela often did.

Never one to be left out, Isabella hurried to join them, wearing princess dress-up clothes.

The man glanced at each of the girls before turning his attention back to her. "Are these your daughters?"

"Yes. Jennifer, Angela and Isabella."

"I mean, they're O'Connells, too?"

"Yes." She frowned in confusion. "Why do you ask?"

He scratched his head. "I used to know someone named Keith O'Connell."

"He's my husband," Reenie said with a laugh and immediately relaxed. No wonder he'd seemed surprised by her name. Evidently, he wasn't a complete stranger, after all. "How do you know Keith?"

"I—" He shoved his hands into his pockets. "I used to work for Softscape."

"You're kidding! Here in Boise or after they moved to L.A.?"

"In Boise."

"That was some years ago." Reenie tried to remember him from some of the social functions she'd attended when the company was still based in Idaho, but couldn't.

"Yeah, I've moved on to other things since then."

She crouched to stop Bailey from sniffing his shoes, glad her dog was acting more like his old self today. "I wish Keith were home. I'm sure he'd be excited to see you."

"We didn't know each other very well." His gaze once again rested on the girls. "You have beautiful children, by the way."

Bailey gave up his halfhearted attempt to act like a more energetic dog, and simply rested his snout on his paws at Reenie's feet. "Thank you." She patted the dog before straightening. "You'll have to leave your card for Keith."

Mr. Russell searched his pockets. "I don't have one with me. Maybe you could just tell him I said hello."

"Of course. Would you like to test-drive the Jeep?"

He glanced across the yard. "Sure. That'd be great."

"Let me get the keys." After a quick trip to the kitchen, Reenie led him across the yard. Old Bailey's collar tags jingled as he and the girls followed.

Reenie felt Mr. Russell's eyes on her as she unlocked the vehicle. She sensed a certain curiosity coming from him, which made her wonder about him, too. She was fairly sure Keith had never mentioned an Isaac Russell. But it'd been nine years. She could easily have forgotten.

"This is in good shape," he said once they reached the Jeep and he'd had a moment or two to check it out. "How much are you asking?"

She'd anticipated selling the Jeep to one of the cowboys around town, or maybe a teenager from the high school. She'd never dreamed someone like Isaac Russell would show any interest. She wasn't even sure what he was doing in town. Dressed in a pair of chinos, a button-down shirt and loafers, he looked like he could afford something much nicer. Something more urban, like a Lexus.

Jennifer started naming the price she'd heard Reenie mention. "Fourteen—"

"Fifteen thousand," Reenie quickly interrupted.

Mr. Russell lifted his eyebrows. "Sounds like I'd better act fast."

"Jennifer wasn't accounting for the new tires."

"I see."

"It's my daddy's," Angela volunteered.

"When will your daddy be home?" he asked.

"Not for a long—"

"Angela, that's enough." Mr. Russell seemed like a nice guy, but Reenie didn't see any reason to tell him she and the girls were alone.

"What brings you to Dundee, Mr. Russell?"

He turned the key in the ignition and the engine roared to life. "I'm, um, here to do a little research," he said above the noise.

"For what?" Angela asked.

He adjusted the seat and tried the windshield wipers.

"For what?" she repeated when he didn't answer.

"I'm writing a novel."

Jennifer brightened immediately, as Reenie knew she would. "What's your book about?" she asked.

He turned off the stereo. "Small-town relationships."

"Well, you've come to the right place for that," Reenie said.

A brief smile indicated he'd marked the sarcasm in her voice. "I'm sure I have."

"So you're only visiting?"

"That's right."

"How long will you be staying?"

"In Dundee?" He shrugged. "A few days. Maybe a week. As long as it takes to get what I need."

"Are you at the motel in town, then?"

"Not yet. I just got in. I was taking a drive to get a feel for the area, and that's when I came across your Jeep." He patted the dashboard. "I love these."

"They're versatile."

"An absolute necessity in the jungle."

"Did you say *jungle?*"

He chuckled. "Never mind."

She pulled the girls away from the idling vehicle. "If you leave your driver's-license number with me, you can take it out on the highway, if you like."

"Not today, thanks. I'll think about it and get back to you, though. Okay?"

"We want to buy a horse," Isabella volunteered.

He smiled at her while turning off the engine. "That sounds like fun."

"What kind of research do you do for a relationship novel?" Reenie asked as he got out and handed her the keys.

"Talk to people, take note of what they say and do."

"Mention that you're writing a book, and half the people in this town will be ready to tell you anything you want to know," she said. "Gossip is their favorite pastime."

He studied her for a moment, and she sensed his curiosity again. "Sounds like you've been a victim of that gossip."

"My family has received more public interest than most."

"You and Keith?"

"No. My parents and my brother."

He cocked one eyebrow at her. "Want to talk about it?"

"I'd rather leave that subject alone. But if you want general information about the area, I can help. I've lived here all my life."

"Thanks, Mrs. O'Connell."

"Call me Reenie," she said. "Everyone else does."

"Okay, Reenie." His unusual golden eyes seemed to absorb every detail of her face. "Since you're willing to help, is there any chance you could meet me at the diner in town later?" He raised a hand and stepped back a foot, as if to assure her that his intentions were honest. "For an interview," he added.

Reenie couldn't see why not. He was acquainted with her husband, which made him an old friend of sorts. And the diner was a public place. She knew practically everyone in town, which meant she'd be surrounded by friends. "When?"

He checked his watch. "Seven? I'll buy you dinner in exchange for your time."

Reenie was hopeful he'd buy more than dinner. She wanted to sell him the Jeep. "It's too bad Keith isn't here," she said. "He's going to be disappointed he missed you."

"I'm sorry I missed him, too," he said. "See you at seven."

"I'll be there."

ISAAC WATCHED the woman he'd just met hustle her children— and her elderly dog—back into the house.

Rena *O'Connell* had given her name as though she'd owned it for a long time and was comfortable using it. But she couldn't be married to Keith. He was already married to Elizabeth.

Maybe they were only living together. This was a small community. Maybe Keith had met Reenie no more than a few months ago. When he moved in with her, she took his name to hide the fact that they weren't officially married. It'd be a good way to avoid the criticism of a small, conservative community, right?

But the three girls... That was where his theory collapsed. Even though Reenie's youngest daughter didn't resemble Keith, there was no doubt that the two older girls were his. Which meant Keith's relationship with Reenie must have predated his relationship with Liz.

It wasn't a reassuring thought.

Isaac needed to investigate a little more, figure out when and how this whole thing had started.

He circled the Jeep to convince anyone who might be watching that he was really interested in it. Then he started toward the car he'd rented in Boise.

The front door of Reenie's house opened before he could reach the curb, and her youngest daughter stepped out. "My mommy said I can give you a cookie," she said, and began clomping toward him in snow boots at least four sizes too big.

He met her halfway up the driveway so she wouldn't trip and accepted an oatmeal cookie. "Thank you."

She shaded her eyes so she could look up at him. "Can I go to the diner with you and Mommy tonight?"

He quickly swallowed a mouthful of cookie. "That's not up to me, honey."

"But my mom said no." She grimaced and put a hand to her belly. "And I'm *hungry.*"

"I'm sure she's planning to give you dinner."

"She's making chicken potpie."

He took another bite of cookie. "You don't like chicken potpie?"

"She puts peas in it!"

Isabella said "peas" as though she meant "bugs."

"Can't you pick them out?" he asked.

She shook her head. "Mommy won't let me."

"Green vegetables are good for you. They make you strong."

Her shoulders slumped. "Don't tell me that. I already know."

Isaac couldn't help grinning at her. He thought about Mica and Christopher, who very likely had three half siblings they knew nothing about. The news would rock their world along with Elizabeth's. But this little imp was particularly appealing. Not only was she pretty, she had a flare for the dramatic that made him laugh.

"What's so funny?" she asked, eyeing him warily.

"You are." he admitted, enjoying his cookie.

Her eyebrows shot up. "I didn't say a joke."

"I know. You're just very cute." He glanced beyond her to the bassett hound that waited dutifully on the porch. "What's your dog's name?"

"Old Bailey."

"Did you name him?"

"No, my daddy did. He gave him to Mommy for her birthday."

"When was that?"

"Oh…a hundred years ago."

He chuckled. Reenie couldn't be much older than thirty. "That many, huh?"

"No, wait. Maybe it was…*two* hundred." She nodded as though she was now positive about her answer.

"Then, it's definitely been a while."

"He's a good doggy."

"I bet he is." Tights covered the thin legs that disappeared into her oversize footwear. "Nice boots," he said.

She grinned proudly. "They're my mom's."

"I see. So…" He lowered his voice, even though he highly doubted anyone inside could hear them. "Where's your dad?"

"At work."

"Where does he work?"

She seemed to have difficulty with this one. "Far away."

Isaac swallowed the last of the cookie. "What's your daddy's name?"

"Keith, silly." She added a giggle for his ignorance. "You know that."

"Right, Keith." Considering the fact that she'd just told him Reenie had received Bailey two centuries ago, he wasn't sure how reliable her answers were. But she was the only one of Reenie's children who wasn't old enough to consider his questions in a critical light. "Is he your *only* daddy?"

She wrinkled her nose. *"What?"*

"Have there been any other…grown men in your mother's life?"

"My Uncle Gabe comes to visit. He can't walk."

"That's too bad."

"If I tease him about it, he dangles me upside down." Another smile.

"Are you sure it's nice to tease him?"

"He doesn't mind. He *likes* it."

"Really. That's difficult to imagine. But I'm not talking about Uncle Gabe."

Her expression reflected her confusion.

He checked the house and saw Jennifer peering out at him but continued to question Isabella. "Don't some of the kids at school have a dad *and* a stepdad?"

"My friend Glenda does. But I don't. Duh." She rolled her eyes and laughed again. "Don't you know anything?"

He pinched his lip. "I admit that I'm a little puzzled."

"About what?"

The whole situation. His brother-in-law seemed to have built two complete families. Two families that existed in different parts of the country. And, from what Isaac could tell, they were completely unaware of each other. How had Keith managed to get away with it for so long?

A *bang* drew Isaac's attention to the house. Isabella's older sister had thrown the door open. "Isabella, it's your turn to put the silverware on the table!"

The little girl sighed dramatically. "I'm coming," she said, and started back up the driveway.

Isaac watched her go. He wasn't sure what he was going to do about the mess Keith had created. He didn't want anyone to be hurt. Not the attractive woman he'd just met. Not her sweet little girls. And certainly not his sister and her children.

In two hours, he'd be having dinner with Keith's *other* wife, the mother of his *other* family. At some point, Isaac would have to tell her—and Elizabeth, too.

God, what was he going to say?

CHAPTER SIX

ISAAC ARRIVED at the diner early. He'd already explored the area and found that there weren't a lot of things to see in Dundee. After about three blocks of businesses, the town fell to quasi-rural residences like Reenie's, where the people enjoyed small acreages and often owned horses or other animals. Once he started climbing into the mountains, he saw mostly large ranches.

"Would you like anything else to drink?" A waitress, wearing a badge that identified her as Judy, set a glass of water in front of him. About forty-five years old, she had a smoker's voice and bleached hair with dark roots.

"Maybe in a minute or two," he said. "I'm waiting for someone to join me."

"Who?"

He'd never had a waitress ask him for the name of the party he was waiting for, at least not as if she had a personal interest. He glanced up to see Judy putting her order pad in one of the pockets of her apron. "Excuse me?"

"Who are you waiting for?"

"Reenie O'Connell." Reenie's last name tasted bitter on his tongue. He didn't want to believe she could be married to Keith. Surely there was some other explanation. He wasn't sure about the ramifications of bigamy, but he knew it was illegal. He needed to do some research, maybe call his friend in Chicago who worked for the Attorney General's office. Part of him wanted to see Keith behind bars. The other part realized that putting his brother-in-law away wouldn't help either family. Which might be the reason, besides the few sensational polygamy cases coming out of Utah, he'd never heard of anyone going to jail for marrying two people at one time.

"How do you know Reenie?" she asked, seemingly unaware that he might consider it rude for her to be so inquisitive.

"I used to work with Keith." He repeated the lie he'd told Reenie while trying to remember what he'd read in the paper about Tom Green. The State of Utah had put Tom Green in jail for bigamy. But, if Isaac remembered right, there'd been other charges as well. Keith hadn't married anyone underage. And what he'd done had nothing to do with collecting welfare. He maintained two relatively "normal" but separate lives, and he seemed to be a good father to his children. Did the state send bigamists like Keith to jail?

"Hel-lo?" The waitress snapped her fingers in front of him, and Isaac belatedly realized that she'd asked him another question.

"I'm sorry," he said. "What'd you say?"

"Did you meet Keith at that computer company?"

"Yes."

She shook her head. "Good thing you got out when you did. Keith's sure gone a lot. If you ask me, he needs to stay home and take care of his family."

Which one? "How well do you know Keith?"

"Well enough. Everybody knows everybody else around here."

"How long has he been living in Dundee?"

"Let's see." She rolled her eyes, which were caked with blue eye shadow, toward the ceiling. "Seems like…gee, his folks must've moved here at least twenty years ago."

Twenty years was a long time. Her answer certainly didn't make Isaac feel any better about who might have come first in Keith's life. "Are his folks still in town?"

"Sure are. They don't live more than a couple miles from Reenie."

Interesting. Apparently, Keith's parents were alive and well, and hadn't been killed in an automobile accident, as Isaac had been told. Keith also purported to be an only child. Elizabeth was always saying how terrible she felt that he had no family.

Me and the kids...we're all he's got, Isaac.

Isaac smoothed his eyebrows with a thumb and finger. "Does he have any siblings?"

He wasn't surprised when she immediately responded in the affirmative. "Two brothers."

"Do *they* still live in town?"

"No. One's away at college. Baylor. The other married and moved to Boise several years ago."

"I see." He hauled in a deep breath. "When did Keith marry Reenie?"

Her trust gave way to skepticism. "I thought you were waiting for Reenie. I thought you were friends."

"Actually, I know Keith." But certainly not as well as he had once believed. "I just met Reenie this morning when I stopped by to look at the Jeep she's selling."

"What brought you to town in the first place?"

"I'm writing a novel about small-town relationships. Reenie's agreed to help me with some of the research."

Judy pursed her lips and nodded as though grudgingly impressed. "Reenie'll be a big help. I'm sure she'll tell you all about how she and Keith met in high school. Got hitched almost as soon as they graduated."

So what he'd suspected was true. *Liz* was the other woman. She'd met Keith on an airplane only eight or nine years ago.

"Reenie's father is Senator Holbrook, you know," the waitress said.

Isaac didn't know. But neither did he care much about Reenie's political connections. He was too busy trying to place events in their proper order. First Keith had married Reenie. Then he'd been hired by Softscape. The company had moved headquarters, and he'd started traveling extensively. Which is how he'd crossed paths with Elizabeth. They began to date, she got pregnant with Mica, they married right away. The only thing that made Keith's extramarital affair so different from those of a lot of men was that he'd married the other woman without divorcing his first wife....

The waitress was still talking, but it took real effort for Isaac to concentrate on anything except his own grim thoughts.

"The senator had big plans for Reenie, hated to see her marry so young," she was saying.

Had Judy just given him a brief history of Reenie's early years? Yes...

"But there was no standing in the way of it," she continued, smiling wistfully. "I've never seen two people more in love. And I gotta hand it to them. They started having babies after the first year, but they worked their way through college. They both graduated with some sort of degree. Even Senator Holbrook's got to be happy with how their relationship has turned out."

Isaac didn't think *anyone* would be happy for long, but there was no time to catalogue the ramifications of what he'd learned from Judy. The bell rang over the door and Reenie walked in, wearing a pair of jeans cut fashionably low on her hips, boots that seemed more city than country, and a thin coral sweater that hugged the slim body beneath her brown leather coat.

As much as Isaac would rather have found her unattractive, he could see why Keith would be drawn to her. She had creamy, flawless skin, beautiful blue eyes, a mouth that was just a little too wide to be perfect, and an energetic, confident air that made him want to look at her much longer. If she was wearing any makeup, he couldn't tell. With the healthy glow of her skin, and the contrast between her light eyes and rich dark hair, she didn't need any.

"Getting started without me?" she said, sliding into the booth.

He forced his eyes to stay on her face as she stripped off her coat. He didn't need to assess her figure. He'd already done that when he'd followed her to the Jeep. "Excuse me?"

The coral sweater had a wide neck that fell off her shoulders slightly—very feminine and appealing. "Are you interviewing Judy?"

He handed her a menu from the clip at the back edge of the table. "I was asking her a few questions."

"Why didn't you *tell* me you know a famous author?" Judy asked.

"Famous?" Reenie had knocked her purse over and was busy collecting all the stuff that had spilled out, but she raised an eyebrow at him when she heard this. "He left that part out when I met him this morning."

"I try not brag," he said with a grin.

She returned his smile as she finished with her purse, then glanced around the diner. "Busy tonight?" she asked Judy.

"Not too bad. I've been telling your new friend here how you and Keith got together." Judy's wistful smile returned, taking the harder edges off her appearance. "Love at first sight."

Reenie shoved her bag and coat farther into the corner of the booth. "And what did he have to say about that?"

"Nothing yet."

"What were you expecting?" Isaac asked.

She tilted her head in a challenging angle. "Most people think that kind of love is a fairy tale."

"It's not?"

Her shoulders lifted in a tiny shrug. "I'm proof that it does happen."

Isaac knew he should say *I'm happy for you,* or some other such thing, but the words wouldn't come. He couldn't make a comment like that knowing what she was going to face in the very near future. "Maybe so," he said.

She put the menu away without looking at it. Isaac figured she could probably recite the diner's offerings from memory. "You sound like a skeptic, Mr. Russell."

"Call me Isaac."

"Isaac. You don't believe in love at first sight?"

He stared into his water glass. "Let's just say it's a phenomenon I've never experienced myself."

"So...you're jaded." She tapped a short fingernail, devoid of polish, against her chin. "Divorced?"

"Never married."

Judy looked appalled at this news. "Handsome guy like you? You're not gay, are you?"

Isaac couldn't help laughing. "Not even a little bit."

"Well—" the waitress made a point of checking him out "—in that case, if you need anyone else to help with your research, let me know. I'm good at small-town relationships." She winked. "And I'm not married."

"Aren't you seeing Billy Jo these days?" Reenie said pointedly.

"What if I am?" She fluffed her hair. "Maybe he'd actually pop the question if he thought he had a little competition."

"I hate to break it to you, but Isaac won't be around long enough to help you reel in Billy Jo," Reenie told her.

"How long will you be here?" Judy asked him.

"Only a few days."

"Figures." She stopped flirting and retrieved her order pad. "What can I get you for dinner?"

He glanced expectantly at Reenie, but she said, "You go first."

"I'll have the chicken-fried steak and mashed potatoes."

Reenie cleared her throat.

"What?" Isaac said when he found her watching him.

"The sirloin is much better."

"Is that what you're having?"

"No, I like the garlic-roasted chicken with sage stuffing."

"But you think I'd like the sirloin?"

"If you're going to order red meat, the sirloin's the best cut they've got."

"Okay." He motioned to Judy. "I'll take the sirloin."

"How do you want that cooked?" she asked.

"Well done."

Disapproval etched several lines on Reenie's forehead, and Isaac hid an amused smile. "What now?" he asked.

"You won't be able to eat it if you order it that way. Mac will turn it to charcoal. Medium would be best, but if you're squeamish, go with medium-well."

Considering some of the things he'd eaten in the past, Isaac doubted anyone could call him squeamish. While in the Congo, he'd sampled a variety of unusual and, sometimes, unpleasant foods. "I just want it *done*."

"If it's a little pink in the center, it'll be more tender." She adjusted her sweater to fall evenly off both shoulders. "Believe me, I know about steak. This is cattle country."

Isaac gave up. "I'll go with your advice. But if it's bloody, you'll have to share your chicken."

She turned her hands up. "I'll take that risk."

This woman had spirit, strength, confidence. He could tell already. "Anything else I should know about dining here?" he asked, teasing her.

"Order the pie."

"What kind of pie?"

"*Any* kind of pie."

"Okay…I'll have pumpkin."

"I'll have the carrot cake," she said to Judy.

"Wait a second," Isaac said with a laugh. "You just told me to order the pie."

"I know. Their carrot cake isn't the best. But I'm in the mood for cream-cheese frosting."

Isaac found his smile lingering. Much as he didn't want to like Rena O'Connell, he couldn't help himself. She was refreshingly quirky and outspoken.

Choosing between Elizabeth and Reenie wouldn't be easy, he decided. No wonder his brother-in-law was working so hard to keep both women. Flying back and forth between Idaho and

California. Splitting his earnings between two households. Making up lies to cover lies to cover lies...

How the hell had he managed it for so long? A double life had to wear a person down after a while. Had Keith planned on leaving Reenie and never gotten around to actually walking out? Had he cheated on her, then let the situation spiral out of control? Or did he consider what he was doing some kind of challenge? Was he laughing at the gullibility of one wife while he was in the arms of the other?

"Can I get you anything else?" Judy asked.

"No, thanks," Isaac replied. He turned back to Reenie as Judy moved away.

"Are you always so direct?" he asked Reenie.

"Pretty much. Why? Does it intimidate you?"

"Not at all."

"That's more than I can say for most men."

"What do you mean by that?"

"Men seem to prefer demure women who let them take the lead, or at least create the illusion of letting them lead."

"You're saying you wear the pants in the family?"

"Not at all. Keith and I are equal partners in our marriage. I'm just saying that I don't hesitate to speak my mind."

"And he's okay with that?"

"He loves that about me." She flashed him another grin.

He chuckled, thinking about the little girl he'd met at the house. Isabella had definitely inherited her mother's spunk. Reenie might be small, but she was a force to be reckoned with. She could probably handle what was coming better than Liz could. But would the crisis rob her of that vital quality he found so unique and appealing? He hated the thought of that.

"What do you want to know about small towns?" she asked.

"First tell me a little about yourself."

"Me?"

"A writer needs to understand the perspective of his source. It shades the meaning of what that source might say."

She briefly considered this. "Okay. I'll be thirty in two months."

Isaac cringed a little at this news. They wouldn't get through her birthday before the truth came out.

"I was born in Dundee." She rearranged the salt-and-pepper shakers and condiments as she talked, even used her napkin to wipe the grime off the salt container. "My parents still live here, along with my only sibling, an older brother." Focusing on someone over his left shoulder, she set her napkin on the edge of the table for Judy to take and waved.

Isaac turned to see that she'd spotted a young cowboy who'd come in earlier. "Friend of yours?"

"A former student."

"You're a teacher?"

"I was until I had Isabella. It was tough enough to work full-time with two kids. Three made it nearly impossible. I prefer to be with them, so I quit."

"Fortunately, your husband seems to make enough to provide for everyone." And he did mean *everyone*. How did Keith support two families without either wife missing the funds he siphoned off? Softscape must pay very well.

"We...squeak by," she said.

Considering the diamond bracelet Keith had given Liz for their anniversary, the four-thousand-square-foot house they lived in, and the expense of belonging to that ritzy tennis club, Keith was obviously not splitting his checks evenly. Why was he spending so much more on one family than the other? Did he prefer Liz to Reenie? Or was he living some sort of yuppie fantasy life with Liz that required fancier trappings? It was even possible that he loved Reenie more than Liz and tried to make up for it with his generosity.

"I'm interested in how couples deal with their finances in small communities," he said, steering the conversation in a direction that might reveal how Keith operated.

She surprised him by wrinkling her nose.

"Is something wrong?"

"I hate to be critical, but I hope that isn't what your book is about."

Once again her frank response tempted him to smile. "Not interesting enough?"

"'Fraid not."

"It's fascinating to me." *Morbidly so,* he thought, and his smile quickly faded.

She accepted the glass of water Judy brought. "You must have been an accountant in a former life."

"A scientist," he said.

"That explains it."

"You're saying accountants—and scientists—are boring?"

"Not boring, exactly. Just preoccupied with the minutiae of life."

Isaac couldn't help being slightly offended. "Someone needs to worry about the details."

"I guess. Anyway, there's hope for you. You're more of a jack-of-all-trades, right? Scientist, computer type and novelist."

He shifted uncomfortably. "Right."

"What do you want to know about small-town couples and their money?" she asked.

Still tempted to defend scientists, Isaac struggled to regain his focus. "Are married couples from rural areas really more traditional in the way they handle their income?" he asked. "Or is that changing? For instance, do you and your husband have joint bank accounts or separates ones?"

"We have a household account that's joint. My husband also has an account of his own."

"Why did you choose that arrangement?" Isaac guessed the idea had originated with Keith, but he was curious to know why she'd gone along with it.

"He likes to invest anything we have left over. He works hard, so I don't begrudge him that. It doesn't amount to much, anyway. We go over the numbers all the time. Especially recently. I've been wanting to buy this farm, and…well…" Her bottom lip came out in a quick pout that reminded him once again of her youngest daughter. "Let's just say we've been talking a lot about money."

"I would think his having his own account would be atypical of couples from around here," he said, hoping for more details.

"It probably is. My parents have always shared everything. But like I said, Keith transfers most of the money over to our household account, anyway. We have bills to pay, you know?"

"So you never actually see his paycheck?"

"It's on automatic deposit. But I know how much he makes."

"How?"

"He tells me."

Right. "What about tax returns? Do you file jointly?"

She grimaced. "You want to hear about my tax returns?"

"It's all part of the various…styles of marriage I'm studying."

"We file separately."

Of course they did.

"But only because a tax consultant told Keith we could save a lot of money that way," she added.

"That isn't true for most people," Isaac couldn't help pointing out.

"It's because of the types of investments he makes—or something like that," she said. "I'm not really sure. I don't like dealing with the IRS. I'm just glad Keith's willing to handle it."

"Generous of him," Isaac murmured.

"What?"

"Nothing." He was beginning to understand how Keith had managed to keep some of the most obvious signs of his double life from becoming apparent to at least one wife. Reenie had married him before they'd had any money, so she didn't expect a lot. Keith gave her enough to support the family, and she didn't ask for more. Simply put, she trusted him. Isaac understood that.

Keith came off as a great guy. Elizabeth trusted him, too. Until last week, Isaac had trusted him as well.

Judy returned with Reenie's soft drink. Reenie leaned back and didn't speak again until the waitress was gone. "Anything else?" A devilish glint entered her eyes. "You might want to include a chapter on how couples around here do their laundry."

He laughed and decided to back off anything to do with Keith, at least for the moment. "Isabella brought me a cookie earlier."

"I know."

"She mentioned you have a brother who can't walk."

Reenie straightened her knife, spoon and fork neatly on her place mat. "That's true."

"I'm sorry to hear it."

"You'll probably be even sorrier when you find out who he is," she said.

"Why's that?"

"Do you like football?"

He slung an arm over the back of the booth. "Let's see...I already have a couple strikes against me for the finance questions and my scientific background. If I want to walk away with my self-esteem intact, I'm guessing yes is a good answer on this. I like football but—" he glanced over at the cowboy who used to be one of her students and let his smile broaden "—rodeo's even better."

"I'd be willing to bet my life savings you've never even *been* to a rodeo," she said.

"I don't look western enough?"

She made a point of leaning over the end of the table to peer down at his loafers.

"These are my city clothes," he said. "I go into a phone booth when I want to become Rodeo Fan."

She laughed and he immediately realized he liked the sound of it. "Okay," she said. "Maybe your book won't be totally dry."

He tried not to feel gratified by her approval. "So who's your brother and what's his connection to football?"

"Gabriel Holbrook. If you're familiar with the NFL, you'll know the connection."

Isaac had been about to take a drink. Now he put his glass down and leaned forward. "*Gabe* Holbrook, the famous quarterback who was paralyzed in a car accident several years ago?"

"That's him."

"Wow." He moved his water glass in small circles on the table. "That must've been very difficult for everyone."

"It was."

"How's he doing?"

"Okay, for the most part. It took some time, but—" she tore the paper off her straw "—he seems to have made the adjustment to his new lifestyle."

"You said he lives around here?"

She suddenly grew leery. "You're not going to chase him down, looking for an autograph, are you?"

"No."

"Okay, then. He has a cabin up in the mountains and a place in town. He coaches football at the high school."

"I read somewhere that Gabe Holbrook was marrying the woman who crashed into him. That's not true, is it?"

She took a sip of her drink, then propped her chin on one fist. "Actually, it is. They're married already. No one thought it'd work out. Even I feared resentment would pop up at one point or another. But the marriage seems solid. They're truly devoted to each other."

"Earlier you said your family has seen more public interest than most. Now I know what you were talking about."

The ice in her glass clinked as she stirred her Coke with her straw. "Actually, that wasn't what I was talking about."

"No?"

"No."

Curiosity prompted Isaac to press her for an explanation, but it really wasn't any of his business. He sobered as his thoughts returned to Keith and Elizabeth and the reason behind his visit. "According to Judy, you married young."

She shrugged. "I knew what I wanted."

"Do you ever regret it? Wish you'd waited? Chosen a different path?"

"Of course not," she responded. "You've seen my kids."

He wiped the condensation from his water glass. "Judy also said Keith travels a lot. That's okay with you?"

A hint of dissatisfaction showed in her expression, the same dissatisfaction he'd noted earlier, but she quickly masked it. "The travel's an issue, but we're dealing with it. When you love someone as much as I love Keith, you do what you can to accommodate their work schedule."

If she suspected that her husband was doing anything wrong, *anything at all,* she didn't show it.

"Is Keith usually home for the holidays?" Isaac didn't remember Elizabeth complaining about Keith being gone for Christmas or Thanksgiving. But Isaac had been out of the country for much of the past three years. And his sister wasn't the type to complain. She felt too grateful for her family.

"Softscape pays him double to work on Thanksgiving, Christmas and Easter. We usually need the money, so he often takes advantage of it. But he doesn't work all three in the same year. He mixes it up, so he gets to be with us for at least one or two of them."

Isaac was willing to bet he was with Elizabeth, Mica and Christopher for the others. Swallowing a sigh, he pinched the bridge of his nose.

"Is something wrong?" Reenie asked.

Isaac met her gaze. He had to tell her. He couldn't go on taking advantage of her friendliness and innocence. She wasn't a woman who'd knowingly tempted a married man into an adulterous affair. She was as innocent as Elizabeth—a good mother, a devoted wife. "I'm afraid I have some bad—"

"Here you go." Judy approached with their dinners, and Isaac clamped his mouth shut.

The waitress put their plates in front of them, gave him the steak sauce she'd been carrying in one of her apron pockets and asked if they wanted anything else. When they assured her they were all set, she moved on to another table.

"What were you about to say?" Reenie asked as she cut into her chicken.

Isaac stared down at his food. He wanted to get the truth out in the open. But now wasn't the time. He needed to be more prepared to counter the devastation he was about to unleash. Besides, he owed it to Elizabeth to speak to her first. "It doesn't matter."

"Maybe you wanted to move on to how folks in this town clean their toilets," she teased.

For a moment, he was tempted to give in to her levity and simply enjoy their meal. She was attractive, easy to be around. But knowing what lay in store for her chased all good feelings away.

"Why not tell me a little about your philosophy on divorce," he said.

She washed her food down with a drink of soda. "Simply put, I don't believe in it."

"Sometimes it's unavoidable," he pointed out.

"That's true. But if you've got kids, you can't give up too easily."

He'd dressed his baked potato. Now he pushed it around his plate.

"That means if Keith did something wrong, you'd probably forgive him?"

"If I could."

He cursed to himself. Elizabeth would probably answer the same way.

"You're not eating," she said, pointing her fork toward his plate. "Is your steak too rare?"

"Actually, it's perfect. I just…I think I feel a migraine coming on."

"Oh boy." Her eyes filled with concern. "Do you have any medication with you?"

"No, but—"

"Then you'd better come back to the house with me. Keith gets migraines all the time. I know how to get rid of them. But it's important to catch it early."

"That's okay," he said. He had a headache, but it wasn't really a migraine. And he'd already learned what he wanted to know. Now he felt guilty for having lied in order to obtain the information. He hadn't expected to admire Reenie so much, to genuinely like her. When he'd appeared at her door, he'd been acting in defense of his sister. "I think I'll go over to the motel, maybe try and get some sleep."

"You won't be able to sleep once the pain really hits."

"I'll live."

She looked as though she might argue with him, but Judy interrupted. "Reenie, your babysitter called. She wants you to call her back."

Worry creased Reenie's forehead. "Is everything okay?"

"She said to tell you the kids are fine. She just needs to talk to you."

Isaac offered to let her use his cell phone, but she shook her head and slid out of the booth. "We don't get good service up here."

Because he'd lost his appetite, Isaac fiddled with his cell phone while she was gone. He'd been so preoccupied with Reenie he hadn't tried to call anyone since arriving in Dundee. He saw now that she was right. He didn't have service, probably because of the mountains.

She returned a few minutes later and started gathering her coat and purse. "I'm sorry, but I've got to go."

"What's wrong?"

"My babysitter has to go home. Her mother isn't feeling well and needs her to watch her younger siblings."

"Is her mother so sick that you can't finish your dinner?"

"I didn't ask. But it's okay. I'll take it with me."

"Of course." He waved for Judy to bring her a container.

"Here." She wrote her number and e-mail address on the back of a napkin. "If you have any more questions on your book, let me know."

"Thanks," he said.

"I'll give you a great deal on the Jeep if you want to make an offer," she added, and tossed him another smile as she hurried out of the diner.

Isaac watched her through the window as she climbed into her minivan. Reenie was something special. No doubt about that. But he was sort of relieved to have her gone. He felt too guilty knowing what he did, too uncomfortable anticipating her pain.

Fortunately, he wouldn't be around to witness her devastation. That thought brought a small measure of relief. Having a front-row seat to Elizabeth's suffering would be bad enough.

Judy came by with his check. He stood, tossed a ten-dollar bill on the table for her tip and paid at the register.

He was about to step outside when Judy intercepted him. "You're not heading out Reenie's way, are you?" she asked.

He hesitated. "No, why?"

She frowned as she held up a brown leather wallet. "I found this on the ground near your table."

"Are you sure it belongs to her?"

She flipped it open to show him Reenie's driver's license.

Isaac kept his hand on the door. He wasn't about to assume responsibility for returning Reenie's wallet. He'd just congratulated himself on the fact that their paths would never cross again. She could come back and pick it up later.

But she had the little kids, who were probably already in bed, and no babysitter.

Certainly he could run it out to her. How long could a quick knock at the door and a simple "Here you go" take?

"Okay, I can drop it by, if you like," he told Judy.

She pressed the wallet into his hand with a grateful smile. "Thanks. I wouldn't want to tempt some of the short-order cooks by leaving it lying around here."

"No problem," he said, and shoved the wallet into his coat pocket.

CHAPTER SEVEN

As much as Isaac would have preferred to slip Reenie's wallet inside the screen door and walk away, he couldn't. If she discovered it was missing, she might panic. Or the dog could get hold of it and chew it to pieces.

He knocked and forced himself to wait on the stoop.

A moment later, the door swung open and Reenie welcomed him with a friendly smile. "Hi. Change your mind about letting me help you get rid of that headache?"

"No." He lifted her wallet into the hazy glow of the porch light. "You left this at the restaurant. I just wanted to drop it by."

"How nice of you."

"It was no trouble," he said as he handed it to her. "Have a good evening."

He started to walk away, but she spoke before he could clear the porch. "While you're here, why not come in and have some peppermint tea? Then I can show you a few exercises that will ease the pain in your head."

Isaac had never tried a home remedy for migraines that actually worked. Fortunately, he didn't suffer from the headaches very often and, when he did, his weren't as severe as those endured by a lot of folks. "I'll be fine."

"Don't be so stubborn." Her eyebrows gathered in annoyance. "It's stupid to suffer when I can help you. It'll only take a minute."

When he hesitated, she opened the door wider. "Come in and sit down."

The expectation in her manner made it difficult for him to refuse. What would it hurt to let her give him a cup of tea and explain her cure for migraines?

With a shrug, he stepped inside her living room. It was only eight-thirty. Now that he knew all he needed to know, he planned on returning to Boise instead of staying in Dundee. But he still had plenty of time to drive there and rent a motel room before it grew too late.

"Make yourself comfortable," she said. "I'll get your tea."

Surrounded by a series of black-and-white photographs of her family, he sat on the couch while waiting for her to return from the kitchen. According to the signature in the bottom right-hand corner of the photos, they'd been taken by someone named Hannah Holbrook. Reenie had told him she had only one sibling, so he guessed Hannah had to be her mother, her brother's new wife or maybe an aunt. On the piano he discovered Keith and Reenie's wedding picture and couldn't help getting up to examine it.

They made a handsome, happy-looking couple. So where had things gone wrong? Had Keith always had a wandering eye? Or had Elizabeth been his first affair?

Footsteps sounded in the hall and Reenie returned carrying a steaming mug. "I can't believe you weren't going to let me help you," she said.

The scent of peppermint tea filled the air. "You did help me."

She handed the mug to him. "With your research?"

He kept his attention on the brown liquid in his cup. "Exactly. I hated to ask you for anything else."

"Hey, you're a friend of my husband's. That makes you a friend of mine."

A friend of her husband's....God, if she only knew.

"You have some nice furniture," he said, because it was true and he wanted to change the subject.

She beamed at him. "Gabe makes it."

"Your brother? The ex-*football* player?"

"Good, isn't he?"

"Very."

"He started working with wood right after the accident. Now he makes all kinds of things. He and Hannah sell certain pieces out of the lobby of her photography studio."

That answered his question about the photographs. "Hannah does nice work, too."

"She does. You should drop by her studio while you're in town."

"Maybe I will." Except he wouldn't be in town after tonight. With Reenie as forthcoming as she'd been, there was no longer any need.

The phone rang. She excused herself to answer it while Isaac sipped his tea and continued to circle the room.

"Can I call you later? I'm with someone," she said, her voice carrying back to him. "He's a friend of Keith's…they used to work together."

Isaac sat on the edge of the couch, feeling uncomfortable again.

"Yeah…at Softscape, several years ago… Okay… Wait, have you called Lucky yet?… Why not?… Jeez, Gabe… The party's next week."

It was her brother.

"A lot of good," she said. "No, but…" At that point, she must've moved into another part of the house, because Isaac could no longer make out what she was saying.

He waited, wondering how many times Keith had sat in this very room. Did his brother-in-law ever regret what he was doing? Fear discovery?

Closing his eyes, Isaac leaned back on the couch and thought about calling Liz. He wanted to get his terrible announcement over with. Tonight. But he decided to wait and tell her in person, so he'd be there to help with the kids, give her a chance to recover. Somehow, he and his sister would get through the coming weeks just like they'd survived the years with Luanna.

Finally he heard Reenie's voice again, saying goodbye. When she came back into the room, he stood to hand her his cup.

"Tea was great," he said. "Thank you. I'm feeling much better already."

"Good."

"I'd better get going."

She blinked in surprise. "But we're not finished yet."

"I still need to rent a room." *In Boise…*

"Give me another minute or two. They're not going to fill up at the Timberline." She set his cup on a neat stack of magazines. "Have you ever heard of One-Eye Integration treatment?"

"No."

"It's usually for people suffering from post-traumatic stress disorder. But someone did a study somewhere that showed it's effective for migraines."

She'd managed to pique his interest in spite of his eagerness to leave. "What does it entail?"

"Eye exercises, basically. By manipulating your field of vision, you can dramatically reduce your headache symptoms. Just cover one eye and—"

The telephone rang again.

"I'm sorry," she said with a helpless shrug. "I'll be right back."

Isaac silently cursed this new delay. He should've left when he had the chance. He wanted a few minutes alone on the Internet to research what might happen to Keith, and to plan what he was going to say to Elizabeth. Maybe he should sit down with his sister *and* his brother-in-law, so Keith would have to admit the truth.

Reenie was coming down the hall. Still preoccupied and anxious to be gone, Isaac turned expectantly toward the entrance of the room, then caught what she was saying into the phone. "No, it'll be better as a surprise. Just a minute…"

Dread filled Isaac as she appeared.

"Guess who I have on the phone?" she said brightly.

"Who?" he replied. But he had a sinking feeling he already knew.

KEITH'S BLOOD RAN COLD the moment he heard the man on the other end of the phone. It was Isaac. He instantly recognized his brother-in-law's voice and could hardly speak for the fear that seized him.

"Wh-what are you d-doing in Dundee?" he asked. He didn't know what else to say. Isaac was supposed to be in Phoenix, golfing this week. How could he have discovered Reenie?

"It's over, Keith," Isaac said simply. "It's all over."

Keith stared bleakly at the other parents in the gymnasium who were watching Mica's gymnastics class. Before he'd withdrawn to return Reenie's "urgent" message, he'd been talking and laughing with them. He'd been one of them, no different. Now they seemed so far removed from him. "What do you mean?" he whispered. "What's over? I don't know what you're talking about." On one level, the significance of finding Isaac at his house in Dundee registered; on another it didn't. The idea of Isaac standing in the same room as Reenie was too horrible to contemplate.

"Of course you do." Isaac's voice came through low and somber. "I'm looking at your wedding picture right now."

"I—oh, God, Isaac, please. What have you told Reenie?"

"Nothing. I wanted to talk to you and Elizabeth first. But…I wasn't expecting… Now I can't—"

"You'll hurt them both," he interrupted. "You know that, don't you? Stay out of it. Leave it alone."

"I can't do that."

Panic shredded Keith's nerves. "Think of the damage you'll do!"

"You caused this, Keith, not me."

The heavy sadness that permeated those words stole Keith's breath. He would have felt better if Isaac had ranted and raved or screamed at him. This unyielding response gave him no room to cajole or justify. "I have kids," he said helplessly.

"I know. That makes the situation even worse, doesn't it? Anyway, I'd—I'd rather not talk about it now. I'm coming to Los Angeles tomorrow. I'll call you when I get in. Make sure you're available."

Keith could've sworn he had a steel ball crushing his chest. Reenie. What must she be thinking? He could hear her in the background, her voice rising as she demanded to know what was going on.

If Isaac told her, Keith knew she'd never forgive him. They'd been together for eleven years. She'd see what he'd done as the worst kind of betrayal. No one would understand how each decision had been forced by the one before it. "You have to let me explain."

"I'd like you to do that, Keith. I really would. I can't help hoping there *is* an explanation. Because Elizabeth doesn't deserve this. From what I can tell, Reenie doesn't deserve it, either. They've both been good…" Keith waited for him to say *wives* and felt a bead of sweat trickle down from his temple. Fortunately, Reenie spoke at that moment, and Isaac veered away from using that word. "They've been good to you."

"I—I didn't mean for it to end up this way. You have to believe me. Think of your sister and Mica and Christopher. Certainly you love them as much as I do."

"Don't try to manipulate me," Isaac warned.

Keith felt like a drowning man clawing at the slippery rocks of a canyon wall. "I couldn't walk away from them, Isaac. I—I didn't know how to tell them. How could I?"

"You should've found a way."

"Don't get involved, please? Stay out of it."

"It's too late."

"No! I'll make up something to explain this to Reenie."

"Keith—"

"Give me the phone!" It was Reenie, sounding almost hysterical.

God... "It would be better to leave things as they are," Keith said, his words coming much faster than usual. "Believe me, I think about the situation all the time, searching for a way out. There isn't one. Not now. Maybe when the kids are older—"

"Are you *joking?*" Isaac interrupted. "You should've told the truth from the beginning. You—"

Suddenly Reenie came on the line, sounding as breathless and panicked as he felt. "Keith, what's happening? Who is Isaac? Why is he here?"

"Honey, I...I love you. I'm coming home. Do you hear me? Don't do anything until I get there. I'm coming home. I'll quit my job. Right now. Buy you the farm as soon as I get there. I won't leave Dundee again. I promise, okay?"

There was a terrified silence as these words sank in. "Keith, what have you done? It's something that will tear our family apart, isn't it?"

"Not if we don't let it, honey."

"There's another woman?"

He cringed at the high pitch of her voice. "There's no other woman for me, Reenie. Just you. I promise. I'm coming. I'll explain everything," he said. But how? He'd lied to her for *nine years.* He had other children to support, other responsibilities. He'd been sleeping with another woman half of every month, a woman who depended on him as much as she did.

A pain-filled cry came through the phone. It traveled through him like a shard of glass. The cover-up was over. He'd known it had to end soon. He was exhausted and had been for the past several years. But not like this....

Maybe once he was back in Dundee he could convince Reenie that it had all been a terrible mistake. If she realized the dilemma he'd faced, maybe she'd forgive him. Reenie was an unusual woman, stronger than most. She'd stay with him for the sake of their girls, right? Which might give him enough time to resurrect their relationship. As much as he loved Elizabeth and

Mica and Christopher, he'd known all along that it couldn't last forever.

Wiping the sweat on his forehead with his sleeve, he tried not to think about them. They'd be devastated. He'd be devastated, too. He already was. But he had no choice now, except to let them go. He'd send them money. Reenie would have to allow that much. The court would mandate it. Eventually, he'd find relief in knowing he had nothing left to hide.

"Reenie, get Isaac out of there. He'll destroy us, destroy our family, do you hear?" he said.

"I don't know what to believe," she whispered.

"Trust me. I'm coming home." He hung up, then told Mica's friend's father that he had an emergency and asked for help getting Mica home.

An expression of concern wilted the man's smile. "Sure, no problem. Are you okay, buddy? It's not Liz, is it?"

"No," Keith muttered.

"You don't look so good—"

Keith didn't wait to hear the rest. He dashed out to his car and headed straight to the airport. He felt terrible for abandoning Elizabeth so suddenly, without a word. Briefly he considered calling her on his cell phone but quickly discarded the idea. What would he say? He couldn't tell her. Not right now. His palms were sweating; his heart was pounding. He was having some kind of anxiety attack. He shouldn't even be driving, but he had no choice. He had to reach Dundee. Isaac would take care of Liz when he arrived tomorrow. She'd be okay. But Keith feared if he waited even a moment longer, he'd lose Reenie.

He prayed it wasn't too late already.

ISAAC WATCHED tears course down Reenie's cheeks as she glared at him. After Keith had hung up, she'd let the phone drop to the floor. It beeped loudly, but he didn't bother to pick it up.

"You lied to me." She spoke softly, but there was a fierce anger in her words. "You're not who you said you were."

He drew a deep breath. "Yes and no." God, this was what he'd hoped to avoid. Elizabeth was his responsibility, not this stranger. But as angry as Reenie was, he couldn't turn away from the pain in her eyes. She was just as innocent, just as hurt as Elizabeth was going to be. "I'm Isaac Russell, but I'm not writing a book on small-town relationships."

"You used me."

"I did what I had to do and now...now that you know this much, you should hear the rest."

Her eyes were wide, frightened. "The rest of what?" she asked, but raised a hand before he could answer. "No, I won't listen. You're lying. You've got to be lying. Again. Like before." Her hands curled into fists. "I want you to leave."

Isaac jammed his fingers through his hair. "Is there someone I can call to stay with you tonight?"

"No. Get out. Get out right now!"

Isaac didn't want to push her any further, but he couldn't leave her alone like this, either.

"Let's call someone," he said. "Your brother. What's Gabe's number?"

"Get out." She grabbed his arm and tried to drag him to the door. "You have no right to be here. I've asked you to leave!"

Her strength surprised him. "I'll go in a minute," he promised, and set her aside as gently as possible.

She grabbed him again. Only this time she seemed less angry. Torn, yes. Panicked, yes. And...hurt. She was shaking so badly, he feared she might be in shock. "Tell me everything," she said, squeezing her eyes closed against the tears that were beginning to fall.

Isaac took her hands. They felt small, cold. "Reenie—"

"Just tell me," she said, her body tensing, as if preparing for a physical blow.

Isaac could almost see the terror rising in her, threatening to take control, could feel the shudders as they passed through her. He had to do something.

Leaning forward, he pushed the hair away from her ear and held her tightly. "It's worse than an affair, Reenie. Your husband is married to my sister."

She tried to jerk away, but he held her to him in an effort to calm her. The quicker he told her the rest, the better. "He met her on a plane, got her pregnant and married her."

She gasped as though he'd just shot her, and he wished there'd been a gentler way to break the news. "I'm so sorry."

She sank onto the couch without responding.

"Reenie?"

"You can go," she said, her voice suddenly deadpan.

Isaac wanted to sit with her, but he knew he wasn't the right person to offer comfort. She'd only fight him. He needed to get someone else over here, someone she trusted, who'd look after her and the girls until Keith arrived.

"How can I reach your brother?"

She didn't answer.

"Reenie?"

Nothing.

She had to have a list of numbers somewhere. Striding briskly from the room, he stood in the hall and tried to orient himself. Where was the damn kitchen?

Through an open doorway to his right, he saw a tiled countertop. But a sleep-tousled Jennifer emerged from another room and nearly stumbled into him just as he started toward it.

"Where's my mother? What's wrong with her?" she asked worriedly.

"She's a little upset right now," he told her. "But she'll be fine." He hoped. "Can you tell me how to reach your Uncle Gabe?"

The girl split a worried look between him and the opening to the living room down the hall, from which they could hear Reenie's muffled crying. Her mother's sobs obviously disturbed her, but she led him to a phone list on the fridge before slipping away.

Isaac found the number he was looking for and dialed.

"Hello?" The person who answered sounded like a young boy.

"Is your father home?"

"Yes. Can I tell him who's calling?"

"Isaac Russell."

"Just a minute, please."

Isaac paced back and forth for several long seconds, listening as Jennifer tried to comfort Reenie. "Are you okay, Mommy? What's wrong? Mommy?"

Blowing out a frustrated sigh, he pivoted and paced back. Finally, a deep voice came across the line. "Hello?"

"Mr. Holbrook?"

"Yes?"

"This is Isaac Russell."

"Who?"

"Who I am doesn't really matter. Your sister needs you. Can you come over right away? Or send someone else in the family?"

"What's wrong?" he asked, his concern apparent.

"Keith's run into some…problems."

"He isn't hurt, is he?"

"Physically, no one's hurt. But it's not a pretty picture. Reenie will explain when you get here," he said. Then he hung up. There wasn't anything else he could do for these people. Now that Keith was on his way to Dundee, Isaac needed to reach his sister as soon as possible.

CHAPTER EIGHT

THE SILENCE FELT ODD, unnatural as Reenie rolled over in bed. She was still half asleep, and yet she knew something was wrong. Something terrible. The wisp of a memory threatened to surface. She attempted to suppress it but heard Isaac Russell murmuring those hateful words in her ear again and was instantly overwhelmed with grief.

For the first time in her life, she wasn't sure she could handle what lay ahead.

Hushed voices coming from the kitchen reached her ears. Her girls. Why were they whispering? What about school? She had to get up. She felt as though she'd been run over by a bus. But she had a responsibility to care for her children.

She tried to shove herself into a sitting position, only to fall back, too weak and exhausted to move. "This can't be happening," she muttered, and tried again. On her second attempt, she managed to sit up and scoot to the edge of the bed, where she blinked against the light filtering through the slats of her blinds. Someone had turned the clock away from her. Who?

As if in answer, she heard a man's voice mingling with her children's. It was Gabe. Of course. Her brother had come over right after Isaac Russell had left.

The other details about last night—the way Keith had sounded on the phone, the palpable guilt in his reaction—started coming back to her in wave upon wave of sickening mental images and sounds. No use resisting. Maybe the truth was too painful to fully embrace, but she couldn't escape it. She already knew the terrible secret Isaac had brought to her door was true. Keith had been cheating on her for years. He had another *wife*, other *children*...a *family* that he went to each time he left her.

Bile rose in her throat. She choked it back while staring at her bare toes. Life-shattering catastrophes didn't happen to her. Her poor brother had lost the use of his legs. Her father had rocked their family with a twenty-four-year-old secret. But she'd always been able to console herself by searching for the bright side. At least Gabe was still alive. At least her father hadn't abandoned them as he could've done.

Where was the bright side in this? She'd been living a lie. And now it was all clear. Why she'd sensed a growing detachment in her husband. Why Keith had fought her so hard when she'd begged him to quit his job. Why he never called when he was away and only responded to urgent messages.

She remembered Isaac's questions in the restaurant. *How do you know how much he makes?... Because he tells me... Do you file your taxes separately?*

She dropped her aching head into her hands. She'd made it easy for her husband to deceive her. She'd been too gullible, too trusting.

But where was Keith's conscience? How could he lie to her so unashamedly? Betray her so completely? Betray their children? And when, exactly, had it all started?

There was so much she didn't know. The news had hit her hard, and she hadn't pressed Isaac for any of the nasty details. Now, question upon question whirled through her mind, along with confusion and doubt and a terrible, seething rage.

A click told her someone had just opened the door. She glanced over her shoulder to see Gabe peek into the room.

"I'm up," she said, wondering how she could sound so normal.

Wearing a sweater and a pair of faded jeans, he rolled a few inches into the room. With his thick black hair, vivid blue eyes and muscular build, he was as strong and handsome as ever. She'd idolized him as a child, was still incredibly proud of him.

"How do you feel?" he asked.

She raked her fingers through her tousled hair. *Like hell.* How would anyone feel? "Fine," she said. "I need to get up, feed the girls."

"Don't worry about the girls. They've eaten. Hannah just left to take them to school."

Thank God for her brother and sister-in-law. Gabe and Hannah had their own children, but maybe Kenny, who was seventeen, had helped out with Brent, his nine-year-old brother. Reenie was grateful they had stepped in for her. She couldn't remember ever needing that kind of help before. She was generally highly functional, efficient. Wouldn't folks be surprised to see that she couldn't put one foot in front of the other today?

"What'd you give me last night?" she asked.

He rolled a little closer, concern a dark shadow on his rugged face. "You wouldn't take any sleeping pills."

"So you put them in the tea you brought me, right?"

When he didn't respond, she grimaced. "My mouth's so dry I can hardly swallow."

"I wanted to make sure you'd sleep," he said. "I thought some rest would help you...cope."

"Cope," she echoed, chuckling mirthlessly. "I guess my life isn't what it seemed, huh?"

"*Keith* isn't what he seemed. That doesn't change anything else."

Gabe was wrong. She'd built her life on the foundation of her marriage. She'd built her children's lives on the same thing. Where did she go from here? "So what do you think?" she asked.

"About what?"

"My sham of a marriage."

"I don't want to tell you what I think."

"Why not?"

"It might make you defensive of Keith."

She grimaced. "I doubt that."

"He called a few minutes ago."

"What'd he say?"

Gabe shifted in his chair. "He's at the airport in Boise, on his way home. He begged me to reserve judgment until he gets here."

"Can you do that?"

"I'll listen to what he has to say, but…"

She waited for the rest. His chest lifted in a deep breath before he continued, "It won't make any difference. Either this other woman exists, or she doesn't."

Exactly. And Reenie already knew she existed. She knew it deep in her bones. "Do you think I'll ever be able to forgive him, Gabe?"

He hesitated, as if choosing his words carefully. "You might be able to forgive him, but trust is another issue entirely. And there'll always be this…other family."

She stared at the tiny slices of light at the edge of her blinds. Odd how the simple things she'd never paid much attention to before suddenly seemed so exaggerated.

"Do you want me to tell him to pack his bags?" Gabe asked at last.

Yesterday she thought she and Keith would spend the rest of their lives together.

"Do you know how to get hold of Isaac Russell?" she asked, not answering his question.

"He left his number on the counter and I put it in my day planner. Why?"

"I need it."

Her brother took his day planner from the pouch on his chair where he always kept it. "Here you go."

She dialed as he read off the number. Then the phone began to ring. Once, twice, three times. Reenie was just about to hang up. She didn't plan on leaving a message. Then Isaac answered.

"Hello?"

She cringed at the voice of the man who'd brought such devastation to her doorstep, the brother of her husband's *other* wife.

God, this can't be real....

"When did it start?" she asked without preamble.

He immediately knew who she was and understood what she wanted. Maybe her question was one he'd been expecting her to ask last night. "Nine years ago."

She'd been prepared for a blow, but nine years still knocked the wind out of her. Nine years was a long time to live a lie. "How many children do—" she struggled to swallow "—do Keith and...and this woman have? One?"

"No, two. And her name's Elizabeth, by the way."

She could sense Isaac's stubborn loyalty and knew it made them enemies. "Two," she repeated, as if venturing out on a ledge she wasn't quite sure could hold her.

"An athletic boy and a very bright girl," he added.

A numbing coldness swept through Reenie. "What—" she took a bolstering breath "—what're the children's names?"

"Reenie, listen—"

"What're their names?"

She heard him sigh into the phone and knew he wasn't enjoying the confrontation any more than she was. "Christopher and Mica."

"Did she know about me? Your sister, I mean?"

"No. She's not that kind of person."

She believed him. But the fact that she couldn't blame his sister somehow made everything worse. The man she loved had done this to her. Keith alone was to blame.

Reenie massaged her temples. She couldn't seem to think straight, to sort out this tragedy.

"He's on his way back to you," Isaac said. "You know that, don't you?"

She remembered Keith's panicked response. *I'll quit my job right now, buy you the farm.* During the past two months, she'd all but begged him for both. He'd made her feel selfish for even asking, then flown off to be with his other family. He'd been lying to her *for nine years*. Lying as he made love to her. Lying as he told Jennifer he couldn't come to her play because of his work. Lying, lying, lying. She couldn't see an end to the lies....

He couldn't love her and hurt her the way that he had.

"Tell your sister she can have him," she said, and hung up.

IN L.A. THE DAY WAS GRAY and drizzly, but Elizabeth was wearing sunglasses when Isaac threw his small bag into the back of her white SUV and climbed in the passenger side. She mumbled a greeting but barely looked at him before checking traffic and pulling away from the curb. Mica and the kids had to be in school because they weren't in the car. Isaac was grateful for that. He wanted to be able to speak candidly, work through this mess one hurdle at a time.

"The weather turned almost the day after you left," his sister said as if the lack of sunshine was important. She was wearing a pair of brown wool slacks with a beige turtleneck sweater and leather boots. If Isaac didn't know what had happened, he wouldn't have guessed from her appearance. Although her face was devoid of makeup and she'd combed her hair into a low ponytail instead of her usual more sophisticated style, she looked as collected as always. The sunglasses, and the strain in her voice, provided the only clues that today wasn't a day like any other.

His sister was a real class act.

What Keith had done was so grossly unfair.

Liz drove past the other terminals and finally swung out of the airport. When they came to a stoplight, she turned her windshield wipers up to combat the falling rain, and Isaac's gaze fell to her hands. He'd been wrong a moment earlier, he realized. There were more clues to her fragility than he'd first noticed. Her fingernails, usually perfectly manicured, had nasty sores around the cuticles. She'd been picking at them. He knew because it was the same nervous habit she'd had as a child. One she'd worked hard to overcome. She also wasn't wearing her wedding ring or the tennis bracelet Keith had given her.

"You okay?" he said.

She nodded, but he couldn't get past those painful-looking fingers. She'd probably paced the floor, digging at herself the entire night. How was she holding herself together? When he'd called her after leaving Reenie's house, he'd found her almost frantic with worry. Since Keith had suddenly disappeared, Isaac had been forced to tell her.

His words had been met with dead silence. Afraid that she'd collapsed, he'd called her name several times, and she'd finally answered—quietly and without tears. Certainly she hadn't reacted to her husband's betrayal in the same vocal, angry way that Reenie had. Reenie was confident enough to acknowledge and express her pain, and to feel justified in doing so.

That was normal; *this* was not.

"Liz." Isaac squeezed her shoulder, hoping to lend her his strength. "I'm so sorry."

"I know," she said softly, but she was still sitting stiffly in her seat, staring at the snake of bumper-to-bumper traffic ahead of them.

"That's it?" he said as they inched their way toward Interstate 10. "That's all you've got to say?"

When there was some space between her and the car in front of her, she eased off the brake and let the SUV roll forward a few feet. "My husband left me last night. What do you want me to say?"

Did she think she could cope with this the same way she'd coped with so many other unfortunate events in her life—by simply absorbing the hurt and shock and carrying on as if nothing was wrong?

"Holding the pain inside will only make it worse, Liz."

When she spoke, he detected a deep reservoir of emotion behind her words. "And letting it out will change what, exactly?"

"Venting might help you to recover."

"How will it do that?"

"I don't know. Most women would cry if they faced what you're facing right now, wouldn't they?"

A slight crease marked her normally smooth, high forehead. "I've never been like most women, Isaac. You know that. Maybe that's why Luanna hated me so much."

The car in front of them slowed, and they came to an abrupt stop.

"Luanna hated you because she was a jealous, coldhearted bitch," he said. "She didn't want to compete for Dad's attention, so she edged you out of the picture as much as possible. What happened after Mom died wasn't your fault. It's just the way things were."

She tore her eyes from the road. "I can't change this, either, Isaac. I have to deal with it whether I want to or not."

She had him there.

"My point is that you did nothing to cause it. Keith was already married when he met you. Had things been the other way around, maybe this would never have happened." Isaac hoped that thought would bring her a small measure of comfort, but if Keith could cheat on a woman as passionate and animated as Reenie, he could probably cheat on anyone. If Isaac had his guess, Keith's behavior had nothing to do with finding either Liz or Reenie inadequate.

"Have you talked to him?" he asked when she didn't respond.

She changed lanes and gunned the SUV, only to slam on the brake two seconds later to avoid crashing into the back of a Suburban. "He finally answered my many messages. This morning. When he arrived in Boise."

The lane they'd abandoned began to move more quickly than the one they were in now, which was in keeping with the luck they were having in general. "What did he say?" Isaac asked.

"That he's going to quit his job. He won't be returning to California."

"Reenie told me she won't take him back. She said you could have him."

"Reenie?"

"That's her name. Remember? I told you last night."

"Yeah, well, maybe he doesn't yet know she won't take him back. Anyway…" She turned on her blinker and switched lanes again.

Isaac wished the traffic would ease before they rearended someone. "Anyway?" he prompted when she didn't immediately continue.

"He said she's an emotional woman, but that she'll calm down and eventually do whatever is necessary to hold her family together."

Isaac had been in such a hurry to reach the airport this morning, he hadn't bothered to shave. Now he rubbed the stubble on his chin as he pictured the spunky woman he'd had dinner with last night. "She might," he admitted.

"I'm sure he knows her pretty well. He's been married to her for eleven years, right?"

Isaac winced. "Right."

They drove in silence for a few seconds. "Have you told Mica and Christopher?" he asked.

"Not yet. I've got to, of course. Soon, so they'll understand what's happening. But…" Her voice finally wobbled. He thought she might break down but, after an extended silence, she lifted her chin and finished as mechanically as she'd begun. "But I've been putting it off. I don't want them suddenly stripped of all security."

As she'd been after their mother had died. "He should give you the house, everything the two of you own."

"I don't care about the house," she said.

"You will once the shock and pain subside."

"No." She shook her head adamantly. "The kids are all that matter to me."

"You don't think he'll fight you for custody?"

"No." Her throat worked for a moment before she got the rest of her words out. "He's not planning on fighting me for anything. He's...walking away, cutting ties. He said he'd send money every month, that he can't promise anything more."

"Money's good," Isaac said, trying to be positive. "After what he's done, that's all you want from him."

Liz looked at him as though he'd just said the most idiotic thing in the world. "Are you kidding me?"

"No. I want you and the kids to have a roof over your heads and food to eat. I'm glad he's willing to acknowledge that responsibility."

"The responsibilities of a father don't end there. If it's only food and rent we're talking about, *I* can work more hours at the dental office or get a better job, and provide that, Isaac. What I can't provide is the relationship Mica and Christopher are losing with their father!"

It was the first time Elizabeth had raised her voice. Isaac waited, hoping she'd give in and really let go. But she quickly reeled in her emotions and spoke calmly again. "They need him."

"They'll...adjust. Eventually," he added, because his response sounded far too trite.

She looked over at him. "You don't understand. Christopher's a very sensitive boy. He worships Keith."

"You didn't choose for this to happen, Liz."

"I don't care. I have to...to protect my son somehow. Do you know how often he—" the furrow in her forehead reappeared "—he asks when his daddy's coming home?"

"I'm sorry about that. You know I am. But there isn't anything you can do about it," he told her honestly.

"Keith can't simply abandon us." Her hands tightened on the steering wheel until he could see the white of her knuckles. "That's not fair. He—he told me he loves me. We...had plans for the future."

"I know."

"Bigamy's illegal. If he won't…if he thinks…anyway, there's always that bit of leverage, right? He won't be able to kiss us off completely."

Isaac scrubbed a hand over his face. Already this wasn't going well. And he had more bad news. "As long as he pays child support, there's a strong possibility he could do just that, Liz."

"What?" She swerved into the other lane, then jerked back before hitting another car. The driver she'd nearly sideswiped honked and flipped her the finger as he passed by, but she did nothing in response, except dig at her cuticles.

Isaac wanted to chase down the other driver. He needed a target for his own anger, and this impatient stranger seemed like the perfect candidate.

"Stop picking at yourself," he said firmly, covering her hand. She scowled but quit.

"And why don't you pull over and let me drive?"

"I'm fine."

"Liz…"

"I said I'm fine."

Rather than argue with her, he went back to their conversation. "Well, even if you eventually decide that you'd like to see him in prison for what he's done, chances are good that won't happen."

"How do you know?"

The cars ahead slowed yet again. Traffic in L.A. drove Isaac crazy. The jammed freeway, the discourteous driver who'd just flipped them off, this horrible situation. He craved the escape of the jungle worse than ever before. But now, even if the grant came through, he couldn't leave. "This morning I called a friend of mine who works in the Attorney General's office in Illinois."

"And?"

Her fingers looked as though he'd need a crowbar to pry them off the steering wheel. "He said we can call the police, but the D.A. probably won't prosecute."

"Why not?"

Isaac fidgeted with his seat belt, bothered, along with everything else, by the chest restraint. "For starters, we have a jurisdiction problem. Because Keith has been living in both Idaho and California, they'd first have to decide which state would take the case."

"For crying out loud. That can't be too hard,"

"In theory. Anyway, the D.A. who ultimately gets the case would have to believe it worthy of his time and effort. And—"

"How can it not be worthy of his time and effort?" she snapped. "Lord knows we have enough proof."

"Bigamy's a felony, but it's not a violent crime."

"So what?"

"Keith wasn't abusive, and he's always provided for his children. Those two things will stand in his favor. Think about it. If he goes to prison, he'll no longer be able to support either family."

"But if the police won't do anything to stop this sort of thing, what's to keep other men from committing the same crime?"

"The kind of man who would do what Keith has done isn't generally the type of man who would also support both families. They'd get him on something else."

"So there's no legal recourse?"

"Not really. Even if the D.A. agrees to prosecute, Keith will likely wind up with nothing worse than a few years of parole and some mandatory community service."

Her fingers twitched, but she left her cuticles alone. "This is... this is unbelievable."

"I know, but we'll work through it together. We'll figure out a fair amount of support and—"

"I don't want to talk about support anymore," she said.

"The whole thing's a shock," he replied. "But you'll recover. I'll stay here in L.A. with you as long as you need me."

"What does she look like?"

The sudden change in subject took Isaac by surprise. "What?"

"You heard me. What does his other wife look like?"

Obviously, her mind was bouncing around, still trying to grasp the full extent of the catastrophe. But Isaac knew she wouldn't like the truth. He hesitated, wondering how to answer.

"Isaac?" she pressed.

"She's...small," he said.

"And?"

"Dark hair."

"Great, we're opposites."

He said nothing.

"Is she beautiful?" she asked.

"Liz..."

"Tell me." She raised her eyebrows expectantly.

"Stop torturing yourself," he said with a scowl.

"She *is* beautiful."

"It doesn't matter. *You're* beautiful."

"But she's the one who's walking away from this with her family intact!"

"You don't really want Keith anymore, do you? Not now. Not after everything he's done."

"This isn't about me, Isaac. Keith now lives in Idaho, which means my kids will never get to see their father."

"In the long run, maybe things are better that way."

"Better for whom?" she cried.

"For you."

"But not for my children!"

"We can make him pay child support. We can't make him visit the kids."

Her eyes darted nervously over the road as she worried her bottom lip. "If we lived closer to him, I know he'd see them. He loves them. That much of what we had *has* to be real!"

"You don't live anywhere near him," he reminded her. "Not anymore."

"We could," she said. "All we have to do is move to Idaho."

CHAPTER NINE

REENIE FELT oddly removed from the situation, as if she was standing outside herself, watching what was taking place in her living room. Yet she'd slept with Keith for eleven years. She'd cooked for him, washed his clothes, planned his birthday parties, borne his children. How could he be facing her right now with tears in his eyes, begging her to believe that he'd merely "screwed up"? That she should give him another chance?

Maybe if he'd had a one-night stand, she could make an allowance. They spent a lot of time apart. She could understand being tempted. But he'd *married* another woman. Whenever she managed to dredge up some hope that they'd be able to salvage their marriage, the image of that other woman and her children waiting for him, kissing him hello, sending him off—everything she'd done herself—created an impenetrable barricade around her heart.

Gabe sat in the doorway leading to the kitchen, a silent but brooding presence. She could sense the rage he felt toward Keith, a man he'd always liked before last night.

Her life had reversed itself so completely. The events of the past fifteen hours seemed absolutely surreal.

She glanced at the clock ticking on top of the piano, conscious of the fact that Jennifer, Angela and Isabella would soon be getting out of school. What would they come home to? Would they have to hear that their parents were splitting up? That their father had been asked to move out? Or could she somehow save them from that?

"Reenie?" Keith looked at her imploringly. "Are you listening to me? I said we'd buy the farm, do anything you want."

She'd heard that part, understood it easily enough. The part she *couldn't* grasp was how he'd kept his actions a secret for so long. And what had made him want to develop a long-term relationship with another woman in the first place. He'd never once mentioned that he was unhappy. He'd never said she was falling short in any way. He'd said only that he loved her, that they'd be together forever, that they were a *family.*

Had he told his other wife the same things? Made the same promises?

"I don't know what to say," she admitted.

He didn't bother to wipe the tears that fell down his cheeks. Sliding off the edge of his chair, he went down on his knees and took hold of her limp hand. "You're just sitting there, staring at me," he said. "Where's the passionate woman I love?"

"She's lost," Reenie said simply. She'd already cried so long and hard, the anger had drained right out of her. In its place was a dull acceptance, like what she'd experienced when little Isabella had broken the handblown vase Reenie's parents had bought her when she'd traveled to Venice with them before her marriage. Of course, this situation was far worse, but underlying her sadness was the same unavoidable truth—tears were useless because there wasn't any way to bring the vase back. Just as there wasn't any way to recover what she and Keith had lost.

"Maybe you should go now," Gabe suggested, speaking for the first time since Keith had begun his profuse and rambling apology.

Keith put up a hand. "Wait, Gabe, please? I know you think you could never make the same mistake, but…I—I'm only human. Sometimes people do…stupid things, really stupid things. I fell. That's all. Then I didn't know how to get out of the mess I'd created. Liz…"

"Liz," Reenie echoed, but it wasn't a question, it was a statement. "Liz," she repeated again, mulling over the casual sound of the other woman's name on her husband's lips—a name she'd never heard from him until now. Who was this woman? What was *she* feeling? And what about her children?

"Her name's Elizabeth," Keith said, his eyebrows drawn as though he was struggling to understand what her response might indicate. "Anyway, she…she got pregnant, Reenie. It was an accident. But once there was a baby, I felt cornered. How could I tell Liz about you, then?"

Imagining Keith making love with another woman—some stewardess he'd met while flying off on one of his many business trips—and conceiving a child with her somehow pierced through the strange numbness that had protected Reenie since his arrival. How long would he have let his affair—*his double life*—go on? Indefinitely? Why hadn't he loved her enough to admit his mistake, so they could somehow deal with it? Instead, he'd waited until Isaac had caught him. And now that he was compelled to admit the truth, he expected her to forgive him?

Nausea roiled in her stomach. Rocking forward, she covered her mouth so she wouldn't be sick. "I've heard enough," she said weakly.

Gabe immediately wheeled toward them. "You need to leave."

"No!" Keith said, his eyes wide, pleading. "I—I can't. I already quit my job. Called them up first thing when I got into Boise this morning. I'm serious about staying put. I won't ever contact Liz again. Anything Reenie wants to do, we'll do. I'll prove that I'm a humbled man, that I never meant for any of this to happen. I'll be so good, she'll have to forgive me eventually. You'll see."

The muscles in Gabe's arms stood out beneath his T-shirt as he shoved himself even closer. Her brother was hurt and disappointed, too, Reenie realized. He'd cared about Keith, welcomed him into the family without reservation.

Reenie wished the anger she'd experienced at first would

come to her rescue. She thought it might stave off the nausea. Keith was right—she typically vented her feelings. But what she'd learned last night had changed her. She couldn't seem to overcome the blow; she'd never felt like this before.

"Get an apartment or go stay with your parents for a while," Gabe said. "What you're trying to do—" he shook his head and glanced at Reenie "—it's too soon."

"Right. Too soon," Keith echoed, making an attempt to be accommodating. "So maybe in a day or two we could talk again?" he asked hopefully.

"Maybe," Gabe said. But Reenie was fairly certain she wouldn't want to see her husband in a few days. Or a month. Or even a year.

Keith climbed to his feet, his head hanging so low he looked almost nothing like the proud, handsome man she'd married. Now he'd agree to almost anything to be on good terms with her again. But what had happened was like the broken vase. Isabella hadn't meant to destroy it. She simply couldn't overcome her desire to handle something she'd been told she couldn't touch.

Keith had done the same thing, hadn't he? Only on a much bigger scale. He hadn't acted with the desire to hurt her or anyone else. She believed that much. He'd just been too selfish, vain, weak or stupid to avoid it. And once he'd gotten involved with this "Liz," his better character traits—his strong sense of responsibility, especially to children—made it impossible for him to escape his own lies.

"What are we going to tell the girls?" he asked.

Reenie finally felt a twinge of sympathy for him. She hated what he'd done to her, guessed the anger she'd felt earlier would reassert itself at some point. But right now, he seemed so pathetic. He'd hurt himself as much as he'd hurt her. "We'll tell them…" Her mind raced through the various scenarios she'd imagined. "We'll tell them the truth," she said at last.

He hesitated. "Really?"

She nodded.

Fresh fear entered his eyes. "About Liz?"

"No. If we can help it, I don't want them to know how badly you let us down."

He blanched at the barb but seemed relieved overall. "Then what?"

"We'll say you made a mistake you didn't mean to make and—" she lifted her eyes to his "—and broke my favorite vase."

"What?" He glanced at Gabe in confusion.

"She needs time," Gabe said.

They didn't understand. But deep down Reenie knew. The relationship she'd had with Keith was lost forever. Like the broken vase, her marriage was beyond repair.

"I STILL SAY THIS IS CRAZY." Isaac couldn't believe he was helping his sister pack and load her belongings into a U-Haul, couldn't believe he'd soon be driving her and her children nine hundred and forty-two miles to Idaho, even though he'd already contacted a real-estate agent there and rented a house. It had been two weeks since Keith had left, but Liz hadn't wavered from her course. She'd quit her job and, if anything, become more determined.

"It's crazy to want my children to be closer to their father?" she responded, turning from the kitchen cupboard, where she was busy wrapping dishes.

Isaac finished sealing the box he'd filled and shoved it toward the door. "You don't know what Dundee is like."

"You've told me about it." She grimaced slightly while stretching her back. Packing up a house this size was no small task. They'd been bending, reaching and lifting for three days. Fortunately, it was easier today because the children were in school instead of trying to help. "It's mountainous there," she recited. "It gets cold and snowy in the winter. And it's small."

"The meaning of small is what I don't think you understand."

"So there won't be any movie theaters or shopping malls." She went back to packing.

Isaac slouched into one of the few chairs left in the room and stretched out his long legs. "Liz, look at me."

"What? It's not like I'm selling the house, Isaac. I'm renting it out on a month-to-month basis, okay? That's not permanent."

"I had to sign a six-month lease in order to get a place in Dundee."

"Six months isn't that long."

"Going there even for a few weeks will be bad enough. Reenie's father is an Idaho state senator and has been for years."

Her eyebrows drew together in an expression of impatience. "So?"

"She's lived in Dundee her whole life and is well entrenched in the community. Everyone likes her."

"Even you," she said, her tone slightly accusing.

Isaac couldn't deny it, so he focused on his point. "I'm saying you won't be welcomed."

"I know what you're saying. But I'm not going there to win any popularity contests."

"You'll be the antithesis of popular. You'll be notorious, a pariah. Are you sure being near Keith will be worth the sacrifice?"

She set two mugs on the counter and stared at them instead of wrapping them in newspaper. "I talked to Chris's teacher yesterday, Isaac."

Isaac could tell by the tone of her voice that this wasn't going to be good. Leaning forward, he rested his elbows on his knees. "And?"

"Since I told the kids that their daddy left us, Chris hasn't been making any progress in school. His teacher said he doesn't even look at the papers she passes out. He sits in his chair, staring out the window, his mind off in some other world. She's worried about him, doesn't know how to reach him. And neither do I."

"He needs time to adjust, Liz," Isaac said gently. "He'll be okay. He's not the first kid to suffer through a parental divorce."

"You mean annulment, right? Divorces are only for legal marriages."

"In this case, after so many years, it amounts to about the same thing. Except it saves you money."

"Lucky me. Well, annulment or divorce or whatever, Christopher isn't coping. This is hitting him as hard as I knew it would."

Isaac understood. He just wasn't sure the risk she was taking would improve the situation. "Keith hasn't returned your calls, Liz. Yesterday, he had his cell-phone service shut off. You can't even leave him a message anymore."

"Which is exactly why I have to go there! Don't you see? I need some type of closure. I need him to face me and tell me he doesn't love me anymore. This silence is…it's like being locked in a dark room. I can't get my bearings. I've been feeling my way around, searching frantically for the light switch. Idaho is that light switch. I'm not sure going there will bring my husband back to me, but I can't extinguish that hope until I see him, talk to him, figure out what happened to us."

"Can't you fly up there and meet with him?"

"For what, a half hour? That's not the same. I have to know he won't change his mind in a week or two."

"If he's back with Reenie, you might have a real fight on your hands. She's probably forbidden him to see you again. Otherwise, he would have kept his cell-phone service."

"You said cell phones don't work there."

"They don't. But it was your only link. He could've kept the service so he could check his voice mail from a land phone. At least then you'd have a discreet way to communicate with him."

"You're saying he doesn't want to talk to me," she said softly.

"Maybe he *can't*."

She considered this for a moment, then lifted her chin. "I don't care. Once we get there, he'll have to acknowledge the children, at least. They need the same kind of closure I'm searching for."

Keith shook his head. "The next few months are going to be a nightmare."

"I'm already living a nightmare," she said.

"Trust me. It's going to get a lot worse before it gets better." *If* it gets better, he thought.

"You can go back to Chicago, if you want." She shoved two more glasses in the box at her feet. "Just because I'm doing this doesn't mean you have to come along."

She'd tried to tell him that at least a dozen times already. But he couldn't leave her. Especially now. Once she arrived in Dundee, she wouldn't have a friend in the world. "Sorry, but you're stuck with me," he said.

"You're too stubborn for your own good."

"Maybe."

"At least you have to go back after Christmas. That's only six weeks away."

He watched her reach for more newspaper. "Actually, I'm not teaching spring semester this year."

She glanced up. "What?"

"I've taken a sabbatical from the university."

Her mouth dropped open. "When?"

"I made it official yesterday."

"But what about your grant? Your trip to the Congo?"

"I forfeited that to Harold Munoz."

Her fingers twitched but she could no longer destroy her cuticles. He'd insisted she use Band-Aids to protect them from further damage.

"Please tell me you didn't really do that," she said.

When he didn't answer, she weaved through the boxes littering the floor and knelt in front of him. Several strands of hair had fallen from her ponytail and there was a smudge of black ink on her cheek. Her dishevelment made her look almost as young as the sixteen-year-old girl who'd been so vulnerable to Luanna. "Isaac, why?"

He scowled so she'd quit making such a big deal out of what he'd done. "Because I wanted to. I needed a break."

"That's not true. You love to teach. And you were desperate to get back to Africa. It was all you could talk about."

"Reginald will send me the applications for next year."

She buried her face in her hands. When she eventually looked up, he could see the tears in her eyes. "Please don't let this ruin your life, too," she whispered.

"It's not ruining my life. I'm taking a sabbatical, okay? A few months off. No big deal."

"But—"

He resecured the Band-Aid that was about to fall off her thumb. "You're my little sister, Liz. I'm not going anywhere until you're back on your feet."

The tears began to spill. "You know, what happened to Mom—"

"Don't think about Mom right now," he interrupted. "You've got enough going on."

"No, it's okay. That's what I want to tell you. I've missed her terribly, but my life would've been a lot worse if—" he wiped away the smudge on her cheek while waiting for her to continue "—if not for you," she finished.

"Hello? Anybody home?" A knock sounded on the front door, which Isaac had left standing open to accommodate his many trips to the truck.

Dashing a hand across her wet cheeks, Liz immediately scrambled to her feet. "Who is it?"

Footsteps started down the entry hall. "Hey, you haven't forgotten me already, have you?"

Isaac stood as a man about five foot eleven, one-hundred-eighty pounds of tanned lean muscle strode confidently into the room. Although it was pretty chilly outside, he wasn't wearing a coat, just a pair of long baggy shorts, flip-flops and a tight-fitting T-shirt—along with a cocky grin that disappeared the moment he saw Isaac.

"Oh, sorry," he said, drawing up short and shooting a glance at Liz. "I didn't realize you already have company."

Liz cleared her throat. "This is my brother, Isaac."

Isaac brushed the dust and dirt off his sweatshirt and jeans while waiting for the other half of the introduction. "This is Dave Shapiro," Liz said. "He's the club pro who's been giving me tennis lessons."

"When she bothers to show up," Dave added with a toothy smile and offered Isaac his hand.

Isaac shook with him while Liz tightened her ponytail in a self-conscious movement that said she wasn't thrilled about being caught looking as she did.

"I'm sorry," she said. "I should've called you. I—I won't be coming back to the club. I'm moving to Idaho."

He frowned at the boxes, wrapping paper and packing tape. "That's what Lauren said."

Isaac nudged Elizabeth. "Lauren?"

"She lives down the street," Elizabeth explained. "We play tennis together."

"She told me what happened," Dave said. "I'm sorry."

Isaac looked from Dave to Liz. What exactly was their relationship? He could feel some sexual tension between them. But he knew Liz had been a faithful wife and was still in love with Keith.

Liz offered Dave a ghost of her usual smile. "You tried to warn me, right?"

"I'm not here to say I told you so. I wish I'd decked Keith when I had the chance."

Isaac stiffened. Those were pretty protective words from a man six or seven years too young for Elizabeth.

Liz tucked the wisps of hair that kept falling forward behind her ears. "Aren't you the one who told me cheating is man's basic nature?"

"If it's not his basic nature, it's definitely his *baser* nature. Just ask my old man." Dave's car keys rattled as he shoved his hands in his pockets. "Anyway, don't hate us all after this, okay? I never would've been stupid enough to walk away from a woman like you."

If Isaac had any choice in the matter, he'd never get close to Liz in the first place. Not only was Dave too young, he seemed... unreliable.

Fortunately, Isaac didn't need to say anything. Liz was already laughing as though her coach hadn't meant a word he'd said. "You wouldn't have married me in the first place. You prefer a bachelor's life, remember? You told me that yourself."

Dave made a careless motion with his hand. "Details, details. Besides, I was speaking hypothetically."

Liz laughed again. "For a womanizer, you really are a pretty nice guy."

For a womanizer... If Liz already knew what Dave was, why did she seem so flattered?.

"What'd I tell you?" Dave flashed her a smile, and Isaac decided that moving his sister out of Southern California might not be such a bad idea. She needed time to recover, get over Keith; she didn't need the attentions of a tennis pro who probably changed women as often as he changed his sheets.

"Is there any way to talk you out of this?" Dave asked, frowning at all the boxes.

"I'm afraid not," she said.

"Her children need to be near their father," Isaac inserted.

Liz blinked at his sudden change of heart but turned her attention back to Dave, who was talking. "So you're going to follow Keith? Give up L.A. for *Idaho?*"

"You have any better ideas?" she asked flippantly.

"You could stay here and have an affair with me to even the score." His wry grin indicated he only was joking. But Isaac suspected he was at least partially serious.

"I appreciate your willingness to help out in the revenge department," she said. "But I don't see how our sleeping together would benefit anyone—"

"Hey!" He pressed a hand to his chest as though she'd wounded him. "Don't knock it till you've tried it."

"And since my brother's in the room, I know you're just being your normal, outrageous self."

The crooked grin reappeared. "Well, there's always tennis. We could keep working on your serve."

"I can't stay," she said. "Isaac's right. My kids need their father."

The club pro sighed heavily. "I'd have to be a jerk to argue with that, right?"

She offered him a sweet smile. "I'm sorry."

He shook his head in apparent regret. "I suppose there's nothing left to do but help you load the truck then, huh?"

At least he'd given in gracefully—and offered to help. Isaac decided to put him to work so he'd quit flirting with Liz. Motioning to several boxes that were ready to go, he said, "You can grab those, if you like."

Dave scratched his head as he ambled toward the closest one. "Idaho. I'll bet you fifty bucks you're gonna hate it there."

Isaac knew better than to take him up on that bet. But at least in Dundee there probably wouldn't be any young tennis pros hitting on his sister.

Hefting one of the heavier boxes into his arms, Dave started out with it, then paused before disappearing down the hall. "Promise me one thing?"

Liz's eyes narrowed with mock wariness. "What's that?"

"Look me up when you move back?"

Her lips curved in another smile, this one a little more genuine than the last. Her response concerned Isaac almost as much as it gave him hope that she'd be okay, that she'd recover.

"You're twenty-four, Dave," she said.

"So?"

"I'm thirty-one. Why would you want to hear from an older woman who's divorced with two kids?"

"What do you think?" he said. "You play a mean game of tennis."

Liz chuckled as his footsteps trailed down the entry hall.

Isaac waited for her to glance over at him and tried not to scowl too darkly when she did. "Who *is* this guy?"

"I told you. He's my tennis coach."

"Why haven't you mentioned him before?"

"Why would I?"

"Because he likes you."

She shook her head. "He likes every woman he meets."

But she still seemed ready to flirt with him. Moving to Idaho was beginning to feel like a good idea. "Okay," he said. "We leave tomorrow."

CHAPTER TEN

"ARE YOU SURE about this?" Reenie's mother whispered.

The smell of books and leather furniture filled Reenie's nostrils as she sat with her mother across from the attorney's wide, neatly organized mahogany desk. She could hear the murmur of Mr. Rosenbaum's voice in the next room, speaking to the secretary who'd just ushered them into his office. Reenie and Celeste had passed him on their way in. He'd greeted them with a warm smile, but she wasn't fooled. The business she had with the attorney would be anything but pleasant.

"I'm sure," she replied stoically.

"But Keith's so contrite," her mother argued.

At first Reenie gaped at Celeste, but on second thought she realized she shouldn't be so surprised by her mother's sympathy for Keith. Celeste was capable of forgiving anything, loving anyone. When Garth had finally admitted his affair, Celeste, who should've been the most offended party, had been one of the first to reach out to Lucky.

"Mom, Keith has another *wife,* another *family.* He's been with her for nine *years.*"

"I know that, dear, but sometimes it's possible to get beyond this kind of thing."

"Dad had a brief fling with a woman who is now dead. The child resulting from that affair is an adult. I don't mean to make light of what happened, but this isn't the same. This is…this is—" *almost unfathomable* "—bigger than I am," she finished helplessly. "It's shown me that the marriage I believed in never really existed in the first place."

The advancing years were beginning to take their toll on Celeste's beauty, but her mother's pale blue eyes were still pretty. They filled with concern. "What about Jennifer, Angela and Isabella? They love their daddy. And Keith's *so* miserable. He came over last night, pleading with me to speak to you."

Reenie dropped her head into her hands. She should've brought Gabe along instead of Celeste. Her brother understood and agreed with her decision to end her marriage. "Why did you wait until we were sitting in the attorney's office to bring this up?" she whispered harshly.

"Because you didn't want to talk about it in the car."

"I still don't want to talk about it," Reenie said. "Anyway, I'm being as kind to Keith as I possibly can be. I'm hiring an attorney in Boise so we don't make a public spectacle out of him, so that we're able to keep his dirty little secret in the family. If I wanted to be vengeful, I would've gone to Warren Slinkerhoff, like almost everyone else in Dundee who's ever filed for divorce. Then every sordid detail would be all over town inside of ten minutes."

"You didn't leave Dundee to protect Keith. You left to protect the girls," she said.

And to protect herself. Reenie felt like a fool for not discovering Keith's deceit years ago. Somehow he'd been able to compartmentalize it all so well. And yet she should've suspected something.

"I'm not sure you want to hire any attorney," her mother was saying. "Do you really want a divorce? You and Keith have always been so in love. Think of your father's birthday last week. Lucky was there and we enjoyed her. Even Gabe was on his best behavior. Time changes perspectives. It's only been two weeks since you found out about this...this affair."

It wasn't just an *affair*. But Reenie refused to explain it all again. What mattered was that she was where she had to be. She knew she wouldn't feel any differently in a year.

"What about the other people involved?" Celeste continued.

"You're asking me about *Liz?*"

"Is that her name?"

"Yes."

"Actually, I'm talking about the O'Connells. They're heartbroken that the two of you are splitting up."

They weren't half as heartbroken as Reenie was. They couldn't be. They only knew what she and Keith had told them—that Keith's traveling had caused some marital strife and they were separating.

"At the very least, give yourself some more time to think," Celeste said.

"I don't want to put off the decision." Reenie couldn't dwell on what had happened any longer or she'd lose her mind. She had to take control and reorganize her life. Except for Keith's visitations with their children—which she intended to make as pleasant as possible for everyone involved—she was going to cut ties with her husband and go back to teaching. Her father had even agreed to help her buy the farm, and to let her pay him back over the next several years.

Maybe she wasn't building the idyllic dream she'd once imagined. But she was facing this challenge squarely. She wasn't about to sit around and cry.

"Keith's quit his job," her mother ventured.

"I know."

"He's now managing the hardware store for Ollie."

"I know that, too." Keith had told her during one of his many phone calls. But Reenie had a hard time imagining her husband among all those tools and cans of paint. He'd always been fabulous on a computer and incredibly bright—but not very handy around the house. "So?"

"So he's not traveling anymore. Chances are good nothing like this will ever happen again."

Reenie wasn't sure what part of that statement offended her most. Her mother's cavalier attitude toward the existence of Keith's other family? The way Celeste overlooked the fact that Elizabeth O'Connell and her children wouldn't simply and conveniently disappear so that Reenie's life could go back to the way it once was? Or the implication that it was all as simple as keeping a tighter rein on her straying husband?

"Chances are?" she echoed incredulously, but the attorney cleared his throat to warn them that he was entering the room. Reenie shot her mother a look that said they'd talk later.

"What can I do for you ladies today?" he asked, his expression a perfect model of professional interest.

The answer to that question was pretty obvious, since he was a divorce attorney and they'd made a formal appointment, but Reenie knew he was *really* asking which one of them wanted to end her marriage.

While he took his seat, she explained that she hoped to get a divorce as soon as possible.

"Most people suing for divorce would like the same thing, Mrs. O'Connell. But I need to be completely honest here. Divorces don't happen overnight."

The expensive-looking cut of Mr. Rosenbaum's short, dark hair and tailored suit told Reenie he was successful in his work and probably knew what he was talking about. But he didn't fully understand her situation. Yet. "This one will be uncontested."

He offered her a patronizing smile. "Anger and greed can complicate the simplest issues. When a divorce turns adversarial, it can take several months to complete, sometimes as long as a year."

"If it is strictly uncontested, how long will it take?" she pressed.

Reenie guessed he didn't run into uncontested divorces very

often, because he steepled his fingers on the desktop and answered somewhat reluctantly, "As little as a month."

A month. She could dissolve what she'd thought was a lifelong commitment in four weeks. In a way, Rosenbaum's answer was a relief but in another way, it was incredibly depressing to think she could so easily end vows she'd considered sacred.

"Do you have children, Mrs. O'Connell?"

"Yes. Three girls."

He put on a pair of glasses and made a few notes on a pad embossed with his name. "Then there'll be custody issues." The tone of his voice seemed to add, *See? The trouble's already starting.*

"I don't think so."

He stopped scribbling long enough to stare at her over the rim of his glasses. "Excuse me?"

"My husband will agree to give me full custody of the girls in exchange for the house and most of the furnishings. The piano that came from my parents, the photographs that were a gift from my sister-in-law, and the furniture my brother made will go with me, of course. And so will the dog. Keith gave Old Bailey to me for my birthday the year we married, so he's been part of the family for a long time. My girls couldn't manage without him right now." Actually, *she* couldn't manage without him, but she refused to admit that to anyone else. "Keith can have the rest," she said. "As for the vehicles, he'll take his SUV and his Jeep. I'll take the van."

Reenie was treated to another glance over the rim of Mr. Rosenbaum's glasses. "He's already agreed to these custody issues and division of property?"

"Not yet. But I have good reason to believe he will."

"How can you be so sure?"

"Because it's a very generous offer, for one. Two, he's guilty of bigamy. If he doesn't fully cooperate, I'll turn him in to the police."

Reenie's mother gasped, but Mr. Rosenbaum acted as though he'd heard it all before. Taking off his glasses, he used a soft cloth from his desk drawer to wipe the lenses before setting them aside.

"Bigamy," he said slowly, leaning back. "Is this a religious thing or…"

"No. This is an adulterous affair that my husband took to the next level."

"So this second marriage is recent?"

She hated admitting the rest. "Actually, it's lasted for nine of the eleven years we've been married. They have two children together. But—" she still couldn't believe it "—I only recently found out."

The human side of Mr. Rosenbaum finally presented itself. He shook his head and leaned forward, his eyes shining with curiosity. "How'd he keep this other family a secret from you for so long?"

"He's a better liar than I ever imagined," she said with a sigh.

"I see."

"Keith's really not as bad as this makes him sound," Reenie's mother piped up.

"And you're…Keith's mother?" he asked Celeste.

Reenie rolled her eyes. "No, she's *my* mother. But every once in a while, she forgets where her loyalties lie."

"I don't forget, dear," Celeste assured her. "I support you one-hundred percent. I just—"

"I know," Reenie interrupted. "You feel terrible for everyone involved."

"I do," her mother said.

"Where does your husband's other wife live?" Rosenbaum asked.

"In California. Which is why our paths never crossed. I guess you could say the distance between us served as a contributing factor to my ignorance." She frowned. "My own innocence and gullibility did the rest."

Rosenbaum rubbed a finger thoughtfully across one eyebrow while she explained the whole situation. When she finished, he scooted forward, reclaimed his glasses and made a few more notes. "I'm afraid I need to explain something to you, Mrs. O'Connell."

Reenie was already raw inside. The gravity in his voice terrified her. "What's that?"

"I can't use the threat of criminal action as a bargaining chip in your divorce."

"Why not? He's guilty!"

"That doesn't matter. I'm an attorney. As such, it would constitute an ethical violation. So, if *you're* going to threaten him, I don't know about it, okay?"

She hesitated, wondering if threatening Keith violated her own ethics, and decided it did not. "Okay."

"And…"

Reenie clenched her hands in her lap. This was probably where things got worse.

"A bigamy charge is not much to stand on, unless…could your husband also be engaged in some kind of fraud?"

"Fraud?" Celeste repeated.

"Like marrying multiple spouses to steal their money?" Reenie asked.

"That would definitely be one form of fraud, yes."

"I don't think so. If he got any money from Liz, he certainly didn't share it with me."

"So…has he broken any other laws that might put him more at risk?"

"Not that I know of."

"Is he a good father?"

"Yes."

"Then, unless we find out something new, most likely it won't be worth the state's time to prosecute him. Do you want to hire a private investigator to see if there might be something you don't already know about?"

"No. I can't imagine there's more."

"Well…" He pursed his lips as he drummed his fingers on the desk. "I guess we can forget about prosecution, then."

No one cared that bigamy was a crime? What Keith had done was fine because he'd never stolen anyone's money?

"Great," Reenie said. "Any more good news?"

"Maybe." Rosenbaum gave her a sly smile. "A man with a guilty bigamy secret wouldn't necessarily know what I've just told you."

"I see."

"You weren't hoping to send him to prison, were you?" he asked.

Reenie rubbed her eyes, which were burning from lack of sleep. She'd spent much of the past several nights sitting at the kitchen table making budgets and projections and plans for her life without Keith and, more than anything else, stewing over her decision to end her marriage. "No, that wouldn't help anyone. I only want custody of the girls."

"Do you plan to allow Mr. O'Connell visitation?"

"Of course!" Celeste cut in. "He can see the girls any time he wants."

"Mo-*ther*," Reenie said.

"I'm sorry, honey. I want to be supportive. I really do. It's just…I'm not sure you'll be any happier with a divorce."

Mr. Rosenbaum arched a thick eyebrow at Celeste. It was easy to tell he thought she was crazy for supporting a bigamist son-in-law. But he seemed to think twice about stating that opinion. "Would you like to ruminate on it for a few weeks and give me a call?" he asked Reenie.

Reenie imagined taking Keith back. Of course she wanted what they'd had before. But that was gone.

"No, I want to file immediately, while he's still repentant," she said. "I'll have a much greater chance of his not contesting anything."

Celeste muttered something Reenie couldn't make out and began wringing her hands, but Reenie kept her spine straight and her focus on Mr. Rosenbaum.

"You're certain?" he said.

"Positive."

"Very good." He stood to shake hands. "I'll draw up the papers and get back to you."

EVERY FEW SECONDS, Keith's eyes darted toward the window. Since Reenie would no longer accept his phone calls or let him come to the house, except to visit the girls while she retreated to her bedroom, he hoped to bump into her somewhere else. Dundee was small enough to make a chance meeting more than a remote possibility. Especially because her sister-in-law owned the photography studio three doors down, and her parents lived only blocks away.

She'd walk by at some point, he told himself, and when she did, maybe she'd see him working at the hardware store and know he was serious about making the changes he'd promised her. Once she realized he was keeping his word, that he was really leaving Liz without looking back, maybe she'd soften and let him come by for dinner once in a while. In a few weeks, she might even let him move in. Eventually, once they were together again and everything was back to normal, he felt certain he could convince her to let him spend a little time with Mica and Christopher. They were innocent in all of this, after all—

"You ever cut those keys for Dot Fisher, Keith?"

Keith stepped aside as Ollie Weston, the owner of the store, slipped behind the cash register and opened the drawer so he could check the levels of their change. Ollie had to be nearing seventy. A taciturn man with a wiry build, a ruddy face and large callused hands, he was beginning to show his age. But he could still explain how to build or fix just about anything. Keith liked him. He'd worked for Ollie before. When he was only sixteen, he'd spent the summer sweeping and straightening the hardware store—which made it pretty fitting to be working here again, since he was starting over.

"Not yet," Keith said. "Peter Granger was ready to check out, so I helped him first."

"What'd Peter want?"

"More lumber for the shed he's building in his backyard."

"He's not done with that yet?"

"Guess not."

"Humph. Well, see what you can do about those keys. Dot's coming by to pick them up as soon as she's done at the beauty parlor."

"You mean the salon?" Keith asked, trying not to smile at Ollie's dated speech.

"That's what I said, ain't it?"

Keith chuckled while ambling to the far corner to use the key machine. In a way, he was glad to be relieved of the pressure, the traveling and the stress of his former job. He knew he wouldn't be satisfied selling tools and insulation forever. But right now, his obsession with getting Reenie and his girls back put anything that required much concentration well beyond his reach. He'd resolve things with Reenie first, then do what he could for Liz and his other kids. Finally, he'd worry about his career.

A flash of movement outside caused him to glance up again. A woman passed by, but he couldn't see her face.

He stopped the noisy key cutter and leaned around a display of car fresheners to get a better look. But as it turned out he didn't need to make the extra effort. A second later, the bell jingled over the door and the woman walked in.

It wasn't Reenie; it was his mother.

"Afternoon, Georgia," Ollie said.

"Afternoon, Ollie," she responded. "Keith here?"

Ollie motioned with his head. "Over there."

Keith started making keys again, pretending he hadn't seen her so she'd have to come to the back to get his attention. The whole town knew he was no longer living with Reenie. There was no way to keep something like that quiet, not when he'd moved in with his parents and was now working for Ollie. But he didn't want Ollie or anyone else to hear what his mother had to say. She was so upset that there was no telling what she might spout off.

"Keith?"

When she touched his arm, he turned off the power switch. The grating of metal on metal instantly fell to a silence broken only by his voice. "Hey, Mom."

"I think Reenie's filing for divorce," she stated bluntly, dabbing at her eyes, which were already red and swollen.

Keith's words seemed to jam at the back of his throat. "Wh-what makes you think that?" he finally managed to say.

"I just ran into Betsy Mann at the grocery store. She said Celeste wasn't able to make it to bridge club today."

"So?" he said, but his mother's tears made his heart pound against his chest.

"She couldn't make it because she was going to Boise with Reenie."

"That doesn't necessarily mean—"

"I didn't think so, either, until I tried calling her an hour ago. She was home but wouldn't come to the phone. Garth said she was too tired, that she was lying down."

He was beginning to break into a cold sweat. "Maybe she *is* tired."

"Too tired to talk to *me?* I've never met with that response in the twenty years I've known her."

He glanced helplessly around the hardware store. He'd done everything the past two weeks to try to win Reenie back.

"Poor little Isabella," his mother said, sniffling. "And Angela, and Jennifer. *How could you let that job come between you and your family?*"

She looked as though she wanted to smack him. He knew she probably *would,* if she ever learned the rest of the story.

"I tried to warn you that you were away too much," she went on. "But you wouldn't listen. You took Reenie for granted, and now you've lost her."

As she started to cry again, Keith thought briefly of Liz. If he couldn't save his first marriage, maybe he should try to save his second. Liz was a good woman. He missed her. But as much as he cared about her and Mica and Chris, as much as he loved them and had enjoyed spending part of each month in L.A., he couldn't imagine leaving Dundee. Just as he knew he couldn't give up on Reenie. She was absolutely vital to his happiness.

He'd known it all along. He just hadn't been able to break out of the mess he'd created. Not when he loved Liz and Mica and Christopher, too. "I screwed up," he admitted.

He must have sounded terribly crestfallen because his mother reacted with some pity. "Oh, honey," she said, putting her hand over his. "Pray it's not too late. You asked me to stay out of it, but—" another sniff "—maybe it's time I got involved."

He could easily guess how much Reenie would appreciate that. But she'd always been close to his family. Maybe a little pressure from the O'Connells would tip the scales in his favor. It wasn't as if he had to worry that she'd reveal the truth. For the sake of the girls, she'd guard his secret with her life. "Okay," he said. "Tell her I'm sorry. Tell her I love her."

His mother nodded. "I will. And I'll remind her of the children and what's best for them. She adores those girls. Surely, she'll listen to reason."

"She has to," he said. He couldn't imagine anything else.

CHAPTER ELEVEN

MICA ADJUSTED the seat belt she shared with Christopher and leaned forward so she could see around Isaac. "This is it?" she said, her voice pregnant with disappointment. "This is where we'll be living?"

Isaac brought the U-Haul to a shuddering stop at the first traffic signal in Dundee—there were only four lights in total—and opened his mouth to respond. But Christopher spoke before Isaac could offer some of the positives he was scrambling to formulate.

"I wanna go home," he said, and started to cry.

Isaac turned down the radio and looked at Liz.

"He's tired," she explained. Her voice held sympathy, but she didn't attempt to comfort her son. She was too busy studying the buildings on both sides of the street, as if someone or something might rush out and attack them.

"We're all tired," Isaac said. They'd been on the road for a day and a half. For most of the trip, Liz had driven the car Isaac was now towing behind them. Having the children squished in the middle, wearing the same seat belt, compromised their safety, but not as badly as leaving Liz behind the wheel. For the past hour, she'd been swerving all over the road. She hadn't been sleeping well enough to weather such a long drive. More often than not, Isaac heard her rambling around as late as three or four o'clock in the morning—and it was starting to show in the dark circles forming under eyes.

"So where's the house?" Liz asked.

Rolling onto his right hip, Isaac pulled the directions out of his pocket. He'd found the house by calling city hall. A secretary there had referred him to a man named Fred Winston, Dundee's only real estate agent. Because they'd handled everything over the phone, Isaac hadn't yet seen the place.

"Just off the main drag, on Mount Marcy Street," he said.

"Mount *Marcy* Street?" Mica echoed. "Sounds stupid."

Mica was generally a happy child, but she'd grown sullen as the miles passed. Chris had been even more morose. Although he was normally very active, he'd sat absolutely still for most of the trip, staring at the dash, unresponsive even when Isaac or Liz spoke to him.

The light turned green and Isaac gave the U-Haul some gas, trying hard not to notice the curious stares they were beginning to attract from strangers on the street. In a town this small, a moving van rolling down Main Street was definitely conspicuous. Folks were probably wondering whether or not they had new neighbors.

"The real estate agent said it's nice," Isaac told Mica encouragingly.

"Don't bother trying to make me feel better," she replied. "It won't work."

"Your father's here," Liz said, clearly hopeful that this information might appease her children.

"So?" Mica replied. "I don't want to see him."

Chris obviously felt differently. Rubbing the tears from his eyes, he sat up. "Where is he?"

"We'll find him," Liz promised. "You'll get to see him soon."

Isaac wasn't looking forward to that moment. But there was one he was dreading even more—facing Reenie again. Without question she wouldn't be happy to know that Isaac, his sister and her children had just become members of her tight-knit community.

He thought about Liz's tennis coach and tried to dredge up

some of the positives of moving to Idaho. But they were long gone. Isaac was back to his original thought. Coming here was crazy.

Liz picked up the directions and began giving instructions. "You need to turn on Third Street. This is Second Street, so that must be it right there." She pointed at the next light.

Two women arranging dried cornstalks at the entrance to Jerry's Diner moved to get a good look at them as they drove by. Isaac recognized one as Judy, the waitress, and quickly averted his face. He wanted to settle in, at least, before the furor started.

"Take a left here," Liz said.

When oncoming traffic cleared, Isaac turned into a neighborhood of older homes sitting on half-acre lots. They passed a street named Mount Glory before turning right on Mount Marcy. According to the address, the house he'd rented was halfway down the block between a rambler of white brick and a rambler of red brick. It wasn't nearly as nice as its two neighbors, but it had potential. Right across the street sat one of the most beautiful homes he'd seen in Dundee.

"This isn't bad," Liz said, but her smile was brittle.

"There isn't a large rental market here," Isaac explained. "It looks a lot better, once you take our other options into account."

"What were our other options?" she asked as he pulled to the curb.

He'd mentioned the choices to her before, when he was making the arrangements. But she'd been too preoccupied with packing and renting the California house to listen. "You decide," she'd said.

"There were three mobile homes available in the trailer park south of town. But I've seen that park and it's not a place you'd want to visit, let alone *live*. Then there was a duplex right behind the school. But Fred—"

"Fred?" she echoed.

"The real-estate agent." Satisfied that he'd positioned the truck the way he wanted it, Isaac cut the engine. "He told me we probably wouldn't like the duplex. The neighbors call the police almost every other week because of domestic disputes. And the man of the house tinkers with cars. There are junkers sitting all over the front lawn."

"Wonderful."

"See? This is looking better all the time." He opened his door and Liz followed suit.

"Who owns this house?" she asked.

"An older couple who are doing missionary work in the Philippines."

"How long will they be gone?"

"I don't know. A couple of years, I think."

She waited for him to come around. "But you said it wasn't furnished."

"It's not."

"What did they do with their furniture?"

"Fred told me they gave some of it to their children and put the rest in storage. Anyway, he promised me that the house was clean and in a good neighborhood, so I signed the lease."

"Sounds like it was our only choice."

"Pretty much."

Mica, who'd climbed out behind them along with Christopher, wrinkled her nose. "It's *ugly!*"

"We're not buying it," Liz told her. "We're only renting."

Mica shook her head sadly. "I can't believe he did this to us."

No one needed to ask who "he" was.

"It won't be as bad as you think," Liz told her and started up the driveway. "Come on. Let's go see the inside."

They skirted the rain-soaked yard and scaled the four steps to the front door, then trooped from room to room, counting bedrooms and planning where the furniture would go. Fortunately, the owners had left an old Ping-Pong table in the basement, which interested Mica. "Want to play, Chris?" she asked, as Isaac and Liz started back upstairs.

"There's lots of room here," Liz said.

Her words rang with false cheer, but Isaac knew it was better to play along. "Fred was right. It *is* clean, if a little dated."

"I'm sure it's better than the duplex or the trailer park."

"No doubt." Isaac was about to head outside. Unless they wanted to sleep on the floor, he needed to get the truck unloaded and the beds put together. They'd called Fred from Boise to tell him that they were getting close, since he'd offered to help with the heavy stuff. He hadn't arrived yet, but Isaac saw no reason not to get started on his own. Except that Liz caught his arm before he could move away from her.

"Coming here…it—it'll be okay, won't it, Isaac?" she asked.

Isaac stared down at her hand. She still had Band-Aids around her nails and a bare spot where her wedding ring used to be. "You knew the move wasn't going to be easy," he said, trying to warm her cold fingers.

She nodded.

"Do you regret it already?" he asked. "Do you want to go back?"

She bit her lip and surveyed the brown shag carpet, the sparkly cottage-cheese-style ceiling, the dark paneling.

"You don't like the house?"

"It's not that. It's…Mica wants one thing, and Chris wants another. I don't know what to do. I feel…torn in two, completely disoriented. Maybe I'm only making things worse by coming here. If I didn't feel such a driving need to be where Keith is, to find my equilibrium by starting where we left off and somehow catching up to where we are now."

"You're thinking too much. Let's keep it simple, okay?"

"How?"

"You feel the need to talk to Keith, to be around him, so we'll do that—for a while."

"The last time I saw him, we were happy," she explained. "We were both smiling and waving goodbye as he drove off to take Mica to gymnastics class. I keep thinking…if only I could see him again, speak to him face-to-face…maybe he'll be able to give me the answers I need, help me figure out *why*."

Her complete bewilderment made Isaac want to break Keith's jaw. "Let's stay until our lease is up," he said. "If you still hate it, we'll figure out Plan B."

She lifted her chin. "Okay. Six months."

He squeezed her shoulders. "Nothing's going to feel good right now, Liz. Nothing, okay?"

"I know."

The doorbell rang. "That's Fred," he said. "I'll get it."

"Wait." She grabbed his arm again.

"What?"

"You haven't given him or anyone else my name, have you?"

"No, I rented the house in my own name. Why?"

"Because I don't want Reenie to know I'm here yet."

"She's going to find out soon enough, Liz."

"I just…I need to talk to Keith first. Okay?"

"And say what?"

"I deserve that much, Isaac. One last private conversation with the man I married before I face the hatred of the whole community."

He couldn't argue with her there. "You don't have to worry about me. I won't volunteer the information to anyone."

She nodded and seemed to relax a bit. "Good."

A dispute over the Ping-Pong game sent Liz hurrying downstairs while he strode through the empty living room and opened the door. But if it was Fred, he was an excellent cross-dresser. A short, plump woman with dark hair, who had to be close to sixty, stood on the porch next to a large wicker basket.

"Hello," she said brightly. "I hope you don't mind my barging in on you so soon."

"Not at all."

"Fred told me you'd arrive this afternoon, so I've been watching for you," she explained with a genuine smile. "I wanted to be the first to welcome you to the neighborhood."

Welcome them? Isaac straightened in surprise. Her simple gesture sure felt good. "Thank you."

"Moving is so difficult. I thought it might make things a little easier for you if I provided dinner tonight." She handed the basket to him. "There's a casserole inside you'll need to heat up before you eat. But the rest is ready."

He could smell cake as he set the basket inside the door. "Smells great," he said. "We really appreciate your generosity."

"It's no trouble."

"Which house is yours?"

"The one across the street." She motioned to the elegant house he'd noticed earlier. "My husband and I live alone now. We have two children, but they're all grown."

"Your home is lovely."

"I enjoy decorating almost as much as I enjoy company," she confided. "We'll have you over as soon as you get settled."

"We'd like that."

"What's your name?" she asked.

"Isaac Russell. And you are…"

"Celeste Holbrook."

"Holbrook?" he repeated, his voice going high on the last syllable.

Faced with his stunned reaction, she hesitated briefly. "Yes, my husband's in the state senate, so he's in Boise a lot. But if you ever need anything, I'm usually home."

"You're very kind," he muttered, but he wasn't concentrating on his words. He was picturing this woman's beautiful daughter—as she'd looked the night they'd had dinner together, and then later, when he'd had to tell her about her husband.

If Celeste was surprised or confused by the sudden drop in Isaac's enthusiasm, she didn't let it show. She had impeccable manners and simply interpreted his response as her cue to leave. "Well, I don't mean to keep you. I know how busy you and your wife must be." She reached into the pocket of her wool coat and withdrew a piece of paper, which she handed to him. "I typed up some information that should be useful."

He thought of Liz in the basement, and her desire to lie low for a few days, as he read what Celeste had provided. She'd listed the day they had garbage pickup, directions to the grocery store and post office, even the number to Ernie's Lawn & Garden Maintenance.

"My number's on the bottom," she said. "Call me if you think of anything else I can do. I noticed you have children. I'm a good babysitter," she added with a wink.

He didn't correct her impression that he was the husband and father of the family. "Thanks," he said again. Then he closed the door and pressed two fingers to his forehead. "Shit."

"What's wrong?"

Isaac lowered his hand to find Liz watching him from the other side of the room. "We just moved in across the street from Reenie's parents."

REENIE SAT in the corner booth at the Arctic Flyer, toying with the ice-cream sundae Lucky had insisted on buying for her and trying to keep Lucky's baby from squirming out of the high chair. Reenie would have met her half sister at Jerry's Diner, where they got together for lunch nearly every week, but word had it that Keith's mother was looking for her. Earlier, Reenie had ducked two of Georgia's calls at home—and slipped out the back of Hannah's photography studio the moment she spotted her mother-in-law coming in the front. She simply wasn't prepared for more of what her own mother had already dished out: *Are you sure you don't want to give Keith another chance? What would it hurt to wait a few months before making a decision? You're letting hurt and anger rule your head. Why does everything have to happen so fast?*

More than anything, Reenie didn't want to explain to Keith's mother that she'd already filed for divorce a week ago. Admitting that she was ending her marriage would make it more difficult to keep what had happened a secret because she would face the inevitable *"Why?"*

But maybe Georgia wanted to talk to her because she already knew about the divorce. Keith could've received the papers this morning, Reenie mused. According to the attorney, if Keith signed them without raising any other issues, everything could be final in three more weeks.

If he'd received the papers, *Keith* would be after her instead of his mother.

"I tried getting hold of your mom to see if she'd like to join us, but she wasn't home," Lucky said when she finally joined Reenie in the booth, carrying a chocolate-dipped ice-cream cone in one hand and a stack of napkins in the other.

"She was probably at her new neighbor's," Reenie said. "They arrived a couple hours ago, while she and I were on the phone, and she hurried off so she could deliver them dinner."

Sabrina squealed for a bite of Lucky's ice cream, and Lucky promptly held it to the child's cherubic mouth. "Celeste is *so* nice," she said.

"Yeah, a real saint." Reenie couldn't help the sarcasm that entered her voice. She admired her mother. But there were times—like the past three weeks—when she wished Celeste could be a little less angelic. Reenie had enough things working against her right now without having to hear about Keith's pain, which was all her mother seemed capable of talking about. Just because Reenie chose not to weep in front of everyone, Celeste assumed her daughter could withstand anything.

Lucky frowned as she watched Reenie destroy her sundae. "You used to like those."

Not anymore. Nothing tasted the way it used to. "I told you I didn't want it. It's too cold for ice cream."

"Are you kidding?" Lucky said. "If Harvey heats this place up any more, he'll have to serve his ice cream in mugs."

Outside, the wind bent the trees and rattled through the eaves. Reenie thought they might get the first snow of the year. But Lucky was right—it was plenty warm inside. "I guess I'm not hungry."

Lucky held her baby's hand to keep Sabrina from knocking the cone to the ground. "You don't have to be hungry to eat ice cream. What have you had today?" she asked. "I mean as far as meals go.

"I don't know," Reenie said.

"Have you eaten?"

"Probably."

"*Probably?* It's after two."

"I've been busy."

"Doing what?"

"Packing, mostly."

Lucky hesitated, then wiped the chocolate from Sabrina's chubby face. "When will you be moving to the farm?"

Reenie was grateful for the change of subject. She'd already heard enough about how she wasn't taking care of herself from just about everyone she knew. "Not for a few more weeks. It'll take that long for escrow to close."

"Can I help you pack?"

"No."

At this unequivocal response, Lucky sat back and arched an eyebrow at her. "No?"

Sabrina began to pound the table of her high chair, so Reenie gave her another bite of ice cream. "Packing gives me something to do," she explained. She'd already scrubbed the house from top to bottom, reorganized the closets and cleaned out the garage.

"Your mother told me you're planning to go back to work."

"I am. I don't have any choice."

"You could always go job hunting while I pack for you."

Reenie continued to stir her sundae. "I've already got a job."

Lucky's hand froze halfway to her baby's mouth. "Really?"

"I'll be teaching math at the high school."

"That was quick," she said, bringing the spoon the rest of the way when Sabrina squealed.

"They've been looking for someone to replace Mrs. Merriweather for two years, so it was easy."

"Mrs. Merriweather? She was an old battle-ax when I had her in high school. Don't tell me she died."

Lucky had been back in town for only a year or so, but she'd grown up in Dundee and, like Reenie, had attended Dundee High. Because she was a few years younger, they hadn't hung out together. Reenie doubted they would've been friends, anyway. Back then, Lucky had been too defensive and angry to make friends. Growing up with Red for a mother hadn't been easy. Reenie, on the other hand, had been blessed with a good family. She'd been loved, even spoiled, and had been one of the most popular girls in school.

"No, she retired," she explained. "Since then some of the other teachers have had to pick up the slack by teaching during their prep hour, so everyone was happy when I called."

"Sounds perfect. When do you start?"

"After Thanksgiving."

"That's next week."

It certainly didn't feel as though the holidays were approaching. "I guess it is."

"No, Sabrina." Lucky guided her child's hand away from the cone before she could crush it. "I'm glad it was that easy," she said to Reenie. "With the year well under way, I thought it might be difficult to get a position before summer."

Reenie thought about how smoothly the call had gone. "It probably didn't hurt that my father helped raise the money to build the new gym."

"Or that your brother was the principal donor, who also happens to be a national celebrity and coaches the varsity football team," Lucky added.

Reenie shrugged. "Being associated with Gabe has its advantages."

"If you say so," Lucky said with a sigh.

Ice cream dripped off the end of Sabrina's double chin. Reenie watched Lucky wipe it again. "He told me he was going to call you and apologize," she said. "I guess he hasn't gotten around to that yet, huh?"

"He called before Dad's birthday."

Reenie felt her eyebrows hike up. "He did? And?"

"I've heard more sincere apologies."

"So you're not willing to forgive him?"

"Why should I? The problem won't go away if I do."

"He was nice at the party," she said, feeding Sabrina when Lucky stopped to wipe her hands. "You have to give him credit for trying."

Lucky set the napkin aside. "No, I don't."

Reenie laughed for the first time in what felt like a really long while. "Poor Gabe."

"Are you kidding me? Your brother's fine," Lucky said. "He's reached career heights other men only dream about. He's richer than Midas. He's one of the handsomest men I've ever met. He gets along great with Dad, as long as I'm not around. And he's happily married. You told me a few weeks ago that Hannah might even be pregnant. Maybe he can't walk, but things could definitely be worse."

"I guess it's okay for you to feel the way you do," Reenie said, letting Lucky take over with Sabrina. "He wouldn't want you to pity him. He hates that."

"He isn't getting any pity from me. I don't even like him."

Reenie could tell that wasn't true. But a woman wearing a plastic hair-protector came in and stole her attention. She recognized that hair-protector; she recognized that coat.

"Oh no." Why the heck had she stopped watching the parking lot?

Lucky twisted to see what had attracted her attention. "Found you, eh?"

Reenie supposed it was inevitable. Dundee wasn't big enough to hide in for long.

"There you are," Georgia said.

"Hi Mom." Reenie managed a small wave.

Georgia's eyes swept over the sticky baby and Reenie's melting sundae before looking pointedly at Lucky. "Could I talk to Reenie alone for a moment?" she asked.

Lucky hesitated, but when Reenie nodded, she slid out of the booth and released her daughter from the high chair. "I'll wash Sabrina up."

"Have a seat, Mom," Reenie said.

Georgia slid into Lucky's place as Lucky headed to the restroom with her daughter. "I'm sure you know why I'm here."

"You want something to eat?"

"I want to talk to you."

"There's nothing to say."

"You and Keith had a good marriage. I think it can be fixed."

"I'm afraid it can't."

"What about counseling?"

Reenie opened her mouth to say that counseling wouldn't help, but Georgia raised a silencing hand before she could get the words out. "I know your budget has always been tight."

Because your son was supporting a whole other family. All the unnecessary penny-pinching was one more reason for Reenie to be bitter. But what good would succumbing to that bitterness do her? Keith had done what he'd done. Her best chance was to put it all behind her. With any luck, she'd be doing that—at least technically—in about three weeks.

"So I'm willing to pay for it," Georgia said. "I can't let your marriage fall apart. I love you and Keith, and my grandchildren, too much."

Reenie felt a sharp stab of the pain she'd been working so hard to avoid. Breaking up with Keith wasn't simple. Their lives had been intertwined for eleven years, fourteen if she counted how long she'd loved him. Her family was his family and vice versa. How did one tear all those relationships apart?

"He quit his job," Georgia was saying. "Now he's working at the hardware store. I think that shows you his intentions are good. He's willing to change, to stay at home and be with you, to support you the way he should have all along."

Don't listen, Reenie told herself. *It's an illusion. She doesn't know.* But Georgia was saying all the things Reenie's heart wanted to hear. And there was always that voice inside her, the one that said this wasn't real, that she'd come out of it okay in the end. "I don't think counseling will work, Mom," she said, but she sounded less convinced than she had a moment ago.

Georgia seemed to take heart at the hesitation in Reenie's response. "How can you say that without giving it a chance, honey?"

"I…I don't know," she said, because she couldn't tell what Keith had done. She didn't want the girls subjected to all the whispering, didn't want them to know how badly their father had let them down.

"Reenie, you and Keith have been happy for years," Georgia said. "Why throw that away?"

Because there was a woman living in California who was also married to Keith. And that woman had two children, which signified a lifelong commitment.

But Reenie hadn't heard a word from Isaac or his sister since Isaac had come to her house. Maybe she was overreacting, assuming the worst. Keith was here, wasn't he? He seemed to have cut ties with Liz just as he said he would.

Reenie supposed it was possible that Liz didn't really love him, that she was willing to let him go. Maybe she had a lover of her own, or was only interested in the financial support Keith could provide.

She rubbed her lip, feeling a brief respite from the tension that had knotted inside her for three weeks. She could tolerate having Keith send off a monthly child-support check, couldn't she? No one else would have to know. They could deal with this on their own, in the privacy of their home. Slowly rebuild the relationship.

She imagined her daughters' faces as she told them their daddy was coming home.

Obviously sensing the fact that she was getting through to her daughter-in-law, Georgia took both her hands. "I'm pleading with you, Reenie. For the sake of your children, try counseling. That's all I ask."

Lucky came from the bathroom, holding a clean and happy Sabrina. When Sabrina caught Reenie's eye, she clapped her hands and kicked her feet and Reenie actually managed a smile. Maybe the life she knew wasn't over yet. Maybe there was still some hope.

"Okay," she said. "Go ahead and set it up."

Georgia squeezed her hands affectionately. "Wonderful, honey. I'll tell Keith you're willing to give it a try."

CHAPTER TWELVE

ISAAC STRETCHED his legs out under the computer and leaned back in his chair, staring down at the napkin where Reenie had written her e-mail address. She'd also left her telephone number, but because it was less intrusive, he was more tempted to write than call. Ever since he'd left Dundee, he'd wondered how she was doing.

"Isaac?" Liz's voice reached him from the top of the stairs.

He stuffed the napkin back into the file where he was keeping copies of his old grant applications and rubbed his eyes. The real-estate agent who'd helped him unload the truck was gone. It was late, too late to be up after a long day of moving, but he couldn't seem to unwind. He kept picturing Reenie's mother standing at the door. His name definitely hadn't registered with her, so he doubted Reenie knew he was in town. But she'd find out soon enough and she wouldn't be happy about it.

Still, Liz's children had a right to be near their father just as much as Reenie's did. Reenie couldn't own the whole town.

"Yes?" he responded.

The stairs creaked as his sister came down. A moment later, she appeared at the door of the small basement bedroom he'd taken as his office, wearing a pair of baggy sweats. He suspected they belonged to Keith. Keith had left all his clothes behind when he'd rushed off three weeks ago. Because he hadn't bothered to collect them, Isaac had wanted to give them to charity. It was Liz who'd insisted they bring them along.

"Here you are," she said. "I thought you'd turned in for the night until I passed your room and saw that the light was on and the bed empty."

"I'm too tired to unpack anything else, but I'm not quite ready for sleep."

"I see you got your computer set up."

He glanced at the glowing screen. "Fortunately, I ordered Internet service when I had the phones turned on a few days ago. I'm good to go."

"That's great. Now you can stay in close contact with your boss at the university while you organize your research notes."

"The research will have to wait until later."

She hesitated. "Why?"

"I'll be working."

"Where?"

That was anybody's guess. Isaac couldn't imagine there were a lot of job opportunities in such a small town, but he had to come up with something. Liz was in no shape to work full-time—not yet. Besides, the kids were better off having her around. With all the emotional changes going on in their lives, they needed her.

"I'll find something," he said. He had a fairly healthy savings account, which meant he wouldn't need to earn a lot. A modest wage to help with the living expenses and keep himself busy until their lease was up would be enough. He hoped that in six months Liz would be ready to move back to L.A. Isaac hated the thought of Chris and Mica losing their father, but Keith was responsible for that. This move was just as much about Liz coming to terms with her sudden abandonment. Once she'd dealt with her loss, she'd be able to offer more support to the kids and they'd all begin to heal.

"I'm hoping to get a job, too," she said. "I can't imagine child support will go very far."

"Especially now that Keith's quit Softscape. We don't even know if he's found anything else."

"True," she said.

"If you go to work, what will you do with the kids?"

"I'll have to arrange child care."

"They'd be better off with you right now."

"But it's not fair to rely on you to support us."

"Why not? It's only temporary. And we're family."

"I should work part-time, at least. Keith might be able to help with the babysitting."

"We'll do perfectly without him."

"We only have one car."

"I'm going to buy a pickup, something fairly inexpensive that I can sell when I leave."

"Sounds good," she said, but she was nibbling worriedly at her bottom lip.

"What is it?" he asked.

"I feel bad for letting you do so much for me. I'm not sure I can deal with the guilt in addition to everything else."

"Then *don't* deal with it. Forget about it and get out of here. You need some sleep."

"I *can't* sleep."

"Take a sedative. Believe me, the world will seem like a better place tomorrow."

She cocked an eyebrow at him. "Somehow I doubt much of anything will change. But I've got to rest, if only for a little while."

"Good night," he said.

She mumbled the same, then disappeared, leaving him alone with his blue screen and the napkin he'd shoved into his file. Reenie... If he wrote to her, would she respond?

After reclaiming the napkin, he typed her address into the send box.

REENIE BLINKED when two new e-mails popped onto her screen. She'd just finished writing to her father, who stayed in Boise during the week when the legislature was in session. He'd be home tomorrow for Thanksgiving. But neither message was from him. One was from Keith. The other was most likely spam, since she didn't recognize the return address: 2871isaac@aol.com

Too tired to deal with her husband, she decided to shut down the computer. It was late, and she'd met with Keith earlier. Things had gone pretty well, considering. He'd insisted he'd left Liz for good and would never hear from her again. All he had to do was send her a check every month. And he'd promised Reenie he loved her more than ever and would be the perfect husband from now on.

Reenie longed to believe him. Only there was an emptiness inside her that had never been there before. She couldn't figure out what was missing, or whether she could go on without it, but worrying about it was keeping her from sleeping.

Indecision...she hated nothing worse.

What do I do? What's best for my children? She was so sick of those two questions, she wanted to scream. Celeste, Georgia and Frank, her father-in-law, thought she should give Keith another chance. Gabe and her own father disagreed. Those who knew the truth supported divorce; those who didn't pushed for reconciliation. Except her mother, of course. Her mother knew, but she couldn't be hard on anyone.

Reenie moved her cursor to the *x* that would sign her off the Internet, then hesitated. The subject line of the second message read, "You okay?"

Maybe this wasn't spam. Maybe it was from an old friend who'd learned of her pending divorce.

She wasn't sure that was much of an improvement over an unwanted advertisement. She was tired of the added attention. But curiosity prompted her to open it.

Hey, she read. Just thought I'd drop you a line to see how you're doing. Did you ever sell the Jeep? Did you take Keith back? How're the girls? Isaac

Isaac? Liz's brother? It had to be him. She'd provided her e-mail address the night they'd met at the diner. He didn't give his last name, but he'd referred to both the Jeep and Keith. Who else could it be?

The hair stood up on her arms as she read the message again. Maybe this wasn't spam, but she sure as heck wasn't any happier to receive it.

Why had he written her?

She closed the message, opened it, then closed it again. She didn't want to talk to anyone even remotely associated with Liz. She was working too hard to convince herself that Liz didn't exist.

But she had a few questions. How was it that Keith had left Liz so quickly and easily? Was Liz terribly hurt? And even though Reenie wished she could ignore the part of her heart that grieved for Keith's other children, she couldn't. How were they accepting the sudden disappearance of their father?

Her pulse raced as she began to type, but she steadied her shaking fingers. We still have the Jeep, but that's way down my list of concerns at the moment, she wrote. How's... she hesitated, almost backed up to erase what she'd written, then forced herself to continue ...your sister?

She didn't bother to sign it. Isaac would know who it was from.

While waiting for his reply, she paced the kitchen, her mind racing. How would Isaac answer her? Would he tell her that Keith was calling Liz? That Keith was still lying to her?

A moment later, a box appeared on the screen from 2871isaac@aol.com. Isaac wanted to instant message.

She froze in front of her computer but didn't sit down. An IM made the conversation more immediate. Did she really want to "talk" to Isaac Russell? A few e-mails were one thing. Active back-and-forth communication was another. Responding to him might encourage further participation in her life. And she couldn't tolerate that.

But what if Keith was playing her for a fool? Again.

Perching on the edge of her seat, she continued to stare at the invitation. Maybe Elizabeth had kicked Keith out. Maybe he'd had nowhere to go and *that* was why he'd returned to Dundee so quickly.

Reenie shook her head. The important thing was that Keith and Liz had split. Did she really want to know if the situation was exactly as Keith had represented it? She was thinking of reconciling with him, of trying again for the sake of her girls.

Isaac could easily tell her something that would blow that to hell and back. Maybe that was what he *intended* to do.

On the other hand, how could she be thinking of getting back with Keith and *not* know the full truth?

The insidious doubt she felt edged closer, making her angry. She wanted to overcome the suspicion, to trust again. But it was no use; she couldn't.

"Damn," she muttered and clicked Yes on the screen.

Isaac's first sentence appeared. What are you doing up so late?

Thinking I must be crazy to accept this message, she typed.

Why?

I'm trying to forget that you and your sister exist.

Classic denial?

Why not?

Funny...you struck me as a realist.

Ah, he'd already hit upon one of her biggest problems. She *was* a realist. But she was also a romantic. And the two sides of her couldn't find common ground when it came to Keith's betrayal. I'm surprised I didn't strike you as an idiot, she wrote.

Why?

You have to ask?

You trusted the one man in your life you should've been able to trust.

For some reason, she didn't want Liz's brother, of all people, to be so sympathetic. Don't be nice to me, she wrote.

Is that a typo?

No.

Didn't think so. There was a long pause. What's the matter? Afraid you might be tempted to like me?

It was her turn to hesitate. No, of course not, she thought. Well…maybe. She'd enjoyed having dinner with him. It wasn't until she found out who he was that she'd crossed him off her list of possible friends. Not beyond my ability to resist, she responded.

I'm an innocent bystander, remember?

We're on opposite teams, remember?

Keith's fault. Not mine.

So why are you e-mailing me? she typed. Are you on some kind of recon mission for your sister?

No.

She waited, but he didn't qualify or explain. Hello?

Just wondering…

What?

Whether you took Keith back.

She tapped her lip as she read his response. So you can help your sister plan her next move?

Not necessarily. But if she asked me…

You'd tell her.

Probably. I'm her brother.

Reenie couldn't fault him for his response. At least he was being straightforward with her. You really think your sister's special.

Yes.

That was quick… Is she very pretty?

Reenie cursed herself the second she'd sent that response. But curiosity about the woman who'd borne Keith two children had been eating at her ever since she'd learned the truth. What had her husband seen in Liz? Was she so beautiful that he couldn't help himself? So incredibly sweet and good that he was drawn to her despite the fact that he had a family?

Reenie knew she was searching for a way to excuse what Keith had done. If Liz was irresistible, maybe Keith wasn't totally responsible. Any man would have done the same.

Very, came his answer.

Does she look like you?

A little.

Then she was probably pretty indeed. Certainly Isaac was more handsome than most men.

Jealousy hit hard, momentarily overriding Reenie's curiosity, doubt, fear, everything else. Closing her eyes, she shook her head, fighting to tamp down the hatefulness it evoked.

She was stupid to make herself so vulnerable, she decided. She needed to remain calm, make good decisions, hold herself together for her children. She did *not* need to talk to Isaac Russell.

Opening her eyes so she could sign off, she saw that he'd already written something else, something that gave her pause: But she's no prettier than you.

A moment earlier, she'd thought he might be trying to hurt her, to strengthen his sister's hand by ruining her self-confidence. But if that were the case, why would he pay her such a compliment?

You're being nice again, she accused, still trying to figure him out.

Not really. You're beautiful—not easy to like. <G>

She laughed in spite of herself. The kind of news you gave me tends to bring out the worst in a person.

Agreed.

I'm usually very likable.

We'll see...

Apprehension swept down Reenie's spine. What's that supposed to mean?

Did you get back with Keith? he asked.

Isaac knew something she didn't; she could tell. Why? Is he calling Liz, too, trying to convince her to forgive him?

My question first.

So he wanted to trade. Fine. It was no secret that Keith wasn't living at home. We're not together.

Is it over, then?

She thought of the divorce papers, which were probably already in the mail; she also thought of her promise to try counseling. Maybe.

Fortunately, he didn't press her for a more definitive answer, because she couldn't give him one.

Your turn, she prompted.

He hasn't called Liz.

At all?

Not once.

Then...I'm confused. What's up?

Nothing. I've gotta go—dead tired. See you around, he said, and signed off.

Reenie frowned at the log box that contained the last of their conversation. "See you around" as in "take it easy"? Or "see you around" as in *"see you someday soon"*?

A LIGHT LAYER OF SNOW had fallen during the night. When Reenie drove the kids to school, the roads were slushy, the fields covered with a thin, white veil. She huddled into her thick sweatshirt while waiting for the heater to warm the chilly van.

"Can we build a snowman when I get home today, Mommy?" Isabella asked.

Reenie glanced back to see her youngest daughter's nose pressed to the window, her breath fogging the glass. "If the sun doesn't come out and melt all the snow, babe."

"What if Daddy wants to help us?" Angela asked, turning away from her own window.

"What if?" Reenie replied, trying to sidestep the challenge in her daughter's voice.

"Will you go inside so you don't have to see him?"

Reenie could feel the interest of all three girls. But she wasn't sure what to tell them. She didn't really want to be around Keith, but maybe counseling would change that. "We'll see," she said.

"You're not mad at him anymore?" Isabella asked.

"I didn't say that. It's more…" Reenie hesitated, picking and choosing her words with care. "I'm trying to get over Daddy's…mistake."

"Mommy, what did Daddy do?" Angela asked.

"I'll explain when you're older. You'll understand it better then."

"If he broke something, can't he buy you a new one?"

"I wish he could, sweetheart."

Jennifer piped up. "Whatever he did, you're trying to forgive him because of us, right?"

Reenie laughed. "How are you old enough to figure that one out?"

"I heard you on the phone with Grandma O'Connell," she admitted.

"Oh. Well, your daddy and I both love you and are trying to work things out so we can all be together."

"Grandma called back after you went to the store," Angela said.

"She did?" Reenie slowed as she came to the line of cars waiting to turn in at the school. "Why didn't you tell me when I got home?"

"She wasn't calling to talk to you."

"She wanted to talk to us," Jennifer supplied.

"What'd she say?" Reenie asked.

"Not to worry. She's going to get you and Daddy some help so that Daddy will be able to come back soon."

Reenie ground her teeth. She knew her mother-in-law meant well, but it was difficult not to resent the interference.

"Is he coming home tonight?" Isabella asked.

"It's a possibility that he could come in a few weeks," she admitted. "But even if he doesn't, you'll all be fine, you know that? Daddy and I will always love you and take good care of you, even if—"

"Hey, who's that?" Angela interrupted.

Momentarily distracted, Reenie turned in the direction her daughter was pointing and saw a tall, beautiful blond woman get out of a white Cadillac Esplanade. Two children tumbled out the opposite side—a girl with dark blond hair and thick glasses, whose willowy build reminded Reenie a great deal of Popeye's Olive Oyl, and an adorable, stocky little boy with golden hair. "I don't know," she said. "They must be new."

"We hardly *ever* get new people," Jennifer said excitedly.

Reenie found herself watching the woman and child as avidly as her children were. "That's true. Do you think they might be the family who moved in across the street from Nanna?"

"Maybe," Angela said. "Nanna told me they have a girl close to my age."

"That girl can't be eight," Jennifer said.

"Why not?" Angela replied.

"She's so tall."

"It's possible," Reenie mused. "She's tall, but so is her mother."

"Her mom's pretty," Isabella breathed.

The woman was pretty—and perfectly assembled, even at this hour and in this weather. "She *must* be new," Reenie grumbled. "No one around here bothers with hair and makeup on a morning like this."

"Hurry so I can catch up with them," Angela said.

Reenie finally drew abreast of the curb and let her children hop out. They waved before running down the sidewalk to catch the woman and her children.

Reenie pulled away, but while waiting for a break in traffic, she noticed that Isabella had left her backpack in the van.

Rolling down her window, she motioned to the person behind her that she needed to get out of line. It was a man in a Lexus. He gave her room, and she managed to reverse until she could double-park. Then she grabbed the backpack and went after her kids.

"Isabella!" she called, dodging traffic as she crossed the crowded lot.

The new woman glanced up when she heard Reenie's voice, saw her hurrying toward them and, grabbing both her children, dragged them off toward the office.

"Who was that?" Reenie asked as her daughters came back to meet her.

"They're new, just like we thought," Isabella said cheerfully.

Angela was only a step behind her little sister and didn't look nearly as happy.

"What is it?" Reenie asked.

Her eyebrows knitted as she shielded her face from the falling snow. "She *is* my age."

"The tall girl?"

"Yeah."

"So what's wrong? I thought you'd be glad."

"I was glad until I asked her if she could come over and play today."

"What'd she say?"

"*She* wanted to. But her mother jerked her hand and said…" Angela hardened her expression as she mimicked what she'd heard, "'I'm afraid not.'"

"Really?" Reenie stared after the woman, who'd disappeared into the office. "That doesn't sound too friendly."

"It wasn't," Angela complained.

"Maybe she reacted that way because we're still strangers. Maybe she wants to get to know us better first. That's understandable, isn't it?"

"I told her that," Jennifer said. "I mean, give them some time. They're gonna like us. We have the same last name."

"What?" Reenie said. But the bell rang right then, and the girls rushed off, leaving her standing at the edge of the parking lot, feeling as though she'd just been zapped with a stun gun.

"They wouldn't have," she murmured, over and over to herself. But her mind was racing. What were the chances that an unrelated family of O'Connells would move to town at this time? Could that blond woman be Liz? And those children… *Keith's?* She remembered Isaac's final words from last night, which now seemed much more than just a turn of phrase: *See you around…*

As Reenie glanced back at the elegant Esplanade, her chest constricted and she took an impulsive step toward the office. She had to find out.

But she couldn't confront Liz at the school. Not with children, teachers and administrators looking on.

"This isn't happening!" she cried, so loud that the last of the departing parents turned to stare.

Rosie Strickland, the crossing guard, was carrying in her sign. "Reenie, are you okay?" she asked.

But Reenie didn't answer. Rushing to her van, she jumped behind the wheel and tore out of the lot.

CHAPTER THIRTEEN

SOMEONE WAS POUNDING on the door.

The noise intruded on Isaac's sleep, dragging him from a pleasant dream he knew he probably wouldn't remember once he opened his eyes. For a moment, he fought consciousness—only to hear the doorbell ring several times in rapid succession.

With a groan, he blinked and stared through his window at the gray, cold-looking day as reality came crashing back. He now lived in a town of only fifteen hundred people in the mountains north of Boise. Three weeks ago, he was waiting to return to the most exotic place in the world. Now he'd be lucky to go to a movie.

"I should've killed Keith when I first figured it out," he muttered. "Then I wouldn't be here."

More pounding. Insistent. Angry.

What the hell could be so urgent? No one even knew who they were yet. Where was his sister, anyway?

"Liz?" he called.

No response. He couldn't hear movement or voices in the house. Even the children seemed to be gone.

Which left him to deal with the visitor.

Maybe it was Keith, presenting him with the perfect opportunity to break his ex-brother-in-law's sorry neck.

That thought was encouraging enough to get him out of bed. Shoving a hand through his unruly hair, he dragged on his jeans, and stumbled down the hall to the living room. His eyes felt like sandpaper; he'd definitely been up too late. But his fatigue fell away the instant he opened the door.

Reenie gasped when she saw him, and rocked back, as if he'd slapped her. "It *is* you," she murmured.

"Reenie—"

"You son of a bitch!"

"Listen to me—"

"You brought her here?" Her eyes darted to the boxes behind him. "You *moved* her here?"

Her voice had escalated considerably. He lowered his, hoping to calm her. "This has nothing to do with you."

"Oh, right," she managed to say, but this time her words were barely audible. She was pressing a hand to her chest and breathing so fast he was afraid she was hyperventilating.

Grabbing her arm, he tried to pull her inside, where she'd at least be warm and dry.

But she reacted as though he was trying to drag her into a grave with a rotting corpse. Yanking out of his grasp, she backed up too fast, slipped off the step and fell.

When she landed awkwardly on one hand, Isaac cursed and darted forward to help her. But she wouldn't let him touch her.

"I already told you—she can have him," she said, scrambling away and climbing to her feet. "My marriage is over. You made sure of that when you came here a few weeks ago. Is that what you wanted to confirm with your friendly little instant message? How hard you were going to have to work to finish things off? Well, pack up your stuff and go back to L.A.—and take my husband with you!"

"It's not that simple, Reenie," he tried to explain. But she wasn't listening. Tears gathered in her eyes and streaked down her face. Only this time, instead of succumbing to them, she lifted her chin and glared through the welling drops.

"Oh yeah?" she said. "It's simple to me. Keith and your sister can spend the rest of their days together. *In California.*"

Except Keith wanted Reenie.

"Will you come in so we can talk?" Isaac asked.

Anger flashed in her eyes, but as she squared off in front of him, he couldn't help admiring her spirit.

"Go to hell," she said. "You can't hurt me, you hear? You can't hurt me! So you might as well leave!" Wincing slightly when she moved her injured hand, she hurried back to the van she'd left running in the driveway.

"Hey, watch where you're going!" he shouted, afraid she'd kill someone, or herself, driving in her current state of mind. But she didn't appear to hear him. Or she was too upset to care. She burned rubber as she backed out of the driveway, and he cringed as she almost hit a Lincoln Town Car that was turning into the driveway across the street.

Celeste Holbrook parked haphazardly as Reenie gunned the engine and rocketed away from them. "Was that *Reenie?*" she called as she stepped out of her car.

He sighed heavily, watching the van screech around the corner. "I'm afraid so," he called back.

"But—why was she at your house?"

She wasn't bringing him a casserole.

"What's wrong with her?" Celeste added before he could respond to her first question.

"She's had a bit of a shock," he said. "Maybe you should go over and make sure she's okay."

Celeste seemed to take in the fact that he was standing outside without a shirt or shoes, freezing in the chill wind. "I will," she said, "right away," and immediately got back into her car.

Isaac turned to go into the house, but just then Liz pulled up, looking a little rattled herself. "What are you doing out here?" she asked as she climbed out of her SUV.

He crossed his arms to garner some warmth. "Reenie came by." There was a long hesitation. "What did she say?"

"She wants us to take Keith with us and go back to L.A."

Liz pursed her lips as she took in this information. "Did you tell her Keith won't even return my calls?"

"No. I didn't get the chance to tell her much of anything."

She threw back her shoulders. "We have a right to be here, too."

"I guess," Isaac said, and went inside.

KEITH'S CHEST CONSTRICTED with fear as he gazed down at the legal-size envelope he'd just retrieved from his parents' mailbox. He'd rushed home over his lunch hour because he was expecting his last check from Softscape and he needed the money. He hadn't sent anything to Liz since he'd left L.A. and their house payment was due on the first. He was sure Reenie was running low on funds, too.

But this was no check. It came from an attorney named Rosenbaum—an attorney in Boise.

In the other room, his father and mother were arguing about where to place a picture Georgia had bought last week.

"Aren't you going to measure it?" Georgia asked impatiently.

"Why?" Frank responded. "I can tell I've got a stud right here. Why not let me hang it and be done?"

"Because I want it centered."

"It *is* centered. I can see that it is. If you don't let me put the nail here, the weight of the picture will pull it right out of the wall."

"Oh, for crying out loud. Keith works at the hardware store. He can get you one of those special doohickeys that works even without a stud, if we need it."

Their voices filtered through his mind as Keith gazed at the envelope. As great as his parents were, living with them was no picnic. He missed Reenie. He missed Liz. He missed his children, clamoring to wrestle with him or climb onto his lap, and he missed the money he used to make...

What about the counseling they'd discussed? he wondered.

That was supposed to save their marriage. She seemed willing to go to a therapist the last time he called. But she hadn't told him to disregard anything he might receive from her attorney.

His heart thumped erratically in his chest as he opened the envelope. He knew what it would contain, and yet the sight of the Divorcement Decree hit him hard. Reenie was divorcing him. The woman who'd always loved him so passionately.

"Doesn't she understand what I'm giving up?" he muttered to himself. What about Liz? And Chris and Mica? His sacrifice had to mean *something* to her.

Vaguely he heard his mother come into the room, but he was so devastated by what he held in his hand that he didn't bother to hide the documents from her.

"What's that?" she asked.

He swallowed hard. "Reenie's divorcing me," he said, his words sounding as hollow as the rest of him.

"What?" She came closer to peer down at the papers. "Honey, she must've started that before she agreed to counseling. Have you called her since you got this?"

"No." The truth was that he was *afraid* to call her, afraid she might say she was going through with the divorce, after all. Until this moment, he never really believed she would.

"Well, don't just stand there, looking like someone shot you," she said. "Get on the phone."

His throat was too dry, too tight. "I'll call her tonight."

"Call her now. This is more important than anything."

"I'll deal with it later." *When he could breathe….*

"If you put it off, you'll lose her for good, Keith. Deal with it now."

Taking a deep breath, he tossed the divorce papers onto the table to get them out of his sight and went to the phone.

Reenie answered on the fourth ring, but she hardly sounded like the woman he knew. "Reenie?" he said.

"What?"

"Have you been crying?"

When she sniffed but didn't answer, the lump in his throat nearly choked him. "I'm sorry, babe. I'm so—"

"Why'd you call?" she asked abruptly.

He blinked, fighting his own tears. "I got the papers."

"Please sign them right away," she said. "I…I want to put this behind me."

Squeezing his eyes closed, he pressed a hand to his aching chest. "What about counseling? You said—"

"I've changed my mind."

"Why?"

"Just go back to Liz, Keith."

"I don't want to go back to Liz. I want to make things right with you. I—"

"There's no way to do that! Don't you understand?"

"I won't sign the papers, Reenie."

"Then I'll go to the police. What you did was illegal, Keith."

He didn't know what to say to that. Would she really turn him in?

The doorbell rang, drawing his mother away from the kitchen.

"You must've loved Liz once," Reenie said.

Grateful for the privacy his mother's absence afforded him, he struggled to come up with an answer for what he'd done that she might understand. He had loved Liz. In many ways, he still did. But not on the same gut level that he loved Reenie.

In the end, he decided there wasn't any way to make Reenie understand. *He* didn't understand, completely. So he tried to take the focus off Liz by putting it back on their own marriage. "You and I have been together since we were in high school, Reenie. That's half our lives. We have three children. You're not going to throw all that away, are you?"

"I'm not the one who threw it away, Keith," she said. "You did. Now I just want to be left alone to raise my daughters. I don't want Liz's kids attending the same school as mine. I don't want to bump into her when I buy gas. I don't want—"

"What are you talking about?" he asked. But Reenie didn't get a chance to explain before his mother interrupted.

"Keith, there's a woman here to see you."

Fresh panic clutched at his throat. "Who is it?"

His mother wore a puzzled, distraught expression. "She says she's your *wife*."

Keith's heartbeat seemed to echo in the room. *Thump, thump. Thump, thump.*

Evidently, Reenie had heard Georgia. "Liz's there?" she asked.

"Yes," he said numbly, amazed to hear no surprise in her voice.

"Maybe you can make your second marriage work, Keith," she said. "For—for your other children. But please, take Liz and her family back to California."

"You can't be serious," he said. "We need to talk…."

Only a dial tone answered him. She'd already disconnected.

Liz HAD NEVER FELT colder in her life. She sat primly on the sofa in Keith's parents' living room, waiting for her husband while staring at her mother-in-law—a woman she'd thought was dead. It was pretty easy to recognize the gleam of animosity in Georgia O'Connell's eyes. Keith's mother didn't want her here. Keith's mother didn't even want to know she existed.

"I'm not trying to cause trouble," Liz said.

"Then what do you want?" she responded coldly. "My son is married to a lovely woman. Together they have three children. His wife's parents are good friends of ours."

Liz had expected Keith's family to know about her—or she would've waited until she could confront him somewhere alone. She'd assumed word would have spread by now, sending shock waves through the whole community. Especially a community the size of Dundee. How could Keith's parents not know? Why wouldn't Reenie have told them?

Maybe Reenie felt as humiliated as Liz did. But at least Keith had really loved Reenie. At least he'd wanted to save his relationship with her.

"So? What do you have to say?" Georgia prompted.

Managing to burrow beneath the Band-Aid covering her thumb, Liz dug even deeper into her cuticle. She'd thought speaking to her husband at his parents' house would be much more private than showing up at the hardware store, where the clerk at the Gas-N-Go had told her Keith worked. But she'd made a terrible mistake coming here. She should've waited....

"I—I realize this is difficult—" she started, but Keith appeared in the doorway at that moment, and the sight of him took Liz's breath away. This was her husband, the man she loved. Surely there had to have been *something* authentic about their relationship.

She stood because she didn't know what else to do. Her natural impulse, even now, was to go to him. She longed to feel his strong arms slide around her, craved his smell, his touch.

But he didn't give her so much as a smile. He looked worried, rumpled, on edge. "Liz," he said with a formal nod.

Georgia O'Connell looked from one to the other. "Who is this woman, Keith?"

Pressing the butt of his hand to his forehead as though he had a terrible headache, he closed his eyes.

Liz held her breath.

"Keith?" his mother repeated.

The shrillness of Georgia's voice seemed to shock him out of his stupor. It also brought an older man to the living room, one close to Keith's height but significantly heavier. "Georgia?" he said. "Are you okay?"

This had to be Keith's father, the man the gas-station attendant had called Frank. Liz could see the family resemblance, the concern underlying his gruff exterior when he saw his wife's distress.

"Mom, Dad, I—I've made a terrible mistake," Keith said.

Liz dug deeper into the cuticle of her thumb, drawing blood. So she was nothing more than a mistake? She should've let Isaac accompany her here, as he'd suggested. But she'd thought, she'd *hoped,* that Keith would come to his senses the moment he saw her, that he'd realize how much he loved her and that they could figure out a positive solution. Why would she want Isaac as a witness to that? He'd never understand why she'd consider taking Keith back.

"You had an affair!" Georgia gasped.

Keith's eyebrows drew together, but his eyes never wavered from Liz's. Liz got the impression that he missed her, too. But something held him back. "It started out that way," he said softly.

At this, Liz's knees nearly buckled. Georgia swooned, and Frank rushed to his wife's side. "Is that why Reenie's divorcing you?" Georgia asked as his father gripped her hand. "Because... because you *cheated* on her?"

Keith blanched but nodded.

The color drained from Georgia's face, leaving her as pale as her son. "So who is this woman? I've never seen her before in my life. But she claims you're married to her."

"He can't be *married* to her," Frank said. "He already has a wife."

"We *are* married," Elizabeth insisted. "And we have two children."

When Keith didn't deny it, Georgia's eyes narrowed. "No! Keith, you wouldn't...you...that's illegal. We brought you up better than that."

"Where are the kids?" Frank asked.

Liz took two pictures from her purse. "Christopher, our son, is with my brother." She handed Chris's picture to Frank and Mica's to Georgia. "Mica, our daughter, is in school."

Stupefied, they stared down at the grandchildren they'd never known they had.

"In school where?" Keith asked, and Liz felt her first flicker of hope. She could tell he was eager to see them.

"Caldwell Elementary."

Georgia managed to pull her attention from the photographs. *"Here in Dundee?"* she cried.

Liz nodded. "I've rented the house across the street from the Holbrooks."

"Oh God," she said, and crumpled into her seat.

THAT AFTERNOON, Reenie let the van idle at the curb as she tapped the steering wheel, waiting nervously for her girls to get out of class. Had Jennifer, Angela and Isabella had any more contact with Mica or Christopher? If so, had Liz's kids mentioned their daddy? Grade-school children didn't generally give names. They said *My mom* or *My dad,* not *Keith.* So there was a chance her daughters still believed having the same last name was a random coincidence.

There was also a chance they didn't....

She should've told them, she thought with a curse. But she hadn't been able to think clearly. In trying to shelter them, she'd left them vulnerable to a terrible surprise.

Jennifer came around the corner of the building, and Reenie held her breath until her oldest daughter spotted her in the van and smiled. Jennifer was fine. But she was two years older than Mica. Once school started, she wouldn't have had much direct contact with the third-grader.

Isabella appeared next. She came bounding down the line of cars, skipping and waving papers at Reenie. Obviously, she was pleased with her performance on some recent assignments.

Mirroring her smile, Reenie told herself to relax as they reached the van.

"Hi, Mom!" Jennifer said, climbing in.

"Hi, honey," she replied, but she was watching Isabella, thinking, *That's two.* Her baby didn't know, either.

"Look! I got a star on all three," Isabella announced as she clambered inside.

"Wow, good for you, sweetheart." Reenie examined each paper. Then Jennifer told them how she nearly beat the whole fifth grade in a basketball shoot-off.

Reenie responded with as much enthusiasm as she could muster, but the crowd of children at the school was beginning to thin and Angela still hadn't come. "Where's your sister?" she asked.

Jennifer pulled the fourth Harry Potter book from her backpack, which she was reading for the fifth time. "I don't know. I haven't seen her."

"Was she at the last recess?"

"Probably." She cracked the book, searching for the place where she'd left off. "But she usually goes to the monkey bars with her friends. I go to the basketball court."

Worry tightened Reenie's stomach into a hard ball. Turning off the motor, she said, "Stay here, I'll be right back," and hurried to the office.

The moment Reenie opened the door she knew her worst fears had been realized. Mica and Angela sat in chairs surrounded by Tom Clovis, the principal, Sherry Foley, the school secretary, and Agnes Scott, Angela's teacher.

"There you are," Tom said with apparent relief as soon as Reenie walked in.

Reenie had grown up with these people, so they'd always been on a first-name basis. She'd even dated Tom, way back in high school.

"We've been waiting for you," he added. "I left you two messages."

Earlier, Reenie had been with her mother, Gabe and Hannah at Jerry's Diner. After that, Celeste had insisted they go to Hannah's studio to call Garth in Boise. Now the entire family was aware of what she faced. It felt good to know they stood behind her. But there'd been no time to run home and check her answering machine. She hadn't even thought of it.

"What's wrong?" she asked.

Tears dripped from Angela's chin. "Mica says *my* daddy is really *her* daddy."

"My mommy told me so," Mica insisted.

Tom laughed awkwardly. "I keep trying to tell them that there must be two Keith O'Connells. But Mica insists her daddy has lived here for a long time, and I know there aren't two Keith O'Connells in Dundee."

The lump growing in Reenie's throat burned. God, how did she explain? What she had to say would humiliate her in front of her friends, in front of the whole town. By tomorrow morning, everyone would know who Liz, Mica and Christopher were. But the pain that knowledge would cause her daughters hurt Reenie even more.

"Angela..." Swallowing hard, she glanced at Mica. The child wasn't nearly as pretty as Angela, but Reenie could see that she'd be a real beauty some day. And there was a bright intelligence shining from her eyes, eyes that were so filled with righteous indignation and pain that Reenie's heart nearly broke all over again. She was tempted to hate this child as she hated Liz— but how could she? The poor thing was as much a victim of Keith's mistakes as she and her own children were.

Kneeling down in front of them, Reenie took Angela's hand, then forced herself to reach out to Mica.

At first, Liz's child's cold fingers repelled Reenie. Mica was the product of Keith's betrayal, a symbol of the most difficult thing Reenie had ever had to face. But the fragility of the girl's thin shoulders and those eyes; which seemed to know too much for her young age, made Reenie grip Mica warmly. "Angela, remember when I told you that Daddy made a mistake?"

Reenie could feel the curiosity of the adults who were watching them, could almost hear their thoughts flying, *What's she doing? Why doesn't she deny it?*

"Yes," Angela replied hesitantly. "You said it was like when Isabella broke your favorite vase."

"It is a lot like that. Daddy's done something that has consequences. We've talked about that, too, right?"

She nodded, but fresh tears gathered in her eyes and fell down
her cheeks. No doubt she could already tell by Reenie's manner
that Mica was right.

Mica flinched as a sob escaped Angela, and somehow, that
made Reenie cry, too. "Well, one time while Daddy was gone
away from me—before you were born—he fell in love with Mica's mother, and…"

Mica's gaze dropped to the carpet.

"Started another family," Reenie finished.

At this pronouncement, Sherry Foley's breath hissed sharply
as she sucked it between her teeth. "Oh, Reenie," she murmured.
Agnes covered her mouth and Tom's eyebrows shot all the way
up to his receding hairline.

Reenie ignored them and managed to smile through her tears.
"Mica's telling the truth. There is only one Keith O'Connell. But
he loves both of you. I know that."

Suddenly the door swung open and Liz stood there, every
hair in place, her clothes without a wrinkle, and sunglasses hiding her eyes.

Immediately, Reenie let go of Mica, and Mica stood and
rushed over to her mother. "I want to go back to California," she
said, breaking into sobs.

Angela sniffed and threw herself into Reenie's arms. "I want
them to go, too."

Reenie slowly stood and faced the woman her husband had
slept with for the past nine years. It was difficult to tell what Liz
was thinking behind those glasses. She seemed so remote, so cool
and collected. But there were bandages on every finger. Surely
that indicated something….

"I'm sorry I was late," she said to the shocked audience,
then led her daughter away as if Reenie and Angela weren't
even there.

Reenie wiped her eyes and kissed the top of Angela's head. "It'll be okay," she promised, but she couldn't hold back the tears when Tom, Sherry and Agnes gathered round to hug them both.

CHAPTER FOURTEEN

IT BECAME APPARENT over the next few days and weeks that the other O'Connells weren't going anywhere. Reenie ran into them all over town. Their presence, and what it signified, made the places she'd always enjoyed going to—the salon, the grocery store, the diner—feel uncomfortable. When she and Liz bumped into each other, they'd exchange quick, uncomfortable glances and move on.

But even if Liz and her family weren't nearby, conversations would stop the moment Reenie entered a room. People she'd known for years and years would look at her sadly. Her in-laws were too embarrassed to even speak to her. And, worst of all, Mr. Rosenbaum turned out to be right. Her four-week divorce stretched into six weeks and then eight as Keith refused to sign the papers. Now that everyone knew the truth and no legal action had been taken, Reenie's threat to go to the police meant nothing to him. He was determined to prove to her that he was a changed man, that he'd do anything to win her back. His actions bothered Reenie so much she decided to demand half the equity in the house instead of giving it to him as she'd originally planned. She also made Keith pick up and drop off the girls at her brother's place.

Fortunately, she had the holidays, her new job and her move to the farm to keep her busy. By January, there was so much going on in her life she hardly had time to think, let alone feel. Keith wanted to move into their old house but Reenie wouldn't allow it—unless he signed the divorce papers. He, in turn, demanded partial custody of the girls.

In February, Reenie finally conceded so she could end the stalemate between them. Keith signed the documents and he had Jennifer, Angela and Isabella every other weekend, Thanksgiving, Christmas Eve and one month in the summer. Sometimes when they were with him, they even spent an afternoon with their half siblings. Not that they were very happy about it. Because Liz's family had moved to town just as everything fell apart, Reenie's daughters believed Mica and Christopher had stolen their daddy. Reenie had tried to explain that the divorce had nothing to do with Liz's children, but Angela, especially, complained about having the intellectually gifted Mica in her class at school.

Fortunately by March, Reenie's friends and neighbors had accepted Reenie's new status. Everyone became accustomed to having the other O'Connells around and, as the scandal turned into old news, life grew easier. Reenie only had to avoid her parents' house, because Liz and Isaac lived across the street, do her grocery shopping on weekends, because Liz worked at Finley's during the week, pick up her girls a few minutes earlier than usual, so all the O'Connell kids wouldn't wind up standing on the curb together. And she had to ignore Isaac Russell, who now worked at the feed store. She would've asked Gabe to pick up her supplies, but didn't feel she could impose on him that much. Since moving to the farm, she had a horse, a cow and several chickens to care for and therefore had to make frequent trips.

She wasn't sure if her visits to Earl's Feed & Tackle prompted Isaac to e-mail her, but he did so every once in a while. Earl, the owner of the store, must've told him when she was in the market for a horse, because the first time he wrote it was to say he could help her find a good buy, if she wanted some help.

She didn't want *his* help, so she deleted his message and didn't reply.

A few weeks later, shortly after she took Bailey to the vet and received the sad news that he had cancer, Isaac had written her again. She wasn't sure what he wanted that time, but she knew he'd heard about Bailey when he said how sorry he was.

Once more, she hit the delete button and didn't respond.

Then, as recently as last month, he'd sent her a message to let her know they were having a sale on the kind of feed she preferred. She was tempted to respond to that one. She carried a heavy load these days when it came to supporting herself and the girls. Because Softscape wouldn't take Keith back if he continued to commute, and Keith refused to move to Los Angeles, he was still at the hardware store. There, he didn't make enough to give her much of anything.

But she didn't respond to Isaac's third message, either. She didn't even go in to buy the feed. She was finished with Isaac, Liz and Keith, although Keith was having a hard time understanding the finality of it all. Her ex-husband still called occasionally, or dropped by with the hope of talking her into coming back to him. He said he'd never get over her, never give up. However, sometimes she saw him around town with Liz or one of Liz's children and knew she would never agree to a reconciliation.

For the most part, Reenie was successful in pretending that Keith, Isaac and Liz didn't exist. She even dated now and then. True, the men she saw were mostly old friends and had no chance of winning her heart. But at least she was moving on. She wouldn't allow what Keith had done to destroy her. If she was more than a little lonely, she ignored it. Between milking the cow in the morning, teaching school during the day and taking care of the kids and the farm at night, she usually dropped into bed around midnight and didn't even dream.

As the snow disappeared and April rolled around, Reenie began to feel as though she was recovering. The resentment in Jennifer's voice when she talked about "smarty-pants" Mica had diminished, leading Reenie to believe that the girls were beginning to adjust, as well. She and Georgia were on distant but not unfriendly terms despite the divorce. And, largely due to Gabe's help, the most rudimentary improvements to the farm, including the repairs to the barn, were complete. Everything was under control. At least, that was what Reenie thought until she walked into the staff meeting at the high school early one Monday and everyone suddenly fell silent.

"What is it?" she asked, gazing around her.

Beth Neilsen, who taught history, was three years older than Reenie and also divorced. Since Reenie had split with Keith, Beth had become one of her closest friends and often hung out with her at The Honky Tonk on a Friday or Saturday night. When Beth stared at the floor instead of responding, Reenie knew something was really wrong.

"Isn't anyone going to answer me?" she said.

The principal, Guy McCauley, stood at the front of the room. "Reenie, um, have a seat, okay?"

Reenie glanced at her watch. It was only 6:55 a.m. Deborah Wheeler was still at the back, filling her coffee cup. "I'm not late," she said, trying to figure out what was going on.

"No."

"Did…a parent of one of my students call to complain? There haven't been any incidents in my classroom—"

"No, no, of course not," he said. "You're doing a super job."

"Then what?"

There were a few murmurs and some restless shifting from everyone else as Guy's lips curved into an awkward smile. "It's nothing, really. I mean, nothing new. You're aware that Ina Guardino goes on maternity leave week after next, right?"

"Yes…"

Deborah carried her coffee to her seat. But she no longer seemed particularly interested in drinking it. She was too busy staring at Reenie.

"And that we've been searching, without any luck, for someone to replace her?" Guy went on.

Reenie scowled. "If you think I can manage another class right now, you're wrong, Guy. I already gave up my lunch hour to take one of Janet Wolfe's computer classes when she broke her hip. And the other periods I'm teaching math, which isn't an elective. Every kid we've got has to pass my class, which means I get up close and personal with *all* the behavioral problems. This semester, I've got both Riley Caywood and Derrick Benson in my sixth period. And you know I have open seventh so I can pick up my kids from school. My hands are full."

"You're busy," he agreed. "And we wouldn't think of overburdening you by asking for more. That's why we're so happy we've managed to find someone else...well, actually Madge found him," he added quickly.

Madge was a history teacher who always sat front and center during staff meetings. At this, she glanced at Reenie with her mouth open, as if she would deny it. Then she gave the principal a scathing look that said, *Big mouth.*

Why she'd respond in such a way, Reenie had no idea. But she was glad they were getting a new teacher. Lord knows they needed one. "Great," she said with a careless shrug. "Who is it?"

She set her bag down and slipped into her usual seat next to Beth. But the ensuing silence felt more than a little stilted. And every pair of eyes remained riveted on her.

Guy cleared his throat. "Isaac Russell."

He'd muttered the words, making them barely audible, but Reenie caught them all the same. "What?" she cried. "No!"

"Now, Reenie, wait a minute." Guy's tone was placating. "Isaac's a *professor* at the University of Chicago. He has a *doctorate,* for crying out loud. We're very lucky to have someone so qualified—"

"He's *overqualified*," she said.

"—who is willing to step in and help us out here."

"But there are only two months left of school," she argued. "We can muddle through without him for two measly months."

"You said yourself that your hands are full. Everyone else feels just as stressed."

"But I didn't know—I was wrong!" she said. "I—I can take on another class."

"What about your kids?"

"I'll arrange for an hour of babysitting after school. It's temporary. Surely there's someone else in this room who can make arrangements, too."

"I will," Beth said, raising her hand like a student.

Guilt stole Reenie's pleasure from this small victory. The last thing her friend needed was more work. Beth was a single mom, too, with four kids at home. But Reenie couldn't think about that right now. She had to make sure she protected *herself* from her enemies. "That's two," she said brightly. "See? Anyone else?"

Suddenly, no one except Madge would meet her eyes.

"Reenie, having Isaac on staff will be better for the students," the history teacher said, glowering at the others as though disgusted with their reluctance to take a stronger stand. "We need a science teacher. And Isaac's *perfect*."

"Looking," someone else volunteered, which was followed by a consenting, appreciative laugh.

Reenie thought it might have been Deborah who'd added this irrelevant detail, but she didn't look over to find out. So what if Isaac was handsome? She didn't want him working at the same school. "But we don't need him," she insisted.

"He's a biologist. Did you know that?" Madge said.

Isaac had told her he used to be a scientist. But he'd also said he was writing a novel. Obviously, he couldn't be trusted. "This is high school," she argued. "We're not teaching college-level classes. No one needs a doctorate to work here."

"*I* don't even have a doctorate," Guy said as if examining the situation from a whole new perspective.

"Maybe Isaac will think he should be principal," Reenie said. She knew she was grasping at straws, but at this point, she was willing to try almost anything. "Maybe *Dr.* Russell will take it upon himself to tell the rest of us country bumpkins how to do our jobs."

"Isaac's only filling in temporarily," Madge said. "He's no threat to Guy or anyone else. Come on, people. He's spent months and months in the jungles of Africa. Think of the knowledge he can share with our student body. He's agreed to take on the academic decathlon team, too."

The oohs and aahs resulting from the announcement of a new academic decathlon coach brought Reenie to her feet. "We have *books* about Africa. And—and *I'll* take on the academic decathlon team."

"Really?" Guy said as if making a mental note. "I told him I'd find him a good assistant."

"No! Isaac already works at the feed store," Reenie said. "They need him. Heaven knows he seems to be the only one available to help me whenever I go in there."

Reenie hadn't meant to shout—but knew she'd gotten a little carried away when everyone blinked at her in surprise. "Come on, people," she said, lowering her voice. "We don't want him here, okay? Please?"

"I agree with Reenie," Beth said, her expression full of sympathy. "Who cares if Isaac Russell is some single hotshot with a doctorate? We don't need him."

"Single?" Reenie said, catching that word amidst all the others. "I mean—"

"We know what you meant," Madge said. "You were as excited about having Isaac on staff as anyone—before Reenie walked in."

Beth suddenly looked deflated. "I said I didn't think it'd be a good thing," she murmured weakly.

"Was that before or after you swooned?" Madge crossed her arms over her enormous chest. "Anyway, I practically had to beg him to take the job. I'm not going back to him now to say that we've changed our minds."

"He's already accepted?" Reenie said.

"I'm afraid so," Guy replied. His expression was apologetic, but she could tell he wasn't going to budge. "We can't rescind the offer, Reenie. But having him teach for two months won't be any big deal. You'll see."

Guy had to be joking, right? *No big deal?* Once Isaac started working at the high school, she'd encounter him every day. Ina's room was right next to hers. God, there was even an adjoining supply closet!

THE MINUTE Reenie walked into the feed store, Isaac could tell that something had changed. He guessed she must've heard that he'd be teaching at the high school, and obviously she wasn't pleased. What else could it be? Over the past several months, her attitude toward him had gradually softened into something more polite than hostile. As recently as last week, she'd exchanged a few formal pleasantries with him when he'd rung up her purchases and loaded her hay.

Today, however, she stood in the corner with Isabella at her side, waiting resolutely for Earl to finish helping Ray White, the foreman from the Running Y Resort. Isaac tried to catch her eye to see if he could get what she needed. There wasn't any reason for him to be twiddling his thumbs while a line formed for Earl. But she wouldn't even look at him.

When Earl noticed her hovering only a few feet away, he glanced at Isaac as if to say, *Can't you take care of her? I'm busy here.* Then he seemed to realize who Reenie was, and sent Ray to Isaac instead.

Four months ago Isaac couldn't have been much help to someone like Ray, who'd grown up on a ranch. When Isaac first started at the feed store, he hadn't known enough about horses and cattle to do much more than run the register. But it hadn't taken him long to learn.

Ray stopped halfway down the aisle to pick up a salt wheel.

While waiting, Isaac breathed in the sweet smell of hay and grain that surrounded him, and realized that he was actually beginning to like Dundee. In a way, it reminded him of the jungle. Not the climate, of course. Because he had to step outdoors regularly, he wore long johns to work under his jeans and a heavy flannel shirt.

But things were simple here, and animals were an important part of life. In Chicago, he hadn't taken the time to get to know a lot of people. The fact that he'd associated mostly with academics who, like him, spent all their energy pursuing their goals, made it more difficult to build deep relationships.

Here that sort of absorption and anonymity was virtually impossible. Everyone knew who he was and had *something* to say to him. At first they'd just wanted to express their indignation about what Keith had done, or appease their curiosity about the new guy in town. But soon they were sharing the problems they experienced with their animals and ranches—sometimes even their neighbors.

"Earl was telling me he thinks I should cut the starches and sugars in the feed for the dude horses," Ray said, carrying the salt wheel under his arm as he sauntered closer.

"Why?" Isaac asked. "You still having trouble with laminitis?"

Ray nodded.

"Has the vet been out?"

"Once, but I knew what it was. You can see the inflammation around their hooves."

"You'll have to watch that, huh?"

"Wouldn't want it to lead to founder."

"Exactly."

"So what do you suggest as far as diet?" he asked.

Isaac couldn't help feeling gratified by the question. Slowly his opinion was coming to mean something, even to tough old cowboys like Ray. "Have you tried the high-fiber cube?"

"Not yet."

"It's got palm kernal, oat feed, wheat feed, grass meal, soya hulls, wheat. With the added vitamins and minerals, it's a real good feed. It may help."

"Worth a try, I suppose." Ray took a can of chew from his back pocket and put a pinch of tobacco between his teeth and gums. "Give me a half-dozen bags, will ya?"

Isaac went after the feed while the Running Y's foreman talked about his latest hand-tooled saddle, which he was trying to finish in time for the rodeo this summer. Isaac responded appropriately, but he wasn't paying much attention. He was too busy trying to hear what Reenie was saying to Earl.

"But I'm afraid she's getting fat," she said.

"Have you noticed changes in her crest, neck or shoulders?" Earl asked.

"It's tough to tell. I haven't had her long enough."

"Do you have a measuring tape?"

"Yes."

"When you get home, measure the length of her from the point of her shoulder to the point of her buttock."

"Jemima's *buttock?*" Isabella laughed. "Is that her *butt?* Her butt's really b-i-g!"

Isaac grinned as he shifted one sack of Ray's feed onto his shoulder and carried it to the register. He enjoyed seeing Reenie and her children's excitement over owning a horse. But he thought she had to be crazy to take on the farm and so many animals when her life was so upside down. Judging from the way her clothes were beginning to hang on her, he doubted she was finding time to take care of herself. Maybe her horse was getting fat, but Reenie was losing weight.

He collected Ray's money while Earl explained to Reenie that she'd also need to measure the heart girth of her horse in order to use the mathematical formula that determined body weight. "Once you know what she weighs, give me a call," he said. "I've got a chart here that'll tell us right where she should fall."

"Do you think I should switch her to a leaner feed, just in case?" she asked.

"Not yet. Give her a little more exercise, if you can. Once you know her weight, we'll determine if we need to change her feed."

"Okay." Reenie sighed as though the world rested on her shoulders, and Isaac couldn't help glancing over at her again. He'd admired her when she was Keith's wife. But now he respected her. As difficult as it must've been to have Liz, Mica and Christopher move to town, she'd behaved admirably. She hadn't tried to make their lives miserable by encouraging her friends to turn against the newcomers. She hadn't stipulated that Keith couldn't see the children—though Lord knows Keith probably would have stayed away had Reenie held out any hope that she might come back to him if he did.

As far as Isaac knew, Reenie hadn't done *anything* petty or mean. According to Mica, who sometimes saw her at school, she even waved occasionally.

For the most part, Reenie's coping mechanism seemed to be avoidance. Which was most likely why she'd never responded to his e-mails. Even the one about Bailey.

"Look, Mom, there's Christopher's uncle!" Isabella said.

Reenie's eyes met Isaac's, then jerked away. Pretending she didn't hear her daughter, she tried to pull the little girl along as she followed Earl to the pallet of feed she wanted. But Isabella managed to wriggle away. A moment later, she came running over to the register. "Hi!"

Isaac thought he saw real annoyance cross Reenie's face, but he grinned in spite of it. Or maybe he grinned *because* of it. Certainly being in her town added a spark of excitement to his life. "What's up?" he asked Isabella.

"My dog's sick again." The corners of her small mouth turned down in a worried frown. "He lies there all day. Mom says his joints hurt too much for him to move."

"I'm afraid dogs don't live as long as people do," he said.

"I know." Her voice dropped. "Do you think he's going to die soon?"

Isaac didn't want to upset her. But he saw no point in lying about something so inevitable. "He could. Maybe you should be prepared for it, just in case. He's old, like your mother said."

Instead of crying, she nodded sagely, and Isaac reached below the counter to retrieve one of the suckers they kept on hand for children. "How 'bout a treat?"

Her face lit up. "Sure."

"Ask your mom first."

"Mom?" she said, turning expectantly.

Reenie's eyebrows knit together as she looked over. "What, honey?"

"Can I have a sucker?"

"Absolutely not."

The answer, so quick and resolute, surprised Isaac and Isabella. "Why not?" Isabella asked indignantly.

"It's too close to dinner."

"School just got out."

In truth, it was only four o'clock.

"I'll buy you something at the grocery store," Reenie said.

"But I don't want to go to the grocery store," Isabella argued. "That takes too long. I want to go home so I can play."

"Ask her if you can have the sucker if Earl gives it to you," Isaac suggested. He knew he was provoking Reenie, but he was tired of allowing her to ignore him. At least now he'd get a reaction.

"She's my daughter, and she doesn't need it," Reenie snapped before Isabella could say anything.

"Yes I do!" Isabella said. "Puh-leeze?"

A muscle moved in Reenie's cheek as she glared at Isaac. "You did that on purpose."

He shrugged, still smiling. "Maybe. But I've done worse,

right? Like moving here? And accepting a teaching position at the high school? It's criminal, really. I should be locked up."

"I'm glad we agree on something," she said tartly.

"Aren't you going a little overboard, Reenie?" Earl said. He glanced between them, but she ignored him.

"She can't accept anything from you," she said to Isaac.

"But Mom-my, *why?*" Isabella asked.

Earl brought the feed sack to the front and dropped it on the counter. "Reenie, it's only a sucker. I would've given it to her myself had I thought of it."

Faced with Earl's support *and* her pleading daughter, Reenie finally seemed to realize she was letting her emotions tempt her into an unnecessary battle. "Fine," she said. But she clenched her jaw as Isabella eagerly unwrapped her candy. Then she paid Earl, waited for him to load the sack, and spun gravel as she drove off.

"That has to be the only woman in town who doesn't like you," Earl said, shaking his head as he came back in.

And the only woman—in town or anywhere else—that Isaac couldn't quit thinking about.

CHAPTER FIFTEEN

"I DON'T UNDERSTAND," Lucky said, her confusion revealing itself in her voice.

Reenie exited the horse site she'd been visiting on the Internet and switched the telephone to her other ear. "I just explained it to you."

"You said Isaac had finally crossed the line."

"He has!"

"By giving Isabella a sucker?"

"It was more than that," Reenie said. "He—he knew I didn't want her to have it."

"I must be missing something," Lucky responded. "I mean, there are worse crimes then trying to make your little girl happy."

"You had to be there," Reenie snapped. "Anyway, he made Earl, who I've known all my life, turn on me, too."

"*Earl* turned on you?"

"Yes, he sided with Isaac."

"How did Isaac *make* him do that?"

"He just did. Isaac's good at winning people over. You know how much everyone likes him. You should've heard the other teachers at school on Monday. 'He has a Ph.D…he's a biologist…I can't believe he'll be working here…God, he's so handsome…' What does handsome have to do with teaching?"

There was a long pause. "Reenie?"

"What?"

"You're too stressed-out for your own good."

"I'm telling you he's stealing all my friends!" Reenie knew she sounded like Isabella instead of a thirty-one-year-old woman. But she couldn't help it. Although subtle, Earl's defection earlier today had really stung.

"Isaac can't steal your friends. Everyone loves you. You're just overwrought. And you're going to drive yourself into a nervous breakdown if you don't relax."

Reenie knew Lucky was right. She was traveling hell-bent for a brick wall. But she didn't know how to stop her forward momentum. She already had more than she could do in a day, yet she kept adding more. She *had* to keep busy—the stress was killing her but saving her at the same time. "I'm managing."

"Why won't you take it easy?"

And give herself a chance to miss what she'd lost? Never. "I'm fine."

"You're not fine. You're whipped. Maybe you should sell your horse and cow and forget about fixing up the farm for a while."

Reenie rubbed her eyes. It was already after eleven. She should be in bed right now, getting a good night's sleep so she could wake refreshed and eager to teach in the morning. But even as hard as she was working, she'd begun to dream occasionally. And when she dreamed, she sometimes felt a pair of strong arms around her. Then the memories would wash over her, reminding her how it felt to be loved by a man, to be desired and protected.

Pure fantasy, she thought. If there was one thing she'd learned from the past year it was that her own arms were the only ones she could depend on.

She bent over to pet Bailey, who'd come to lie at her feet, and tried not to notice how quickly his health seemed to be failing. He couldn't die on top of everything else. Not now. "You're okay, boy, aren't you?" she said.

His eyebrows twitched as he looked up at her with his liquid brown eyes. "Don't go anywhere," she whispered to him. "Please?"

"Will you do me a favor?" Lucky asked.

Bailey affectionately nosed her bare feet as Reenie returned to her conversation. "What?"

"Take a few days off and sleep, okay?"

Running her toes lightly over the dog's back, Reenie surfed through a few more horse sites. Her problems weren't as easily solved as taking a vacation. But everyone seemed to give her the same advice. "Sure, good idea," she said drily.

Lucky sighed on the other end of the line. "You're really scaring me."

"I told you, I'm fine."

"Is Keith still calling?"

"Not so much. From what I hear, he's trying to get back with Liz."

"I guess it doesn't make much sense to lose *both* families."

"I think that's the logic he's using."

"Is she responding?"

Reenie remembered seeing them leave the diner together the other day. "She goes out with him occasionally."

"If they reunite, do you think he'll move her and her kids into your old house?"

"Hopefully not. That would be too creepy."

"He could. He's already living there. And if he sells, he's going to have to pay you half the equity."

"True. But maybe Liz has some money stashed away somewhere."

"She wouldn't be working at the grocery store if that was the case."

"Thanks for cheering me up."

"Sorry. Would you mind if they got back together?"

Reenie had certainly spent some time thinking about it. "Probably," she admitted. "Besides the whole jealousy thing, it would make the girls' visitations so much more awkward. Especially if Keith was taking them back to our old house every other weekend."

"Yikes, I see your point."

Reenie glanced at the clock in the corner of her computer screen. "I gotta go. We're starting a new unit in my math classes tomorrow, and I still have to prepare the rest of my lecture." She didn't mention the stack of papers she had yet to grade, because she didn't want Lucky to go back to telling her how she was running herself into the ground.

Lucky covered the phone and said something to her husband. "When does Isaac start at the high school?" she asked when she returned.

"A week from next Monday. At least, that's when Ina goes on maternity leave."

"Today's Wednesday. Which means you have almost two weeks to get used to the idea."

That was supposed to help?

"Does Keith have the girls this weekend?" Lucky asked, suddenly switching topics.

"Yes."

"Would you like to go out to dinner with Mike and me this Friday? Get out of the house?"

"I can't. I told Beth I'd go dancing with her."

"Well, that's hopeful, at least. Maybe you'll meet someone new." *"Here?"*

"You never know. There're always new people coming to stay at the Running Y. Sometimes they go into town to kick back with the locals."

"That would be exciting," Reenie lied.

Lucky hesitated, making Reenie suspect she saw through her inflated response. If so, at least she didn't call Reenie on it. "Okay, I'll talk to you tomorrow."

Reenie sagged in relief as she hung up. She was growing to love Lucky like the sister she was. But even simple conversations with anyone seemed like hard work these days.

Wondering if Tara Benson, an old friend from high school

who'd married and moved to California, had written her back, she clicked over to e-mail.

There weren't any messages from Tara, but her mother had sent her a new cake recipe, her father had written to say he'd be home early on Friday and would like to take her to lunch, and Beth wanted to know if she could borrow something to wear on Friday night.

She told Beth she could borrow anything she wanted, then started to grade papers. A moment later, however, she noticed an instant message request on her screen. It was from 2781isaac@aol.com.

"Speak of the devil," Reenie grumbled. She immediately hit the reject button and smiled in satisfaction. "Take that, *Dr.* Russell."

She graded more quizzes, then glanced up to see that he'd sent her another request. "What do you think, Bailey?" she asked. "Do we want to hear from him?"

Bailey opened one eye and nuzzled closer before dozing off again.

"My thoughts exactly. No way," she said and hit the reject button again. She knew there was a way to block certain senders, but she'd never blocked anyone before and didn't know how. Just as she was trying to figure out the process, the telephone rang.

The caller ID said *I. Russell.* How dare he call her! Especially at this hour. He had no business even e-mailing her. Sure, she'd given him her address. But that was before she'd known who he was.

She picked up the phone because she had a few things she wanted to say to him. "Hello?"

"I've found you the perfect puppy," he announced.

It was Isaac all right, but his words, and the childish enthusiasm in his voice, took her off guard. *"What?"*

"He's at an animal shelter in Boise. They just got him, and he's great, so you'd better act fast. Do you have a pencil?"

"I don't want a new puppy," she said. How could she replace Bailey before he was even gone?

"I was thinking it might distract the girls from…you know, what's to come."

Isaac had a point there. She had been worried about how her girls would respond to the death of their beloved pet. And Bailey was so mild tempered and tired, she doubted he'd mind the company. He was getting to the point he didn't want to be bothered by Jennifer, Angela and Isabella. He preferred to lie by Reenie all the time.

But Reenie didn't have a chance to explain all that. Isaac gave her the URL, then, before she could say anything more, hung up.

She blinked at the handset. Was he right? Would it soften the blow?

Bailey wheezed as he shifted in his sleep. As she listened to him, her eyes filled with tears. The vet said he didn't have much longer. They were going to have to say goodbye to him soon, and then the house would seem so empty.

Maybe it wouldn't hurt to take a look.

She typed the address and hit enter, and her computer conjured a picture of the cutest puppy she'd ever seen. The caption below said he was a black Lab/chow mix only ten weeks old. But the fact that he wasn't a bassett hound surprised her. Isaac had said he'd found her the perfect puppy. Wouldn't he think she'd want another bassett?

Maybe he was as smart as everyone said. Maybe he understood that if she got a different breed, she wouldn't be replacing Old Bailey.

She sighed, unwilling to give Isaac any credit for his insight.

"You're darling," she said—grudgingly because in her mind the puppy was connected to Isaac Russell—and clicked on the link below the picture. It would be nice to surprise the girls with a puppy on Sunday, when they returned from their father's house after the weekend….

But as she read about all the fees associated with the adoption, she knew better than to waste her time. She couldn't afford to spend $160 on a dog right now, not when she could still be facing a stack of vet bills for the pet she already loved.

"Too bad," she said, and closed the window.

The good manners her mother had instilled in her as a child dictated she thank Isaac for trying to help. But she wasn't convinced he'd done it for the right reasons. She preferred to believe he considered her some kind of challenge. If he could win her friendship, his takeover of the town would be complete.

She wasn't going to allow him such a victory. If she held out, maybe he'd eventually pack up his sister and her children and take them all back to California.

LIZ SAT in the darkened living room, staring at the moonlight spilling through a crack in the drapes and onto the carpet. The four and a half months she'd been living in Dundee had been the most difficult of her life. Too guarded to make friends as easily as Isaac, she felt isolated and alone. She was always on the defense in case she ran into Reenie or a member of Reenie's family. And now her renters in California had presented her with an offer to purchase the house, and she had to decide whether or not to let it go.

Sometimes, when the stress of her current situation really got to her, she called Dave Shapiro. He made her laugh, which eased the tension. She wanted to call him tonight but thought better of it. Isaac was still awake and would be coming up to bed in a few minutes. She didn't want her brother to know she was speaking to Dave as often as she was. She knew getting involved with a twenty-four-year-old womanizer wasn't the wisest thing in the world for an older, brokenhearted divorcée to do. Besides, he'd probably try to convince her to keep the house just so she'd eventually come back. But she knew returning wouldn't be best for her kids. They were doing well here, where they could see their father regularly.

Their father... With a grimace, she finished her tea and set

the empty cup on the side table. Once Keith had begun to realize that he couldn't save his first marriage, he'd started calling and coming over more often. He claimed he wanted to see
the children. But Liz could sense the not-so-subtle change in
his focus. Soon he was bringing her gifts, taking her out to eat,
touching her. Although their marriage had been annulled, she'd
welcomed his attention at first. The last time they'd been together, she'd even gone home with him—and had soon found
herself in Reenie's old bed, staring up at the ceiling while he
moved on top of her. She'd felt very disconnected from their
lovemaking. She'd missed him terribly. But she could never
completely escape the knowledge that he'd chosen Reenie over
her, that she'd always be second-best. That night was when she
realized she was worth more than what he'd given her. That
was also when she'd caught her mind drifting, imagining he
was Dave.

"Liz? You still up?"

She turned at the sound of Isaac's voice coming from the
doorway and smiled. "Yeah."

"What are you doing?"

"Just thinking."

"About what?"

"Keith. Reenie. This town."

He slipped into the room and sat across from her. "Keith's
been calling here a lot," he said, watching her carefully.

Folding her arms, she leaned back in the chair. "The kids are
getting to see a great deal of him. Which is good."

"*You've* been seeing a lot of him, too," he pointed out.

"Not so much," she said. "At least not anymore." She'd told
Keith the night they made love at Reenie's old house that she'd
never let him touch her again.

"What does that mean?" Isaac asked.

"It means that there's no danger I'll ever go back to him."

Isaac's smile revealed a certain amount of relief. "I'm glad to hear that. For a while, I was really regretting the fact we came here."

"I'm glad we did. If we hadn't, it would've taken me much longer to get over him."

Isaac's eyebrows arched up. "You sound pretty definite."

"I am. He's tried to get back with me, and I've tried to resurrect what I once felt. It's just...not there, anymore."

"That's great."

She felt a flicker of guilt when he responded so positively, knowing he wouldn't approve of her being in contact with Dave Shapiro. But after everything she'd been through, her late-night talks with her old tennis coach were a guilty pleasure she wasn't ready to give up. She couldn't move back to L.A. without tearing her children away from their father, which she didn't have the heart to do. So maybe she was worried about nothing. She couldn't get herself into too much trouble with Dave nearly a thousand miles away.

The images she'd begun to entertain of him called her a liar, but she knew nothing would come of their relationship. She'd never get involved with a man who was so much younger than she was. Especially one nowhere near ready to make a permanent commitment.

"I received an offer on the house in L.A.," she told him. "The renters want to buy it."

"Really? Are you going to sell?"

She shrugged. "I could use the money."

"Do you have much equity?"

"Not a lot. But it'd get me through a year or so."

"You don't have to sell," he said. "We're managing."

"Thanks to you."

"I'm happy to help."

She twirled a lock of hair around her finger. "But you won't be here forever."

"No."

"I ran into Reenie the other day," she said.

"You always run into Reenie." He stretched out in the chair and crossed his legs at the ankle. "In this small a town, it's tough to avoid her."

"This time I ran into her in the literal sense."

He scowled. "Not with your car…"

"No. When I dropped Christopher and Mica off at school last Wednesday, I realized that I'd forgotten it was Chris's turn to share snacks with the class. So I ran over to the grocery store, gathered several boxes of cookies and rushed toward the checkout. Next thing I know, Reenie comes around the corner and, *bam,* we collide."

"You're kidding."

"No."

"What'd you do?"

"I'd dropped everything, so I stooped to pick it all up."

"What'd *she* do?"

Liz clasped her hands in her lap and stared down at her cuticles, which were finally beginning to heal. "She could've gone merrily on her way, but…."

"What?"

"She didn't. She helped me gather what I'd dropped."

For a moment, Isaac seemed deep in his own thoughts. Then he said, "She's a good person, Liz."

"I know." Leaning forward, she toyed with the handle of her empty cup and changed the subject. She knew her brother liked Reenie. She suspected he might be attracted to her in a romantic sense. But she couldn't dwell on that. She couldn't lose both Keith and Isaac to the same woman. "Have you already sent in your grant applications?"

He nodded and stood. "What are you going to do about the offer on the house?"

"I'd like to move back to L.A." She couldn't help thinking of Dave again. "But I can't as long as Keith's here. Maybe when the kids are older."

"So you're going to sell."

"Yeah."

"Mica and Christopher are very lucky they have a mother like you," he said softly, and squeezed her shoulder as he passed by on his way to bed.

Liz knew she should retire, too. Instead, she slipped downstairs and picked up the phone.

WILEY DURANGO, the owner of The Honky Tonk had remodeled and expanded shortly after Conner Armstrong had opened the Running Y Resort. Now, in the spring and summer, young families, executives, nature lovers, even college students came to Dundee to sample the Western experience. To capitalize on the influx, Wiley had added an extra room to his bar, with a mechanical bull. On weekends, he hosted live bands, and on Saturday mornings he had his waitresses give line-dancing lessons.

Tonight, the bar was particularly busy, but Reenie couldn't say she was having much fun.

"You look distracted," Beth said, drawing her attention from the people on the dance floor.

Reenie took a sip of her Long Island Iced Tea so she wouldn't have to bother gathering the willpower to smile. "Not really. I'm just listening to the music."

Shania Twain's latest played so loudly Reenie's ears were ringing, but at least the volume made it difficult to talk. She didn't feel inclined toward conversation tonight. At the last minute, Keith's parents had decided to take the girls to Texas to see Keith's brother, who was at Baylor, and although Reenie had never particularly liked this brother, she was feeling a little left out. Texas should've been a family trip. But her divorce had changed things all the way around.

It was good the kids were getting away with their grandparents, she told herself. Certainly she wouldn't be able to provide the same experience. She wouldn't be traveling anywhere in the near future, not alone with three children. For one thing, she didn't have the money.

"Are you missing your girls?" Beth said.

"I'm trying not to think about the fact that they're so far away," Reenie replied.

"When did they leave?"

"This morning."

"They missed school today?"

Reenie nodded. "But their grades are good. One day won't hurt them."

"So shake off the doldrums. Sunday will be here before you know it."

"It's not the girls," Reenie insisted.

Beth stirred her gin and tonic with her straw. "Is it Isaac Russell?"

Remembering the picture of the adorable puppy Isaac had found, Reenie frowned.

"Reenie? Are you still upset that Liz's brother will be teaching at the school with us?"

"No, I don't care about that," she lied.

"Are you going to assist him with the academic decathlon team?"

The arch Reenie put into her eyebrows probably answered that question clearly enough. But she didn't stop there. "What do you think?"

"Right. Of course not."

Alex Riley, one of the more handsome cowboys who worked at the Running Y, approached their table. Anticipation lit Beth's eyes the moment she saw him. She'd had her heart set on Alex for months, so much so that Reenie could almost hear her chanting *Pick me, pick me!*

But Alex turned toward Reenie instead. "Would you like to dance?"

Sensing Beth's disappointment, Reenie felt too guilty to accept. "Actually, I think I'm going to—"

The door opened and Keith stepped in, along with Jon Small. As recently as a year ago, Jon and Keith had barely known each other. Growing up, they'd never traveled in the same circles. Jon had liked cars and motorcycles; Keith had liked computers and sports. But times had changed. Now they were both divorced, and when Jon wasn't with his older brother, Smalley, he was hanging out with Keith, even though he wasn't half as smart, half as talented or half as handsome. He'd always reminded Reenie of a weasel.

"Reenie?" Alex prompted when she paused.

Reenie had been about to suggest he dance with Beth while she finished her drink. But seeing her ex-husband come into the bar changed her mind. She did not want Keith to find her alone at a table. She knew he'd spend the entire night trying to talk her into going home with him, especially since the girls were out of town. Although her feelings had definitely changed toward him, he was still the only man she'd ever slept with, and she was beginning to miss having a sex life. She didn't want to do anything she'd regret in the morning.

"I'd love to dance," she said, and took Alex's hand.

"Boot Scootin' Boogie" came on as Alex led her through the crowd. An old Dundee favorite, this song had people lining up to do a dance one of the waitresses had choreographed.

"You don't think Keith minds that we're dancing, do you?" Alex said as they started moving to the music.

Reenie opened her mouth to say he probably did, then realized Alex already knew that. Keith was standing at the edge of the dance floor, glaring at them both while shifting impatiently from foot to foot.

"He has no right to object," she said indifferently.

They stomped and turned along with everyone else. "I'm not worried," Alex said. "Give me a few more beers and I'll be ready for a good barroom brawl."

Just what she needed, Reenie thought sarcastically, the father of her kids getting busted up at The Honky Tonk.

Unless—she missed the next step and hurried to catch up—there was a chance he'd have time enough to recover before the girls returned on Sunday night.

"That grin looks mighty devilish," Alex said.

Reenie laughed. "For a moment there, I was tempted."

"I could be careful. Just fatten his lip a little. After what he did to you, he deserves it."

Reenie agreed. But revenge wouldn't solve anything. "No fighting."

"Since he essentially did the same thing to Liz, I bet Isaac would like a piece of that action."

"Isaac doesn't strike me as particularly violent. Anyway, he's not here, so it's a moot point."

"What are you talking about?" Alex said. They pivoted, rocked forward, then back and stomped again. "Isaac and Earl are playing pool in back."

Reenie stopped dancing and started searching the crowd in the other room. "Where?"

Alex pointed. "Right there."

She leaned to one side and then the other, trying to see through the crush of bodies. Sure enough, she eventually caught a glimpse of him. He stood at the side of a pool table, completely immersed in conversation.

CHAPTER SIXTEEN

"LET'S GO," Reenie said the moment she returned to the table.

Beth glanced up at her in surprise. "But we just got here thirty minutes ago. And I was hoping to—"

"Hey, Beth. How 'bout you?" Alex said. "You ready to dance?"

Reenie hadn't realized Alex was still on her heel.

Beth gave her a quick pleading look, then turned a radiant smile on the handsome cowboy. "Sure," she said, and hopped right up.

As they disappeared into the crowd, Reenie cursed silently, immediately regretting the fact that she'd let Beth drive tonight. They should've come separately, she decided. Then neither would have had to wait for the other.

But how was she to know? They'd gone dancing several times already and never run into Keith or Isaac before. It was simply bad luck that both men were here tonight.

So what now? she wondered, taking a good long drink. She couldn't sit at the table. Keith was already making his way over. She couldn't go into the back without bumping into Isaac. And it was too cold to wait outside. The Honky Tonk was usually so crowded and so hot, she'd seen little point in bothering to bring a coat for the five-minute car ride.

She decided the restroom was her best recourse, but Keith cut her off before she could reach the hall.

"What were you doin' dancing with Alex?" he asked, his eyes glittery, his jaw hard.

Reenie told herself to ignore him and keep walking. But he wouldn't let her. As soon as she tried, he grabbed her wrist and pulled her back.

"I've been patient, Reenie," he said. "It's been months. When are you going to stop punishing me for what happened and take me back?"

Reenie's jaw dropped. "What *happened?*" she echoed. "How can you say it like that? As if 'what happened' was out of your control?"

"It *was* out of my control. I wasn't capable—never mind. I've already apologized. Thousands of times," he said. "It hasn't done any good. You wanted me to stay in Dundee, I'm here. You wanted the farm, you have it. The only thing keeping our family apart is you. When are you going to let bygones be bygones?"

"When did you become so *clingy,*" she said, throwing his own words back at him.

His voice dropped to a grating rumble. "I never took you for a coldhearted bitch, Reenie."

"If I'm a bitch, you made me this way," she retorted. "But I don't want an argument. You and I are over, and I'm moving on. That means I can dance with any man I want."

He paled. "Don't say that. We're in love."

"Not anymore, Keith."

"You promised me for better or worse!" he snapped.

"What about your own promises?"

"I haven't slept with anyone since I came clean!"

"You didn't come clean. You were *caught.*"

"Since I was caught, then."

"Maybe I'll ask Liz if that's true," she challenged.

He didn't respond right away, and his momentary hesitation was enough to tell her she didn't need to ask Liz.

"I don't care," she said. "Let me go."

"No, you have to listen to me."

"There's nothing more to say."

He rubbed a hand over his face. "Reenie—"

"Because You Loved Me" by Celine Dion began to play. It was an old song, but the lyrics were particularly poignant, considering what they'd once been to each together.

"Dance with me," he said suddenly.

"I don't want to dance with you," she said.

"Damn it, we have three children together. You owe me that much."

"I don't owe you anything!"

"Especially because she's already promised this dance to me."

Reenie felt a man's firm grip on her elbow and turned gratefully toward him, until she saw that it was Isaac Russell.

"Like hell," Keith said.

Isaac's gaze flicked over Keith's face, as if he welcomed the possibility of a fight. "What'd you say?"

"Stay out of this, Isaac," Keith said.

Isaac released Reenie's elbow. "I'll go if Reenie tells me to."

"Reenie?" Keith said.

Reenie couldn't let her ex-husband win this battle. He'd caused so much pain to her, Liz, Isaac, everyone who was part of either family. She wanted him to know she'd rather stand with Isaac and Liz, than with him. Then maybe he'd get it through his head that they were finished as a couple.

"Like Isaac said, I've already promised this dance to him," she muttered, and let Liz's brother lead her onto the floor.

FEELING AWKWARD and uncomfortable, Reenie looped her arms loosely around Isaac's neck. They were scarcely touching and yet she felt as though they were dancing too close. How could that be? She danced with men all the time. No one else made her so…aware of her body in relation to his. Where her hands were. Where *his* hands were. Where her legs were. Where *his* legs were.

She bit her bottom lip to help her tolerate the contact. Why did Isaac have to rescue her at the onset of a slow song? Celine Dion seemed to be going on forever.

"Did you like the puppy?" he asked.

Clearing her throat, she let go of her lip. "He was cute," she said, but she kept her eyes on the other dancers, the old scuffed boots lining the high shelf going around the room, the lassos and beer-slogan mirrors hanging on the gray wood walls.

Isaac shifted slightly, turning her. But again she found things to look at besides his face: Bear, the bartender, serving up drinks; Jon Small talking low but anxiously to Keith; the constant influx of people coming or going at the door.

"Are you going to adopt him?" he asked.

His voice was just deep enough to resonate below the music. "No," she said simply.

He leaned back so she *had* to look up at him. "Why not? I think it'd be a good distraction for the girls. Bailey can't last much longer."

"I know, but…" She didn't want to tell him she couldn't afford the fees. "Maybe later."

"Would you rather get a different kind of puppy?"

"No."

He frowned slightly as they went back to dancing, and Reenie glanced over his shoulder to see Beth cozying up with Alex. Beth and Alex had only danced twice so far, but they were definitely making the most of the chance to get intimate. From what Reenie could tell, neither of them wanted to go home alone tonight.

She wondered if that meant she'd be able to borrow Beth's car. Of all nights for her friend to finally catch Alex's interest.

"What's wrong?" Isaac asked.

"Nothing."

"What didn't you like about the puppy?"

"Would you give up on the puppy?" she said. "I loved him! I just…I can't afford him right now, okay?"

"He's at a shelter."

"The fees still amount to a hundred sixty dollars. But…I'll get a new dog, someday."

He tried to move her closer, but she resisted and, finally, he sighed. "You know, you're going to put my back out if you don't relax."

"You were expecting a warmer reception?" she asked.

"Maybe not warm, exactly. But I thought dancing with you would be a *little* more fun than holding a cardboard cutout."

"I'm not that stiff!"

He cocked a doubtful eyebrow at her.

"If you were someone else, I wouldn't be like this," she said.

"Prove it."

"How?"

"Pretend I *am* someone else."

Reenie saw Keith waiting at the edge of the dance floor with Jon, his new shadow. She knew her ex-husband would harangue her again as soon as Isaac let her go.

At the moment, she didn't have any better option than to make the most of the situation. Telling herself to relax, she let the music carry her away and, a moment later, she had her head tucked under Isaac's chin, her lips not far from the pulse at his neck. She could feel his hard chest against her own, his hips moving in an erotic rhythm with hers.

She thought he might tease her about getting a little more than he'd bargained for, but he didn't. He didn't talk at all. His hands were at the small of her back, strong and sure as he guided her along, and she could smell cologne on his nice cotton sweater.

Closing her eyes, she let herself nuzzle closer. God, he felt good. And she was so weary, weary of the hurt and disappointment, weary of the responsibility, weary of trying to look into the future far enough to decide what would be best for her little family. For right now, she only wanted to feel the music and forget.

When the song ended and Isaac stepped away, the loss of his

body heat felt as though someone had stripped her of a warm blanket.

Reenie told herself to thank him for his help with Keith and walk off, to forget the way he'd held her. She missed having a man in her life way too much.

But her ex-husband hadn't given up his vigil at the edge of the dance floor. And Alex had his arm draped around Beth, his head bent to hers. Already they were in their own little world. But it was still early, and Beth probably wouldn't be presumptuous enough to let Reenie borrow her car.

Instinctively, Reenie grabbed Isaac's arm before he could walk away. "Will you take me home?"

The question had come out of nowhere and obviously took him off guard. "Are you ready to go now?"

She nodded.

Evidently Celine Dion had a big fan in the crowd because the theme song from *Titanic* came on next—another slow one.

"On second thought, after this dance," she said, and slipped into his arms before he could even respond. She didn't care if she was being too bold. He'd told her to pretend he was someone else—and it was working. For some reason, she felt as though she could dance with him all night.

AS HE DROVE HER HOME, the memory of Reenie clinging to him on the dance floor swirled through Isaac's blood like an aphrodisiac, making his nerves hum with sexual awareness. He hadn't held a woman so closely since he'd left the Congo. There, he'd enjoyed the company of a female field assistant, had even spent a few nights in her bed. But their interaction had been casual. In fact just dancing with Reenie felt like a more intimate experience.

"You have a sitter for the girls?" he asked conversationally. He hoped small talk might help him keep his thoughts moving in the right direction because, even if Reenie would allow it, he couldn't get involved with her. It'd be too hard on Liz. Plus he knew Reenie wasn't the type to welcome a brief affair, and he'd be leaving as soon as his grant came through.

"No," she said. "They're in Texas with their grandparents." She stretched her chest restraint as though she might turn to face him but continued to stare out the window instead.

"Why Texas?"

"They're visiting Keith's brother."

"At Baylor?"

She nodded and finally looked over at him—and he couldn't help admiring the sweep of her long lashes. He loved her eyes, thought they had to be the most beautiful pair he'd ever seen.

An unbidden picture suddenly flashed through his mind—Reenie looking up at him, those eyes filled with desire as he stripped off her shirt—

He cleared his throat. "Have you ever been to Texas?"

"No."

They came to the stoplight where he needed to turn in order to go to her house, but he didn't give his truck any gas even after the light turned green. He squinted into his side mirror. Unless he was mistaken, the headlights behind him belonged to a Jeep.

"You can go now," she said.

"I think Keith's following us," he responded as he finally made the turn.

Keith knew Reenie wouldn't be happy to hear this news, but *he* was slightly relieved. He sensed that, tonight, Reenie's defenses weren't what they usually were. Maybe she'd had a little too much to drink. He wasn't sure, but with Keith around, Isaac wouldn't be tempted to take advantage of her in any way.

She grimaced. "You're kidding."

"No."

"Of course you're not kidding," she muttered to herself, and turned in her seat to see for herself.

"Am I right?" Isaac asked.

"'Fraid so."

"Is Jon with him?"

"No, he's alone. He must've left Jon at The Honky Tonk."

Isaac didn't need to keep checking his mirrors. Keith wasn't making his presence too much of a secret. At times he was nearly riding Isaac's bumper.

When Isaac finally swung into Reenie's driveway, Keith parked on the road.

Reenie didn't get out.

"What do you think?" Isaac asked her. "You want me to tell him to leave?"

She stared at her house, which sat dark and empty, then twisted to see her ex-husband again. Keith hadn't turned off his engine. He sat there, letting it idle while he glowered at them.

"No, I want you to come in," she said.

Isaac blinked in surprise. "I don't think that's such a good idea."

"Why not? You gave my kid a sucker. You want to be my friend, don't you?" She tempted him with a smile.

Her *friend?* That was like saying the Big Bad Wolf wanted to jump rope with Little Red Riding Hood. Right now, Isaac's feelings ran much hotter. He wanted to take her to bed. But that was more information than she needed.

Besides, if she wasn't experiencing the same attraction, he was probably okay.

"I'll give you a glass of wine, and you can tell me all about Africa," she said.

He imagined the quiet, empty house. "I don't think so, Reenie. Not with Liz and everything that's gone before." *And the fact that you appeal to me more than any woman I've met in a long time.*

Her smile turned challenging. "I thought we were each pretending to be someone else tonight."

That approach had wound up being a little *too* effective, especially on the dance floor. But Isaac hated to leave Reenie to the mercy of Keith, who had no right to be bothering her, anyway. With the girls gone, there wasn't anything to keep him in check.

"Okay," he said, "for a few minutes," and gave Keith a quick glance as he followed her to the door.

KEITH SAT OUTSIDE in the Jeep long enough for Isaac to build a fire and for Reenie to get them each a glass of wine. But a couple of quick checks at the window told her he'd turned off the engine. She suspected he wasn't planning on going anywhere until Isaac left. She knew that was the case when she heard a loud knock at the door and saw her ex-husband through the peephole.

Taking a deep breath, she pulled the door open and stood in the opening.

Her ex tried to see over her head. He was looking for Isaac, of course, but she held the door close to her body so that, at most, he could make out the glow of the fire coming from the living room. "What do you want, Keith?" she asked.

"I want to know how long he's going to stay here alone with you."

Bailey managed to join her at the door, but she gently moved him aside with one foot. "As long we're enjoying ourselves," she replied.

Keith's expression darkened. "What kind of game are you playing with me, Reenie?"

"No games," she said. "I have a friend over, that's all."

"Isaac's your *friend* now, is he? What about Liz? She your friend, too?"

Reenie gritted her teeth. "I'm beginning to believe she'd be a truer friend to me than you've been," she said. "Anyway, you're the reason they came to town."

His mouth dropped open. "That's not fair! I asked them to go back to L.A. I knew you didn't want them here. I *begged* Liz. She wouldn't go because of the kids."

Closing her eyes, Reenie shook her head. "So she's more concerned about Mica and Christopher's welfare than you are. Somehow that doesn't make me admire you any more."

"But I knew you'd never come back to me if... How was I supposed to know...to expect... I mean, I love all my kids, but—"

"Not as much as you love yourself, right?"

He looked so stricken when she said that, Reenie wished she'd bitten her tongue. Maybe it was the truth, but she wasn't out to hurt anyone. Keith had done enough to himself. She only wanted him to leave her alone so she could get on with her life.

"Not as much as I love *you,*" he whispered.

"You'll get over me," she said.

"I don't want to get over you."

Reenie heard Isaac's footsteps, then felt his reassuring presence as he came up behind her. "Go home, Keith," he said.

Keith's eyes darted between them. "How dare you think you can interfere. This is none of your business. You have no right to—"

"What?" Isaac challenged.

"Don't touch her," he said. "Don't you dare touch her!"

"We're adults, Keith. We'll make love until dawn if we want to," Reenie said, and shut the door. She could feel Isaac's eyes on her, but she didn't try to read his expression. Instead, she patted Bailey, then parted the drapes to see what Keith would do next.

Her ex-husband paced across the front lawn for a few minutes. Finally, after shouting a curse at them and giving a finger to the house, he got into his Jeep and tore off.

"I bet he'll be back later," Isaac said, still standing behind her.

Reenie straightened and turned. "I know."

"He doesn't have a key to the house, does he?"

"No."

"Good."

She offered Isaac a feeble smile. "He makes it pretty hard to pretend I'm someone else, huh?"

"That's a good thing," he replied. "Because your eyes make it too damn easy."

Reenie's heart began to pound against her chest as her gaze locked with his, and she realized that some of the anger she'd felt toward Isaac in the past stemmed from the fact that she found him far too attractive. No woman felt good about desiring her enemy.

But was Isaac really the enemy?

"This is going to be complicated," she whispered.

"Not if we don't let it get that way," he insisted.

"Right." Taking a deep breath, she nodded.

"Are you ready for me to go?" he asked.

"No." She studied him for another moment, taking in his curly dark hair, his golden irises, the clean angles of his face. Then she held out her hand. Would he take it? He was attracted to her, too; she felt it.

He hesitated for only a moment before cursing softly and curling his strong, tanned fingers through hers. "This isn't going to help, Reenie," he said.

"I don't care," she responded, and smiled as his warmth seemed to glide right through her. "Just tell me about Africa."

CHAPTER SEVENTEEN

KEITH'S ANGER MADE IT almost impossible for him to stand in one spot as he waited for Liz to open the door. He kept picturing Isaac and Reenie at the farm alone, imagining what they might be doing right now. And it made him want to hit someone.

When Liz finally appeared, he shoved his way into the house and tried to kiss her. He knew he was being too aggressive, but he couldn't contain his frustration any longer. He was so sick of having no control over his life, no ability to bring what he wanted most back to him. If he couldn't have Reenie, he'd take Liz. He couldn't lose both families. Not for good! He'd paid his price!

But Liz turned her face away so that he couldn't reach her lips and pushed on his chest until he finally let her go. "What's wrong with you?" she breathed, her eyes snapping. She didn't raise her voice—but he knew that was only because she didn't want to wake the children.

"I've been humbled, okay? I—I regret what I did with every breath I take. It's time to forgive me."

She shook her head as though he'd just said something absolutely insane. But it didn't sound insane to him. He couldn't understand how Liz *and* Reenie, who'd both loved him so much, could turn their backs on him now. He spent half his time rambling around the empty house he'd shared with Reenie and his girls, marveling that he could suffer such a quick and immediate reversal.

"I'm afraid you don't get to decide what I do or do not feel," she said.

"But I'm available now, Liz. There's nothing standing between us. I have no one else to worry about, no secrets. You could have my complete attention."

"It's too late," she said.

"Why?"

She lifted her hands in a helpless gesture. "It just is."

"I'll be good to you. I'll—I'll make it so that you never have to think of Reenie again."

"That's impossible, and you know it. What you did has very far-reaching consequences, Keith. I can't change that."

He grabbed her hand. "You could forgive me."

She pulled away. "Even if I could, you really want Reenie, not me. You've made that very clear."

"That's not true." He feared she'd easily recognize that statement for the lie that it was, but he was desperate enough to use almost anything to convince her. At least he could live a semblance of the life he once knew if she'd come back to him. At least he could walk away from Reenie with a *little* of his dignity left. "I love you, Liz. Look at everything I gave you. I never bought Reenie a diamond tennis bracelet. I gave you a better house, paid for a part-time nanny—"

"I was working, too, Keith. Except for the bracelet, *we* bought those things."

"I gave you more of my paycheck than I did her!"

"The question is why?"

"To make you happy."

"No." She shook her head. "To make *you* happy. You were trying to maintain a certain lifestyle, Keith. You were living your fantasy life, weren't you? A nice house, a pretty wife, a nanny for the two kids, a membership at the club. You were taking advantage of the chance to be something completely different than you are when you're here in Dundee. I think you got a kick out of putting on a show for our friends."

"That's not fair. I bought those things, did those things for you."

"If you were thinking of me, what happened would never have occurred," she said softly. "Now, I'm going to ask you to leave."

"What?"

"I don't want you here. You can call when the kids are awake, but don't come over here again without permission."

"I can stay as long as I please," he said.

"No, you can't. Isaac's asleep down the hall. I'll call him if you won't go."

"That's bullshit," he scoffed. "Your big bad brother isn't even home."

She lifted her chin but didn't respond.

"Don't you want to know where he is?" he taunted.

"Not necessarily."

"He's with Reenie," he said. "Isn't that a bitch? He's probably screwing her brains out right now."

"Get out." Her hands curled into fists, and the loathing that filled her face finally registered.

"Forget I even came here," he said. "When Isaac leaves, Reenie's bound to realize what she's throwing away. Then she'll come back to me. You'll see. And you'll be sorry you didn't act when you had the chance!"

With that he marched out and slammed the door. Part of him hoped she'd follow him, beg him to come back in so they could work things out. She used to do that kind of thing when they had a disagreement. But she didn't. Instead, he heard her lock the door behind him.

ISAAC LAY on the floor with a pillow, staring up at the ceiling while trying to keep from touching Reenie, who had her head on his chest and was lying perpendicular to him. The fire flickered in front of them, crackling, popping, and smelling like smoke and sap.

"So they still speak French in Africa?"

They'd drawn the drapes in case Keith returned. The house

felt warm, close and private, and although they were both relaxed, there was a subtle yet undeniable tension in the air—tension that came from restraint.

"Early colonization made a lasting impact on the whole continent," he explained, allowing himself the small concession of playing with her hair.

"But I thought the people in Central Africa spoke mostly Bantu."

"Many do—but there are a lot of different languages."

Bailey had snuggled close to her body. She petted him as she spoke. "Do *you* know French?"

"Oui, je parle français," he said with a grin. He was tempted to tell her a few other things in his second language—how beautiful she was, for one—but he knew she'd only press him for the interpretation. "And I can understand Bantu, but I can't speak it very well."

"So why must a biologist from America travel to Africa on behalf of the forest elephant?" she asked.

"They're an endangered species. Seventy years ago three to five million elephants inhabited Africa. Today only about five hundred thousand remain. Roughly one-third are forest elephants. With so few left, it's important to monitor them."

"But with the human population growing, and the forest being destroyed, can monitoring really do any good?"

"You bet. It lets us know where they live and how they travel, so we can determine how much land must be protected to give them enough space. Also, a vet generally comes along and collects samples."

"Blood samples? That sort of thing?"

"Blood, ectoparasites, feces, skin biopsies. That way we can create some baseline data and perform health assessments of the animals."

Reenie lay quiet for several seconds, still petting Bailey. Isaac wondered if she was listening to the classical music she'd turned on, or thinking. "I'm not sure I've ever heard of the forest elephant before tonight," she finally mused.

"Sometimes they're called pygmy elephants."

"Haven't heard of that either. But Africa isn't a very popular subject up here. I don't know one other person who's ever been there."

"Typically when people hear the word *elephant*, they picture the savanna elephant," he said.

"The big ones you see walking across grassy plains in the movies."

"Exactly. At one time we thought there were only two types of elephants in the world. The African savanna and the Asian." He wasn't sure why he was going into so much detail. She probably didn't care about the different species of elephant. But he was afraid the temptation to let his hands wander might get the best of him if he didn't keep talking. "But when a DNA identification system was set up to trace the origin of poached ivory, we found that the forest elephant is actually a third species, as different from the others as lions are from tigers."

"Do they look that different?" she asked.

"Definitely. Savanna elephants can be as tall as thirteen feet."

"Forest elephants are smaller?"

"By quite a bit. The largest of the bulls might reach eight feet. They also have more rounded ears—" Reenie leaned up to take another sip of her wine and offered him a drink. He loved the half smile she gave him when he accepted her glass. It let him know she was feeling the same tugging awareness he was. He nearly reached up to bring her down on top of him so he could meet her mouth with his, but he knew a relationship between them was just too…impossible.

"You were saying they have more rounded ears," she said.

"Right." Isaac found it difficult to concentrate when he looked at her. He waited for her to relax against him again before continuing. "Their tusks aren't curved like the savanna. They're straight and thin with a pinkish tinge to the ivory. A forest elephant's lower jaw is longer than the other two species, giving it a narrow face. And forest elephants are a few shades darker in color."

"You love them," she said, rolling over and propping herself up on her elbows.

He grinned. "They're incredible animals."

Her responding smile faded. "But they might not be around much longer because they're losing their habitat, right?"

He sobered. "That, and because poachers kill them for their ivory."

"Okay, let's not go in that direction," she said, and took another sip of wine. "Tell me what's involved when a biologist decides to track a forest elephant."

He folded his arms behind his head. "Well…we base out of Ouesso, in the north. From there, we move into and around the forest by boat or land rover, or we hike to different campsites, searching for elephants."

Bailey lifted his head, licked Reenie's hand, then rested his muzzle on his paws again. "How's he doing?" Isaac said, changing subjects.

"Not so good," Reenie said. "I'm afraid he's not going to last much longer. I should probably have him put to sleep, but I'm hoping he can make it a few more months."

He leaned toward her and cupped her chin. "I'm sorry."

"It's part of life," she said. "One I don't want to deal with, especially in the near future, but—don't make me sad. We were talking about finding elephants."

He dropped his hand before he could try making her forget about Bailey in more physical ways. "Right. Well, they might weigh twenty-five-hundred kilograms but they're still very difficult to find."

"You're kidding. That's over five thousand pounds. It's hard to imagine something that big being hard to find."

"The jungle is incredibly dense."

"It must be. So what do you do when you come upon one?"

"I immobilize and anesthetize it so I can place a GPS telemetry collar on it."

"A collar?"

His eyes focused on her lips. "You are so…"

"What?" she prompted.

"Gorgeous."

She laughed. "You don't think that's stating things a little too strongly?"

"Hell, no."

"I think you've had too much to drink."

"Not by a long shot. Anyway—" he cleared his throat "—what was I talking about?"

"Collars."

"Right. GPS collars. They weigh nearly thirty pounds."

"Sounds like you have a fun job."

He took a drink from his own glass. "It's exciting. You never know when you're going to find one."

"If I ever had to face an animal that weighed over five thousand pounds, I'd want an army with me. Tell me you don't take these elephants down all by yourself."

"No. I have a whole team of scientists to help me. Last trip, there was someone from the Wildlife Conservation Society, someone from the Fossil Rim Wildlife Center, a veterinarian from the National Zoo, local trackers who were members of the Bambenjelle people, a Bantu-speaking Kaka—"

"Kaka?"

"Another local people."

"That's it?"

He moved her hair over her shoulder. "I also had a field assistant." With whom he'd had a brief sexual relationship. But he didn't add that. It was only relevant to him in that it had been a long time ago and was seeming more remote by the second.

"Still, it's got to be dangerous," she said.

"It's worth it."

"How close do you have to get?"

"To within fifty meters. The first bull I ever anesthetized was standing in a bai—"

"What's a bai?"

"A big wet, grassy clearing in the forest. They go there to drink. Anyway, the water was about three feet deep, and I had to walk into it to hide behind a small bush so he wouldn't know where I was when I shot him." He chuckled, remembering. "As soon as the dart struck, he splashed water all over us with his trunk and body, drenching everyone. And the next three minutes felt like hours as we waited to see where he'd go."

"Where did he go?"

"He ran to the water's edge and into the forest, and we rushed behind him. Our Bambenjelle trackers led the way. We ran for fifteen minutes before we caught sight of him again. It was quite a chase."

"And you've given up all that to work in Earl's feed store?"

She spoke lightly, but he could tell there was something more serious underlying her tone. He suspected she wanted to know what he was really doing here, how long he'd be staying. He also suspected she'd already guessed the answer.

"I've recently improved my situation, remember?" he said. "I'll soon be working at the high school with you."

"But you could never really be happy with either job, could you?"

He sat up, finished his wine and stood. It was getting late. If she was still awake, Liz would be wondering where he was. "Probably not," he admitted. He wanted to make love to Reenie, to wake up in the morning with her naked in his arms, to have breakfast together.

But he knew he couldn't have a casual relationship with Reenie. She had three children. She deserved someone who could offer her a commitment.

And then there was Liz and Keith and the past…

"That's what I thought," she said.

He reached out and took her hands. "Reenie, if things were different—"

She pulled away. "Don't explain. I understand."

"I don't want to hurt you."

She grinned and managed a little shrug. "I don't want to hurt you, either."

Had she possessed a little less spunk, he probably could've walked away from her right then. But she had the spark of a fighter in her eyes, one that said she might be down but she was far from out.

Bringing her to him, he ran his hands up her backside, pressing their bodies tightly together. He was looking for a good excuse, anything that might let him bend his own rules a bit.

Her defiance offered him that.

He meant to lower his mouth to hers, to at least leave with a taste of her on his lips. Wise or not, he refused to begrudge himself such a small concession. But he'd underestimated her. Giving him a devilish grin, she turned her face away at the last second so that he barely caught her cheek.

"Good night," she said, stepping out of his reach.

He hesitated for a second, wondering if she knew what she'd just done to him. He had a feeling she did.

"Don't challenge me," he murmured.

"Why not?" she responded flippantly.

"Because you already know what I want."

"And?"

"Getting it wouldn't be good for either one of us."

"Maybe I'm tired of being good," she said. "But I'll respect your wishes. Good night."

Before Isaac could even blink, he was standing out on her front stoop with the door closed firmly behind him. *Maybe I'm tired of being good?* If she wanted a torrid affair and was taking volunteers, he wanted to be the first in line. But—

Remember Liz. I should be happy the evening has ended so benignly.

Only he wasn't happy at all. All he could think about was how hungry he was to feel Reenie beneath him.

He knocked.

When she opened the door, it was only by a few inches. "Did you forget something?" she asked innocently.

He pushed the door open wider. "Yeah, this." Taking hold of her shirt, he pulled her to him, and kissed her, *really* kissed her. This time he didn't give her the chance to turn away, but neither did she try. She put her arms around his neck and arched into him. One of them moaned; or maybe they both did. Then she parted her lips, letting him drink deeply, until desire burned through him like a good shot of whiskey.

When he finally let her go, they were both shaken and breathless. "Some people just don't know what's good for them," he muttered, his eyes taking in her flushed face, her half-lowered eyelids.

"Are you talking about me or you?" she challenged.

He met her gaze. "Maybe both."

"Then consider that kiss something to remember me by," she said.

The door clicked closed once again.

Isaac frowned at the panel, then stabbed a hand through his hair. Damn, she was frustrating. Why couldn't she simply agree that they had some type of powerful attraction going on that was better left alone—for everyone's sake—*and then leave it alone?* Instead she had to make him feel as though he was missing out on something he might later regret.

Go home. Complete your grant applications. Get the hell out of Dundee. This woman could stand between him and the future he had scripted for himself. He'd never run into anyone else like her.

On the other hand, if *she* could take the heat, why was *he* the one backing away?

He pounded the door again. "There's more where that came from," he called. "But you'd better be damn sure you know what you're asking for if you ever invite me back."

Then he walked away.

LIZ WAS UP. Isaac could see the kitchen light burning through the front window when he pulled into the driveway, and sighed before letting himself into the house.

"Isaac?" his sister called as he closed the front door.

"Yeah, it's me."

She came to stand at the threshold of the kitchen, wearing an elegant cream-colored silk robe. She looked as though she'd been losing even more weight. She didn't seem to be doing well in Dundee. She had no friends. Keith called her occasionally, but she was distant even with him.

Not that Isaac hoped she'd be warmer to Keith. He just wanted her to recover, be the person she'd been before Keith undid all the good of the past several years.

Somehow Isaac needed to get her to *engage* again. To care about people besides her kids.

"Have fun?" she said.

The strain in her shoulders and face told him she knew where he'd been. "Sort of. Why? Keith call?"

She watched him. "Stopped by, actually. He was furious."

"He had no right to bother you."

"I finally told him I'd have to call you out of your bedroom if he didn't leave."

"I'm sorry."

She said nothing.

"I would've told you about Reenie myself. You know that, don't you?" he said.

"You have the right to decide who you want to see."

"I know, but…I can understand how you must feel toward her, Liz. I wish—" he shoved his hands into his pockets "—I wish I wasn't so attracted to her."

His sister opened her mouth, then closed it again and disappeared into the kitchen.

"Say it," he said to her retreating back.

"Say what?"

He followed her to find that she was busy sewing the curtains she'd promised Mica for her bedroom. She spent all her time, when she wasn't at the grocery store, working on projects that included her children or served them in some way. "Whatever you want to say. I'm tired of feeling as though you might shatter at any moment. Can't we just—" he thought of Reenie and how honestly she faced the world "—talk frankly?"

"There's nothing to say. You like her, I don't."

"You don't really know her."

"We're not in the position to become good friends."

He sat at the table. "I'll be leaving for Africa soon."

"Which is why I can't understand what you're doing. It's not fair of me to expect you not to see her for my sake. But God, Isaac, what about *her?* As much as I hate her for the jealousy she inspires in me, as much as I hate her because Keith *still* wants her more than he ever wanted me, I know she's been through a lot. Why would you get involved with her if you know that you're leaving?"

"Because…there's something about her, Liz. I don't know how to explain it."

"She's the other woman in my life!"

"You don't think I realize that?"

"Is she aware of how you feel?"

"She knows I'll be leaving in a few months," he said in lieu of an answer.

Only the sound of Liz's scissors cutting through fabric broke the silence. Finally she said, "How do you think she feels about you?"

He shrugged. He was pretty certain Reenie would have made

love with him tonight, had he handled the situation differently. But he didn't volunteer that. There was honesty, and then there was stupidity.

"Is she over Keith?"

"She acts like it."

"Keith said the girls are in Texas."

"She told me the same thing."

Liz set her scissors down and straightened. "Isaac, I—"

"What?" he said.

"You told me you wanted me to say what was on my mind."

"Go ahead."

"Since you're leaving Dundee soon anyway, could you just... stay away from her?" she asked. Her expression turned beseeching. "Please?"

He stared at his sister, wondering why he found agreeing to her request so difficult. His libido had to be the problem, right? What else could it be? He and Reenie had very little in common other than having a close connection to Keith, which wasn't a favorable thing. She was still recovering from her divorce. She had three children. The word *commitment* might as well be stamped across her forehead.

When he considered all those factors, he thought he could overcome his physical desire. "I'll make you a deal," he said at last.

"What?"

"You quit calling Dave Shapiro, and I'll stop seeing Reenie."

A frown creased her brow. "You know about Dave?"

"I knew there had to be some reason you waited for the phone bill every month, snatched it out of the pile and paid it before I could."

"We just talk like friends. It's nothing, really. He—he gives me something I need right now, Isaac, that's all."

"Reenie felt pretty necessary to me tonight, too," he admitted. When he remembered her and that kiss, she still did.

"Did you sleep with her?" she asked, her eyes widening.

"No."

"Good," she said. "If I fall for Dave, it isn't as though he's going to love me back. They're both dead-end relationships."

"So we have nothing to lose by giving them up."

"Right." She finally nodded. "Okay."

REENIE HAD WANTED to arrive early, so she could get a good seat for Caldwell Elementary's Annual Talent Show and be settled before Liz or Isaac arrived. But she'd forgotten her video camera and had gone home for it at the last minute. Now Liz and her brother were already standing at the back of the multipurpose room, and Agnes Scott, who was in charge of the talent show this year, was addressing the audience.

"The children have worked so hard. I think this will be one of Caldwell's best talent shows ever. When I first held the auditions…"

The place was packed to overflowing. Almost immediately, Reenie removed her lightweight black jacket and slung it over one arm. The weather was cool and mellow, a perfect spring evening, but it was stifling inside. Especially because a few folks still turned to stare when she and Liz were in a room together. She hated the extra attention, wished people would mind their own business. But she couldn't escape it tonight. Jennifer would soon be on stage doing a cheer she'd choreographed herself. Angela would perform a tap-dance routine. And Isabella would be singing "Somewhere Over the Rainbow."

"Reenie!"

Reenie glanced up to see Keith waving at her. He'd told her he probably wouldn't be coming, that he had to drive his dad to Boise for a doctor's appointment in the late afternoon. Evidently he'd managed to get back in time.

I've got a seat for you right here! he mouthed, pointing to the chair next to him. But Reenie didn't want to sit there. She didn't want to hear what he had to say about Isaac coming to her house last Friday. Keith had tried to call her several times already, had even stopped by the farm again after Isaac had left that night, and then the next day. But she'd managed to brush him off with the threat that she'd call Gabe if he didn't leave her alone. Gabe might be in a wheelchair, but no one messed with him. He could make people back off with a single raised eyebrow.

Wishing her mother wasn't away with her father, getting ready for a fund-raiser in the Panhandle, she held up her video camera and motioned to tell her ex-husband she had other plans. Then she hurried across the room and stood against the wall. She felt Isaac's eyes on her as she moved, but refused to look at him. She could also feel Liz's cool disdain.

The lights lowered and a spotlight illuminated the stage as two kindergarteners came out to do a magic trick. They stuffed one scarf into a hat and pulled out a whole string of them in many different colors. Afterward, they made a ball disappear and re-appear using various cups.

Everyone clapped when they finished. Then Mica came out in a pretty dress and black patent leather pumps, walking with the perfect poise of her mother. "I'm going to play *Moonlight Sonata* by Ludwig van Beethoven," she said into the microphone and headed for the piano someone had rolled into the center of the stage.

Reenie put her video camera down. Angela rarely talked about Mica anymore—when she did it was with a certain amount of respect—but Reenie didn't see any need to make Mica part of her family's permanent record of this event.

Still, as Mica situated herself on the piano bench, Reenie began to feel very ungenerous. Mica was no different from any other child; Liz was no different than any other woman. They had suffered, too. Probably just as much as Reenie and her children, maybe more.

With a sigh, Reenie raised her camera again and pressed the record button. She was going to fight the jealousy, overcome it, she decided. Surely she could be a better person than she'd been.

Mica played strictly from memory, and not some simplified version of the sonata, as Reenie had expected. The piece was obviously very difficult, yet the girl didn't miss a note.

When she finished, the audience erupted in enthusiastic applause. Reenie held her video recorder with her legs so she could join in. She even found herself smiling broadly. What an amazing child. Angela had mentioned, here and there, the kind of test scores Mica always received. Evidently, Liz's daughter had a number of talents.

Smiling shyly, Mica bowed and walked offstage, and Reenie couldn't help looking back at Isaac. She expected him to be accepting the accolades of those around him. *She can really play... Wow, is she only eight?... I've never heard such a young girl master the piano like that...* Certainly Liz was smiling proudly and responding to those around her. But her brother had his arms folded and was leaning against the wall—looking directly at Reenie.

When their eyes met, Reenie felt her stomach lift as though she'd just been swept into the ocean by a particularly strong wave. What had happened last Friday seemed to play between them—the hours of comfortable companionship, the images he'd painted of Africa, the kiss at the door, even his final comment: *There's more where that came from. But you'd better be damned sure you know what you're asking for if you ever invite me back.*

They hadn't contacted each other since, but the attraction hadn't fizzled. If anything, it had grown stronger. She could tell he wanted to be with her now as badly as he had then. And she wanted to be with him every bit as much.

"What are you doing?" Keith snapped.

Reenie blinked and pulled her attention away from Isaac to see her ex-husband looming over her. "Nothing, why?"

"You're staring at Isaac."

"No, I'm not."

"Who were you looking at, then?"

"Nobody. Stop it," Reenie said. "I'm happy for him and Liz, that's all. Mica did a great job."

"You're happy that *Mica* did well?"

"Aren't you?"

"Of course, but…" Keith's expression grew tortured. "You don't care about me anymore, do you. You want Isaac."

"I don't want anyone."

"He loves his work, Reenie. He loves being free to spend *months at a time* in Africa. He won't stay here with you."

"Like you did?" she said, unable to resist the barb.

"Like I'm willing to do now," he said earnestly.

"You'd better sit down," she said. "You're making it hard for people to see."

"He won't treat you right, Reenie."

"I can worry about myself, Keith."

Mrs. Devonish, one of the teachers at the school, made her way over to them. "Keith, do you mind?" she whispered. "You're disrupting the show."

With a final frown for Reenie, he nodded and moved away, and Reenie went back to videotaping what was happening on-stage, wondering if Keith could be right. *Did* she want Isaac? Since last Friday, she'd watched her AOL account religiously, hoping for a response to the e-mail she'd sent him, thanking him for taking her home and telling him she'd had a good time. She'd begun to look for him or his truck almost everywhere she went. And the unhappiness she'd felt about having him work at the high school had changed into something much more akin to excitement. She knew he wasn't long-term boyfriend material, but a girl deserved to have a *little* fun, didn't she?

Isabella came out and began to sing her song. As usual, every *r* sounded like a *w*. "Somewhere over the wainbow, dweams come twue…"

Reenie couldn't help grinning as she watched proudly. When Isabella came to the end of her song, Reenie applauded wildly.

Then her thoughts returned to Isaac. As much as she wanted to, she couldn't avoid the truth. She'd be a fool to get involved with Liz's brother. With the farm and her job and her girls, she had more than she could handle already. The very last thing she needed was a quick fling with a man who'd soon be flying off to the jungles of Africa.

CHAPTER EIGHTEEN

"YOU'RE INFATUATED," Liz said as Mica and Christopher raced off to get another cookie from the refreshment table.

Isaac scowled, but even as she accused him, he couldn't help letting his focus follow Reenie as she moved about the room, talking to friends, trying to gather up her girls. She was wearing a low-cut pair of jeans he particularly liked, with a tight-fitting sweater and a sexy pair of boots. He enjoyed watching her walk. "No, I'm not."

"You're acting very predatory, like some big cat or something. Maybe you're not ready to pounce, but you can't take your eyes off your prey."

To prove his sister wrong, he forced himself to turn his back to the entire room. "I agreed not to see her, and I haven't." He hadn't even responded to the e-mail she'd sent him, which hadn't been easy to ignore. "What about you? Any calls I don't know about?"

Her eyebrows knit as though she wasn't finding their agreement any easier to abide by than he was. "He left me a message last night."

"Did you return it?"

"No."

"Good girl."

"He's not quite as bad as you think. And he lives a thousand miles away. What difference could it possibly make if—"

"Liz?"

Reenie's voice. An invisible current swept through Isaac as he turned and found her standing right beside him, along with her three daughters.

Liz quickly masked her surprise. "Yes?" she said warily.

"I just wanted to tell you how much I enjoyed Mica's performance. She's very talented," she said.

Liz blinked several times before managing to find her voice. "Thank you. I—Your girls did a great job, too."

Reenie smiled triumphantly. Isaac knew she was proud of her children, but he could also tell that the triumph in her smile had very little to do with the talent show. "Good night."

"Good night," Liz repeated, then, when they were out of earshot, she turned questioningly to Isaac. "Evidently she likes you, too," she murmured.

Isaac watched Reenie walk out. "She didn't do that for me," he said.

REENIE SAT in front of her computer. The kids were in bed, happily exhausted after the talent show. They had school in the morning, and she had to teach. But it was Thursday night, so the weekend was drawing close. She could handle one more short night. It was the cold shoulder she was getting from Isaac that really bothered her.

Why hadn't he written her back? Or called? She knew he found her attractive. He'd stared at her so much tonight he'd probably missed half the show.

Her buddy list showed him as being online, so she clicked on Read Mail. Nothing.

Old Bailey lay in the corner by the couch. Apparently, he didn't even feel good enough to come over and snuggle with her anymore. She was going to have to face reality one of these days....

The lift she'd felt earlier when she'd spoken to Liz and praised Mica slowly disappeared. Bailey was dying. She needed to talk to someone. She thought of her parents and Gabe. Lucky. Beth. Any one of them would be supportive. But she wanted Isaac.

With a sigh, she typed him an instant message. Where are you?

There was a long pause. Either he'd walked away from his computer, or he was thinking about rejecting her offer to chat. Finally she got a response.

Right here.

Bailey's not doing so well.

Is it that time?

I think it might be. I need you… She stared at the words on her screen. She meant them just the way they stood, but she knew she couldn't send Isaac something *that* revealing. So she added a bit more. I need you to tell me some more about Africa.

You think that'll help?

I like hearing about it.

There was another long pause, then, Have I mentioned the Pygmy tribes?

No.

Well, there are quite a few different ones—the Bambuti, the Batwa, the Bayaka, the Bagyeli.

They all start with *b*?

Ba means people.

I see.

Pygmies live in some of the most inhospitable forests of Eastern Congo.

What are they like?

Textbooks will tell you they're hunter/gatherers, that they have dark skin and stand about fifty-nine inches high.

What would *you* tell me?

They're a struggling people who are fighting hard to protect their culture and their homes. They're playful, spiritual. They like to sing.

What's their music like?

Vocal and rich...sort of like harmonic yodeling with a hypnotic rhythm.

Again, she felt his love of Africa and his work. Do you miss the Pygmy tribes when you're in the States?

Sometimes.

It's hard to imagine they're really so small.

Anthropologists have automatically assumed that they're the most primitive members of the human race. But...

The ellipses meant he was e-mailing more. She waited.
I'm not sure, he went on. Races of true Pygmy size in pre-

history are unknown to archeologists. Where they come from is a bit of a mystery.

She shot another glance at Bailey, wishing Isaac would come over. Tell me about how they live, she typed.

Pygmy women look after the tribe's general welfare. They search for food in the forest. They gather a lot of vegetables and a mixture of yam, fruit, mushrooms and tubers that they call manioc. In some seasons they collect termites, caterpillars and snails.

To eat?

Yum, huh? :)

That helps take my mind off my own troubles.

LOL Are you okay?

I don't want Bailey to die.

I know. I'm sorry.

She felt a lump rising in her throat and didn't know how to respond.

What you did tonight...complimenting Mica to Liz... that was nice, he wrote.

She smiled through her tears. I have my better moments.

Has Keith been bothering you about last Friday?

Here and there. Tonight he accused me of staring at you.

You were staring at me. :)

Only because I want your body. :)

You love to flirt with danger.

I've always played it pretty safe in the past. Are you dangerous?

In ways. Did you know that the food the Pygmy women gather is shared equally by the community?

LOL—We're back to Pygmies?

And that Pygmies practice alloparenting? he asked.

No. What's alloparenting?

Group parenting, more or less.

The whole tribe raises the young? Something like that?

Pretty much.

You were staring at me, too, Isaac, she wrote.

No kidding. I couldn't take my eyes off you.

Reenie felt quite a bit warmer when she read that. So why hadn't he responded to her e-mail? You know my number.... Nothing.

Never mind, she wrote.

I'm leaving town at some point, Reenie. There's no-where for us to go.

I know. It's getting late, she said. I have to get to bed.

But we haven't talked about the role of Pygmy men.

Maybe some other time. Night.

Reenie... he wrote, but she signed off and went over to hug her dog.

"You have lousy timing, you know that, Bailey?" she said.

He licked her face, and she decided that, as much as it hurt to do it, she'd take him to the vet after school. It was time to put her beloved dog out of his misery.

ISAAC SIGHED as he stared at the screen. He'd known that answering Reenie's instant message would be going against his agreement with Liz. But her dog was dying.

"Hear anything from Reg?" Liz asked, surprising him at the door.

"You're still up?" He swiveled toward her. "Evidently we're all a bunch of night owls."

"Who else is up?"

"No one."

"I'm sure I can guess."

He didn't answer.

"Any word on your grants?"

"Not yet. You anxious for me to go?"

"If it'll save you from falling in love with Reenie."

"You hate her that much?"

"Not hate."

"What, then?"

"Where she's concerned, I feel too many emotions to untangle them." She leaned against the doorjamb. "Mica really admires her. She was thrilled to hear that Reenie liked her performance."

"How does Mica feel about Angela?"

"I think she's as jealous of her as I am of Reenie."

"Mica's a very bright girl. What's there to be jealous of?"

"Angela's as popular as Reenie is. See the parallel?"

"Mica and Angela each have their own unique talents."

"Had we all met under different circumstances, I'm sure we wouldn't have had any trouble."

Isaac wrote Reenie's number on a pad of paper, stood and handed it to his sister.

"What's this?" she asked.

"Call Reenie. Invite her out to lunch."

"You've got to be kidding me."

"I'm not."

"Why would I do that?"

"Because her dog is dying. And because she's worth getting to know."

Liz's hair fell in front of her face as she stared down at the number he'd written. "She makes me feel...inadequate, Isaac."

"She made the first move, Liz. Give it a shot. It could be good for Mica and Christopher." When his sister looked up at him, he grinned. "You're worth getting to know, too."

"Her dog is dying?"

"It's breaking her heart."

She studied the slip of paper a minute longer. "I'll think about it," she said.

THE NEXT MORNING Isaac drove Mica and Christopher to school. Liz had to work earlier than usual because Marge Finley was having knee surgery and wasn't able to come in.

Christopher climbed out of the truck first. "Thanks," he said.

"Yeah, thanks." Mica gave him a peck on the cheek before sliding toward her brother and the open door.

"No problem, guys," Isaac said.

"Will you be picking us up?" Christopher asked eagerly, craning his head to see around his sister.

Isaac knew the kid wanted to go out for ice cream. A trip to the Arctic Flyer had become standard operating procedure when Isaac picked them up from school. "Sorry, bud, I'll be at the feed store until dinnertime."

"I thought you were quitting that job," Mica said.

"Today's my last day, although I've agreed to help now and then."

"Maybe Mom will take us out for a treat," Christopher said to Mica.

"She thinks we eat too much sugar already," Mica grumbled.

They slammed the door and Isaac nearly pulled away. He would have, except something caught his attention. Angela and Isabella were standing under the big oak tree near the front entrance to the school, and they appeared to be waiting for Mica. At least they were watching her pretty intently.

Halfway to the tree and her two half sisters, Mica's footsteps slowed and she glanced back at him. Isaac got the distinct impression she didn't want him to see her meet up with Reenie's girls. So he quickly looked down, as though he was fiddling with the radio. When he checked again, Mica and Angela had their heads bent close together and were talking and smiling. Eventually, they walked off together, leaving Isabella to tag along behind.

The person in the car behind Isaac tapped her horn. He was holding up traffic. Pulling out of line, he rolled down his window.

"Isabella!"

She turned, then smiled broadly when she recognized him. He waved her over to the truck. Letting Mica and Angela, who seemed to be in their own little world anyway, go on without her, she skipped toward him.

"Hi!" she said, trying to see him by hanging on to the window opening and standing on tiptoe.

He reached across the seat to open the door.

"You drove Mica and Christopher to school today?" she asked, slipping inside.

"Yep."

"Where's their mom?"

"Working at the grocery store."

"Oh."

He looked around the playground but could no longer spot Mica and Angela. "What are Mica and Angela doing?" he asked.

She shrugged. "I don't know. Probably playing on the monkey bars. They always do that."

"Every morning?"

"And at recess."

Interesting, Isaac thought. Mica never mentioned Reenie's girls. Certainly she hadn't told him or Liz that they played together at school. "How's your mom doing today?" he asked.

"Okay, I guess. She's a little sad."

"Why?"

"Because Bailey's not feeling good. He's too old. Mom told us the vet's going to put him to sleep today. And he won't wake up," she added.

"Did you say goodbye to him?" he asked.

She nodded.

"I'm sorry you had to do that."

Big tears filled her blue eyes, eyes that reminded Isaac so much of Reenie's. "I'm going to miss him."

"So is your mother, sweetie."

She sniffed and nodded, and he reached out to squeeze her little hand. "It'll be okay. I know it hurts, but sometimes we have to say goodbye to animals and even people we love. It's part of life."

"I know," she said. "We're going to have a funeral for him tonight and bury him by the barn so he'll still be close to us."

"That's a good idea."

The bell rang. Wiping her eyes, she offered him a final watery smile. "I gotta go."

"Bye," he said, and watched her run safely to class. He started off toward the feed store, but when he was only halfway there, he stopped at the Arctic Flyer so he could use the payphone to call Earl. Then he headed to Boise.

REENIE PULLED into her driveway, put the transmission in Park and turned off the engine. She hadn't wanted to go to the vet alone, but she hadn't wanted any of her children to have to suffer through the experience, either. So she'd picked up her mother and her half sister earlier.

"Want me to get the shovel?" Lucky asked from the back seat.

"No, Keith can do it."

"When's he coming over?"

"In a few minutes." Reenie had told her ex-husband she wouldn't be home until four-thirty because she'd wanted to have plenty of time to collect herself before facing the rest of the family.

"Will he be bringing the girls?" Celeste asked.

"Yeah, he picked them up from school so I could…you know, do this."

"I'm glad he'll be here," Celeste said. "He gave you that dog before you had any kids. He loved Bailey, too."

Reenie nodded and opened her door. "Let's carry him into the back, okay?"

Lucky helped her lift the crate containing Bailey's body, and together they headed around the side of the house. Reenie hated the fact that her dog wouldn't be around to greet her when she came home each day. If he hadn't been so miserable, she would've let his life run its course. But the cancer was getting too painful for him.

"This has been such a tough year for you," Celeste said, following behind. "I was telling Garth just last night that I'm very proud of the way you've handled—"

The jingle of a collar and a *yap, yap, yap* interrupted.

"What's that?" Lucky asked.

"I don't know," Reenie answered honestly.

Celeste skirted around them. "Sounds like a dog."

When they reached the gate, they saw that it *was* a dog. A puppy. He had a big red bow around his neck and was straining against a rope tied to a stake in the ground. The moment he saw he had company, he wiggled and barked and whined for attention.

Celeste crossed over to him, walking gingerly because her high heels kept sinking into the wet lawn. "Who's this little guy?"

Reenie's jaw had fallen open. Quickly clamping her mouth shut, she realized it was the dog from the shelter in Boise. Isaac must've brought him. But she didn't want her mother and Lucky to know that Liz's brother had given her anything. She didn't see any need to put herself in the awkward position of trying to explain why he might do so. As far as anyone else knew, family included, she and Isaac barely spoke to each other. "I—I thought it would be a good idea to get a new puppy for the girls, to distract them from the sadness of losing Bailey," she said.

Celeste bent to pat the puppy's head. "Why didn't you tell us he was here?"

"I thought you wanted to wait a few weeks," Lucky said. "But I can see why you changed your mind. Boy, is he cute."

Reenie didn't answer either one of them. "Let's put Bailey over here," she said.

Once they'd set the crate on the ground, she turned to find Celeste wearing a puzzled expression.

"There's a gift card tied to his collar," she said. "And it has *your* name on it."

Damn. The card had been hidden by the bow. "I'll get that."

Reenie started forward, but it was too late. Her mother read the brief message aloud. "'Think of me now and then, okay? Isaac.'"

"Russell?" Lucky said.

Reenie cringed at Lucky's loud voice. "I—I don't think so," she said.

Her half sister gaped at her. "We only know one Isaac, Reenie. If this dog didn't come from him, where did it come from?"

What could she say? She'd met an Isaac on the Internet who'd shipped her a dog? No way would that work. "Okay, Isaac and I have become...friends."

"Friends," Lucky repeated skeptically.

It hardly helped to convince them to take her relationship with Isaac as lightly as she was presenting it when, a moment earlier, she'd lied about even *having* a relationship. But she tried anyway. "Yes, friends."

"Buying you this puppy was a very nice thing to do," Celeste said. "And this card..."

"He didn't mean anything by the card."

"Of course he did," Celeste insisted. "But Reenie, Isaac is Liz's brother."

"Don't jump to conclusions," she said. "It's nothing. Nothing at all." The way they kept staring at her prompted a little more. "We...we danced one night."

"And?" Lucky said.

"And then he gave me a ride home. End of story."

Lucky began to smile.

"Quit it," Reenie said, her voice rising. "So what if Isaac gave me a dog!"

Lucky's eyes suddenly moved to something behind her, and a sick feeling settled in the pit of her stomach. Keith was there. She could tell by her sister's expression.

"Mommy, did you say Isaac bought us a puppy?" Isabella came running toward them, along with the other girls. But Keith didn't move. He stood at the open gate, wearing a dark glower.

Reenie quickly ripped the card off the puppy's collar and stuffed it in her pocket. "I'll get the shovel out of the barn," she said, and hurried away.

By the time she returned, Angela had untied the puppy. The girls were kneeling down, laughing and petting him as he jumped and tried to lick their faces. Keith had joined Lucky and Celeste, but he didn't look happy, and both Lucky and Celeste seemed uncomfortable.

"You're really broken up about Old Bailey, huh?" he said, his words dripping with sarcasm as she handed him the shovel.

"I loved Old Bailey. I'm going to miss him a lot."

"Yeah, right. Like you miss me?"

Celeste and Lucky exchanged glances and Reenie cleared her throat. "Let's not make this any harder than it has to be, Keith," she murmured. "Dig the grave, okay? The girls will say their goodbyes and I'll offer a final prayer."

"Isaac gets to buy a new puppy and be a hero. I get to dig the grave."

"I didn't ask him to buy me a puppy."

"You don't have to accept it," he said earnestly.

Reenie waved at the girls to remind him that they weren't alone. Jennifer had clued in to the fact that an argument was brewing and was watching them closely, but Angela and Isabella were completely enthralled with the puppy. "He got it from a shelter. We can't take it back even if I wanted to. Which I don't."

"Tell him to come pick it up," he insisted. "I'll buy you another dog tonight. A bassett."

The deep sense of loss Reenie felt at Bailey's passing suddenly reasserted itself, and the tears began to flow. "I don't want another bassett," she whispered.

"Then, I'll get you whatever you want. Just—"

"Keith, stop," Lucky interrupted. "Reenie's already grieving enough."

Celeste put her arm around Reenie and patted her sympathetically. "I know how much you loved Bailey, honey," she said. "I know."

After feeling older than her years for so many months, Reenie suddenly felt very young. She wanted to turn her face into her mother's shoulder, to cry in the brokenhearted way of a child. For everything. For Liz and Mica and Christopher. For Bailey. Even for the fact that living at the farm was nothing like she'd imagined it when she'd pictured buying the property with Keith.

"I'm sorry," her mother said, but before anyone could add anything else, a new voice rose from the direction of the driveway.

"Hello? Anyone home?"

It was Isaac.

CHAPTER NINETEEN

A SPLIT SECOND AFTER he spoke, Isaac rounded the corner of the house to find himself facing not only Reenie and the girls, but Celeste, Lucky and Keith, as well. Keith's being there came as no surprise. His Jeep was parked in the driveway. But Isaac hadn't expected Celeste or Lucky.

Not good timing. He knew that instantly and hesitated, but only for a half step. He'd committed himself when he'd called out his greeting, couldn't turn back now. Besides, he'd worried about Reenie all day. He wanted to make sure she was okay no matter who was around.

He took in the fact that she was crying, and that her mother was trying to console her. "You okay?"

He got the impression she wanted to come to him and bury her face in his chest. Or maybe that was what *he* wanted. Regardless, she couldn't do it, and he couldn't invite it. Not with the girls and everyone else around. Besides, he'd already stretched his agreement with Liz about as far as he could.

Pulling away from her mother, she nodded.

"I'm glad you're here," Keith said, breaking the awkward silence. "Now, you can take your puppy home with you."

Jennifer sidled closer to her mother. Isabella paused from her play. "Take the puppy? No, Daddy. He's *ours*."

"I'll get you one myself," he insisted. "A better one."

"We like this one," Jennifer said softly.

"He's funny," Angela added.

"He's a gift," Isaac said. "He stays here unless Reenie doesn't want him."

"You think you can give my family a dog, even if I say no?" Keith snapped.

"I think that's up to Reenie," Isaac said.

"Well, you're wrong. I still have a say. You come around here again and I'll—"

"What, Keith? Maybe it's time you and I slip off somewhere alone and set a few things straight?" He spoke as amiably as possible and kept a smile on his face for the benefit of the children, but he knew the adults weren't fooled. A direct confrontation between him and his ex-brother-in-law was long overdue.

Celeste grabbed Keith's arm to keep him by her side. "No. I'm sure that won't solve anything."

"Keith, isn't the situation bad enough without letting your jealousy make things worse?" Lucky asked.

Jerking away from Celeste, Keith whirled around to glare at her. "What makes you think you can stick your nose into it, Lucky?" he challenged. "You're no sister to Reenie. You didn't even know her until—"

"Keith!" Reenie shouted, but he wasn't finished yet.

"This isn't fair. Garth is your husband," he said to Celeste. "And your father," he said to Reenie and Lucky. "All three of you love him."

"This doesn't have anything to do with—" Reenie started.

"You're *proud* to be connected to him," he went on, ignoring the interruption. "Yet he made a mistake twenty-something years ago, the same mistake I made. He screwed another woman."

Reenie's eyes darted quickly to their children, but he didn't stop.

"So what? It was bad. But no one crucified *him* for it. You stuck by him even after you found out!"

Screwed another woman? A red haze descended over Isaac's vision and his right hand curled into a fist. "Be careful," he warned. "That's my sister you're talking about."

Reenie moved closer to him. "Isaac, no. The girls are here."

He struggled to control his anger.

"It was *her* fault," Keith continued. "Liz…Liz wouldn't go away. She got pregnant, and then…"

"You're blaming *her?*" Isaac cried. "God, Keith, she didn't even know you were—" Feeling Reenie's hand on his arm, and the attention of all three girls as well, Isaac bit back the rest of that statement. "You have a lot of nerve," he said, keeping his voice low.

Keith jutted out his chest in a challenging, belligerent stance and glanced from Celeste to Lucky to Reenie. But when he finally looked at Isaac, and their eyes met, he lowered his head. "No, it's not her fault," he said softly. "Maybe that's the worst part of it." Throwing the shovel on the ground, he started for the gate.

"He's hurting so badly he can't help himself," Celeste explained, obviously torn.

Reenie's expression was unreadable as she watched him go. But Isabella jumped up and ran after him. "Are you leaving, Daddy?" she called. "Daddy?"

Isaac thought Keith was going to ignore her and continue on his way. But he paused near the gate, swung his daughter up in his arms and buried his face in her neck. Isaac's own anger dissipated as he sensed Keith's recognition of his tremendous loss.

After a few moments, Keith put Isabella down again and disappeared around the side of the house.

"He knows it's over," Celeste said sadly.

Isaac agreed. He'd seen the realization in Keith's eyes.

They fell silent as the Jeep's engine started up, then listened to the sound fade as Keith drove away.

Isaac let his breath out. "Do you want me to take the puppy back?" he asked.

Reenie crouched to pat the dog. "No. I, for one, am happy he's here." She closed her eyes as he licked her cheeks. "And I'm even happier that you're here."

Lucky's eyes widened as if the candidness of Reenie's statement came as quite a surprise. But she quickly recovered. "Me, too," she said brightly. "Now that Keith's gone, we could use your help."

THE NEXT DAY, Elizabeth and her children were coming out of the Arctic Flyer when they passed Reenie and her girls going in. As soon as Liz realized who it was, she averted her eyes, expecting to walk on by as though Reenie and her children didn't exist, as usual. Their relationship had changed slightly since the talent show, but they'd been ignoring each other for so long it had become habit.

To Liz's surprise, Reenie touched her arm and offered her a tired smile. "Hi, Liz."

Liz hesitated for a brief moment. Dressed in a coral-colored sweater, dark denim jeans and a pair of stylish boots, Reenie looked nice. But there were dark smudges under her eyes that indicated she might not be feeling as good as she looked. Remembering what Isaac had said about her dog, Liz considered offering some words of comfort, but settled for nodding politely. "Hello."

Simple though this exchange was, Mica, Christopher, Jennifer, Angela and Isabella gaped at each other as though fireworks had just burst across the sky. Then Isabella giggled behind her hand at a funny face Christopher made and Mica and Angela exchanged smiles.

"Why are you acting so smug?" Liz asked Mica after the door to the restaurant swung shut and they made their way to the Esplanade.

"What's smug?" Mica asked.

"Pleased with yourself."

"I'm not...pleased with myself."

"What's going on, then?"

"Nothing."

They climbed into the SUV and Liz backed out of her parking space. As she twisted to check behind her, she saw her daughter give a little finger wave to Angela, who was still inside the restaurant. Glancing over to see how this action might be received, she watched Angela wave in return.

Reenie wasn't around to see it. Liz guessed she was in line to order.

Stopping immediately, even though she was blocking the entrance to the drive-through, Liz studied her daughter. "Are you and Angela becoming friends?" she asked.

Mica continued to stare out the window, twirling the ends of her hair, which she often did when concentrating.

"Mica?"

Finally her eyes darted to Liz's face, but she wouldn't maintain eye contact. "If we were, would that make you unhappy?" she asked.

How to respond? *Would* it make her unhappy? Reenie was her rival. At the same time, Liz wanted to let go of the past and live again, didn't she? To quit hovering at the edges of this community and become part of it?

She just wasn't confident she could do that. "I don't think so."

"But you're not sure?"

"Not quite," she admitted.

"They had to put their dog to sleep," Mica said.

"Now you're trying to play on my sympathy?" Liz replied.

"To sleep? What does that mean?" Christopher asked.

"He was old and very sick," Liz explained. "They had to put him out of his misery."

"You mean *kill* him?" he cried.

Liz searched for a softer way to state it. "He was dying. They stopped his pain."

"How did it go?" Mica asked.

"I have no idea," Liz replied. "Do you?"

"Not yet."

"Because you haven't been to school since it happened?"

She nodded. "I feel bad for them."

Someone turned into the parking lot, and Liz pulled up to get out of the way. "So you *are* friends," she said, adjusting her rearview mirror to be able to see her daughter's face.

"Isaac likes her, too," Mica said defensively. "And he likes Isabella and Jennifer. Even Reenie."

"How can you tell?" Liz asked.

She took a moment to consider. "Never mind."

"Come on, Mica."

She blew out an exaggerated sigh. "I saw a message on his computer."

Liz knew she had no business delving into her brother's personal affairs, but she couldn't help asking. "From Reenie?"

"The address had her name in it."

"What'd it say?"

"Thanks for the puppy."

Liz told herself she should be upset. She'd asked Isaac not to have any contact with Reenie, and he'd gone ahead and given her a puppy.

But she wasn't angry. She only wondered if that was a big enough breach of The Agreement to justify letting herself call Dave.

"I HEARD YOU GAVE Reenie a dog," Liz said, putting coffee on to brew.

Isaac glanced up from the newspaper he'd been reading while eating a quick bowl of cold cereal. It had been a long weekend. Other than stopping by to check on Reenie after her visit to the vet, Isaac had managed to get back on track and keep his distance from the "other woman" in Liz's life. But he couldn't give himself a lot of credit for that. He'd spent much of his time replaying those few seconds when he was kissing Reenie at her doorstep—and longing to do it again. He'd lain awake at night, thinking about how she might respond if he were to kiss her again. And on Saturday, he'd gone to The Honky Tonk, then the diner, then the Arctic Flyer, and the new Dundee Inn & Steakhouse, in the hope of "accidentally" bumping into her. Liz couldn't blame him for a random meeting, right?

Fortunately for his conscience, that hadn't worked out. He'd made it all the way to Monday without so much as responding to Reenie's quick note of thanks for the puppy. But maybe that was because he knew he'd be seeing her this morning, regardless. It was his first day teaching at the high school.

"Who told you that? Keith?" he asked.

"Does *he* know?"

"He was there. So were Celeste and Lucky. Between the three of them, I'm sure half the town has heard by now."

"What made you get involved?" she asked.

He rattled his paper as he turned the page, hoping she'd get the hint that he really didn't want to examine the reasons behind his actions. "It wasn't a big deal." He checked his watch. "Want me to wake the kids? It's getting pretty late."

"No, I'll take care of that." She moved to the table and gently pulled his paper down. "We were talking about Reenie. I want you to know that I consider puppy-giving a significant breach of our agreement."

"She had to put her dog to sleep, Liz."

"Don't play on my sympathy. It's still a *significant* breach."

Of course he knew that, but… "How significant?"

"I get to call Dave."

"No way!"

"Why not? You bought her a puppy! And you gave it to her in front of three other people."

She had a point. "Okay," he said. "One call. But that's it. Then we're even, and we start fresh."

When she smiled, the relief he saw in her face made him more than a little nervous. He couldn't let her get hurt yet again. "Liz, he's too young for you."

"And Reenie's perfect for you? What, are you going to write her from Africa, and then from Chicago after that? Or are you just going to have a fling with her whenever you come to visit me?"

He drew a deep breath, finished his orange juice and stood. "Right. It's good we have these little talks every now and then."

She laughed, which made her eyes sparkle, and he realized that he hadn't seen her looking so happy for months—not since she'd found out about Keith and Reenie. He was glad to know she was healing, that she'd be okay after he left. But for him, her recovery meant both good and bad news. The good news was that, when his grant came through, he could really go.

Unfortunately, that was also the bad news.

AT THE MONDAY-MORNING staff meeting, Reenie gave up her usual seat next to Beth for a spot at the back of the room, as far away from Isaac as possible. In the past week, she'd been excited to work with him. But now she wasn't so sure it'd be a good thing. At least for her. She'd e-mailed him twice after he gave her the puppy, and he hadn't responded.

What was going on with him? Why would he do something so nice, then immediately withdraw? Was he playing games? When he'd brought her home from The Honky Tonk, he'd done the same thing—led her to believe he was interested in her, then backed away.

Oh well, it was all for the best, Reenie told herself. Maybe life at the farm was lonely, and maybe Isaac made her heart race, but he'd never give up his research for anyone. The most Reenie could hope for from him was a few months of stimulating conversation, comfortable companionship and hot sex—

Wait a second...that wouldn't be too bad, would it?

"I was thinking we should hold an assembly where Isaac puts on a slide show to give the students a taste of what field research is like," Guy was saying, at the front. "We need to take advantage of having a man like him on staff. We may never have such an opportunity again. So if you can think of anything else along these lines, please don't hesitate to suggest it."

The principal had been heaping praise on Isaac for ten straight minutes. Reenie clenched her jaw as her patience grew thin.

"We're so lucky Isaac—or I should say *Dr.* Russell—feels our little school is worthy of his assistance," Guy continued. "Not many high schools in our state can claim a teacher of such renown."

Suddenly Reenie couldn't take any more. "Oh, for crying out loud, working here beats hauling sacks at the feed store, doesn't it?" she said.

Everyone turned to gape at her. "Reenie!" Deborah whispered harshly.

"What?" she said. "Can we get on with the meeting? I have things to do in my classroom."

Isaac looked over his shoulder. He should've been offended by her tone, if not her words, but when their eyes met, a slow grin curved his lips.

"Don't mind Reenie," said Deborah, who was sitting directly behind him. "She didn't want you to work here in the first place."

His eyebrows lifted. "Somehow that doesn't surprise me."

There were a few chuckles. Reenie felt her cheeks flush but she challenged Isaac's gaze anyway. She'd almost fallen for him. She'd been thinking of him constantly, waiting for the phone to ring, checking her e-mail….

"Maybe I'll be able to convince her that I'm not so bad," he added mildly.

"Well, if you can't, don't beat yourself up over it," Deborah said. "No one's as stubborn as Reenie."

Reenie narrowed her eyes. Obviously, Deborah was trying to impress Isaac. "Why don't you mind your own business, Deborah?" she said.

"This *is* my business," she responded. "I work here, too. And

I, for one, am glad that Dr. Russell has joined our staff." She grinned sweetly at him.

"Come on, people," Guy said. "Let's...uh...let's..." Flustered by the sudden conflict, he shuffled through his papers as though searching for where he'd left off.

"Go?" Reenie volunteered. "The bell's about to ring."

He checked the clock. "Right. Let's get to work. Deborah, would you show Isaac to his room?"

"Of course," she said, beaming. "I teach *Honors* English, so I'm in the building across from you."

Reenie swallowed a sigh. It was only mid-April. This was going to be a long two months after all.

ISAAC COULD HEAR Reenie's voice in the next room, lecturing about geometric proofs. Earlier, she'd closed the doors that led into their adjoining supply closet, on both sides, but he didn't have any classes the last two periods of the day so he'd opened them up again. He liked listening to her, enjoyed the passion in her voice when she tried to convince her students of the necessity to study hard for the SAT's. She was a good teacher.

Swiveling to face his computer, he logged onto the Internet. He'd sent home a syllabus, showing what he'd be covering with his students, but he wanted to post the same information on the school's Web site for those parents who might never receive the hard copy. Before typing in the URL, however, he checked his mailbox, sorted through a few messages from old students and professional acquaintances, and found Reenie's thank-you still waiting there, unreturned. He guessed that was what had upset her. No doubt she could sense the attraction and tension between them, and it frustrated her as much as it did him to leave the situation unresolved.

But he couldn't do anything about it. There was Liz, of course, but also something more. Last Friday, standing in the prayer circle at Bailey's funeral, along with Reenie, her daughters, her mother and her half sister, had made a profound impact on him. He'd felt so...protective of the whole family. He'd actually been able to see himself living at the farm, painting the barn, riding horses with the girls, going to Thanksgiving dinner at the Holbrooks. He'd never had the desire to make any relationship permanent before—and that scared the hell out of him. Especially because he'd been thinking of hanging up his field clothes in order to write the book he wanted to write, the one he'd always planned to tackle later, when he retired.

Which was why he chose to dwell on last week's kiss. Physical desire he could understand. He'd experienced it often; he'd experience it again. It never interfered too much with his work or changed his life. But that odd sense of wanting to connect with Reenie in other ways, as well, even when her nose was running and her eyes were red and swollen was disconcerting. If he wasn't careful, he could wind up going from bachelor to stepfather of three almost overnight. Then he'd have to say goodbye to Africa *and* Chicago. He'd have to deal with Keith on a much more personal level, because Keith had partial custody of the girls. And it'd be very awkward for Liz. For all of them, really.

No matter how he looked at it, pursuing a relationship with Reenie, any kind of relationship, was not a good idea.

So why couldn't he get her off his mind?

With a sigh, he dropped his head in his hands. He should've stayed at the feed store. He'd tried, at first, to refuse the offer to teach. But at the time, getting closer to Reenie hadn't sounded half-bad. He'd never dreamed she'd respond positively enough to become a true temptation.

The bell rang and Reenie's class erupted in a loud babble as the students gathered their books and backpacks and filed outside.

Seven minutes later, the bell rang again, signaling the start of the final period of the day. When everything remained quiet next door, Isaac went to stand in the doorway.

He had a feeling Reenie could sense his presence, but she

wouldn't turn. She sat at her own computer, where she was busy entering test scores or something.

"You don't have a class this period?" he asked.

"It's my prep hour."

He glanced at the clock on the wall. "That's why you're able to pick the girls up from school every day."

No answer. But then, he didn't need one. He'd been stating the obvious. "When do you have to leave?" he asked.

She kept working. "In about fifteen minutes."

Folding his arms across his chest, he stayed where he was, admiring the silky sheen of her hair, her profile.

"What do you want?" she finally asked, her voice brisk, impatient.

"How honestly do you want me to answer that question?"

Pulling away from the computer, she whirled to face him. "Stop, okay? Just stop with all the…the flirting, and the games."

"What *games?*" he said.

"You want to be with me. You don't want to be with me. You want to be with me. You don't want to be with me. It's confusing. I don't understand what you're after, but if it's revenge for your sister's sake—"

"*Revenge?*" He scowled. "Come on, Reenie. You know better than that."

She marched closer, close enough that he could reach out and touch her, and propped her hands on her hips. "Then what? Why did you buy that puppy?"

"You know why."

"Explain it to me."

"I wanted to make you feel better," he said with a shrug. "There's nothing complicated about that."

"So you were being my friend? We're *friends?*"

He rubbed a hand over his jaw. "More or less."

"I think the lack of definition in our relationship is what I'm struggling with. It doesn't *feel* like we're friends, Isaac."

As she stepped even closer, his body tensed with sudden arousal. Certainly he'd never had another friend who affected him the same way. "What does it feel like?" he asked, his attention falling to her lips.

"Hot and cold, all at the same time," she murmured, her voice growing husky. "As though I'm free-falling through space. Maybe I'm in trouble, but I don't mind the descent. I can't breathe when I look at you, yet I can't see anyone else when I close my eyes."

"Reenie." His own voice came out a hoarse whisper, and his hands moved almost of their own volition, circling her waist, drawing her up against him. He knew there was a whole list of reasons to head straight back to his own room, but he couldn't— he craved her too badly.

"Tell me you don't feel it, too," she whispered, covering his pounding heart with her palm.

Closing his eyes, he kissed her forehead, drinking in the scent and feel of her. "I'm trying to imagine what it'll be like in a month or two," he explained, struggling to keep his thoughts clear.

"How can you do that?" she whispered, her lips moving against his neck as she spoke. "You never know what's going to happen."

"I'm going to leave Dundee."

"I know."

"And that's okay?"

"Later will take care of itself." She pulled back to look at him. "Anyway, you didn't seem so hesitant a week ago. You said I'd better be damned sure what I was asking for if I ever invited you back."

"That was sexual frustration and testosterone."

"In other words, all talk?"

When he hesitated, she dipped her head again. Her tongue, warm and wet, slid against his neck. His groin tightened instantly, and he knew in that moment what he'd said was far more than talk. He was going to have a lot of explaining to do when he saw Liz. "Not by a long shot," he said, and pulled her into the supply closet.

CHAPTER TWENTY

THERE WERE no windows. With both doors shut, it was quiet and almost pitch-black. Reenie couldn't see Isaac, but she could hear him breathing. And she could feel him. His mouth was hot and wet on hers as his hands sought places only Keith had touched.

"We're at school. We can't go too far," she murmured.

"Everyone's in class."

"It's still not right," she said, but the strength of her desire threatened to overcome all resistance.

"We won't go too far," he promised. "Anyway, I locked the doors."

Good thing they had to guard against the theft of their science supplies or they probably wouldn't have had the locks to begin with. "We can't lose any more petrie dishes."

"Thank God."

They chuckled together as he released her bra. Reenie moved to stop him, but his mouth covered hers again, coaxing her without words to give him a little leeway. Then his hand moved around front, and pleasure shot through every nerve as his palm covered her breast.

"Oh boy," she whispered. "We're in trouble."

"No, we're great," he answered. "Everything's great."

"But I want to make love. Here. Now."

"See what I mean?" His lips were running over her neck. "Everything's great. Perfect. Heaven..."

"No, Isaac. Not here."

"Right. I know. Just…" He lowered his head to suckle her, and she thought her legs might give out on her.

"Just what?" she managed to ask.

"Trust me for one second."

Feeling the strength of the arms that held her, she let her eyes drift closed. Five minutes in a dark supply closet with Isaac wasn't going to hurt anyone. He wouldn't take it too far. He'd just said she could trust him….

"Isaac? Isaac, are you in there?"

Isaac froze, his mouth still on Reenie's breast, his hands under her skirt, cupping her behind. His shirt was starting to stick to him as a thin sheen of sweat rose on his body from the restraint it had required not to take what they were doing to the next level. "Oh, *that's* why we can't do it in a supply closet," he whispered in her ear.

Reenie gave a weak laugh. "What do you think Deborah wants?" she asked, her voice barely audible as she drew away.

He grimaced even though she couldn't see him. "Is that who it is?"

She chuckled. "Yeah," she whispered. "Your new admirer."

"Do you think I could tell her to come back in a little bit? That I'm not finished in here yet?"

She slugged him in the arm as she scrambled to right her clothes, and he began to miss, already, the taste of her. It was more than a little jarring to have her panting against him one minute, then torn away the next. "I'll see what she wants. You wait here, okay?"

"Are you kidding? I've got to go. It's time to pick up the girls."

"We could have Liz do that."

"Yeah, right."

"It was worth a shot," he said sheepishly.

The doorknob clicked as someone tried to open it. "Isaac?" Deborah sounded frustrated. "What're you doing in there?"

Waiting for his erection to go away. "Just organizing a few things."

"Do you know where Reenie is?"

He leaned forward long enough to pull Reenie's earlobe into his mouth while she finished buttoning her blouse. "Haven't seen her," he said when he lifted his head.

"Stop it," Reenie whispered, muffling a laugh. "You're going to get us caught."

"Her car's still in the lot," Deborah mused.

"Check the ladies' room."

"I did."

"Bummer," he muttered to Reenie, and slipped his hand under her skirt again. "I'm sure she'll turn up," he said in a louder voice.

Reenie shoved his hands away, fixed her skirt and cracked open the other door. Then Isaac caught her arm so he could peek out to make sure it was safe. He didn't want to see her suffer any backlash from what had just happened.

The room was empty. But when she tried to slip out, he pulled her back yet again. "What about goodbye?"

She combed her fingers through her long hair. "You're crazy. Go see what Deborah wants."

"We're not finished," he said. "Not by a long shot."

Her eyes met his. "I know."

"*I-saac?*" Deborah again.

"Go talk to her." Reenie pushed at him but grabbed his shirt when he turned away. "Wait."

"What?"

"I—I don't want my kids to know about you. There isn't any reason for them to get attached."

He agreed but, inexplicably, felt his euphoria dim. "What about everyone else?"

"It's our little secret. You're leaving, remember?"

"I remember."

"Considering that, it's best to…to keep this to ourselves."

"Got it." He started to go, then hesitated again. "That means we'll have to sneak. And we can't go anywhere together. I hate that."

"*There* you are!" Deborah said, marching into Reenie's room. Evidently, she'd given up on him and decided to go around. "I thought you said you didn't know where she was!"

Isaac jammed a hand through his own hair, knowing it had to be mussed after his and Reenie's whirlwind encounter. "I didn't. I just heard her come in and—"

"Where was she?"

"Did you need something?" Reenie countered.

Curiosity and a touch of suspicion entered Deborah's eyes as she glanced from him to Reenie. "Guy's looking for you."

"Why?"

"He wants to know if you'll feel better about things if Isaac takes over the computer class you're teaching for Janet Wolfe."

Reenie turned to Isaac. "Do you know anything about this?"

"Of course he does. He volunteered," Deborah piped up before he could answer. "I wanted to confirm with him, since it means he'll be as busy as the rest of us, but I couldn't get him to come out of the dumb closet."

"It's an incredible mess in there," Isaac said.

He could tell that Reenie was having a difficult time not smiling at his answer, and couldn't help grinning himself. He could still smell Reenie, taste her, feel her. He wanted more…a lot more.

"You must like to clean," Deborah grumbled.

Isaac let his eyes linger briefly on Reenie. "I do. As a matter of fact, I'm anxious to get back to it as soon as possible."

MICA AND CHRISTOPHER WERE riding bikes out front when Isaac got home. Liz was making dinner.

"How was your first day?" she asked, as he joined her in the kitchen.

He thought of Reenie and the supply closet and felt like whistling. "Not bad. Not bad at all."

"So you think you're going to like it at Dundee High?"

"Definitely." He stuck his head into the refrigerator and pulled out a can of beer while she put the meat loaf she'd made into a pan. He could already smell her homemade rolls. They were cooling beneath a towel on the counter.

"What was so great about it?" she asked.

The can hissed as he popped the top. "It's just good to be teaching again."

"Did you see Reenie?"

He remembered the smooth texture of Reenie's breast. "A couple of times. Her room is right next door to mine."

His sister put the meat loaf into the oven and gave him a funny look. "That's not good news."

"Why?"

"Because you have an odd expression on your face, and it's giving me the impression that you've broken our little agreement. Again," she added pointedly.

He stretched his neck, uncomfortable beneath her close regard. "Yeah, well, I need to talk to you about the *agreement*."

She propped a hand on her hip. "Okay…"

"Have you called Dave lately?"

"Just the one time since we last talked."

No help there. "Too bad."

"I thought you *didn't* want me to call him."

"I don't." He blew out a long sigh. "But I *hate* being the weak link here."

She chuckled, which surprised him. "Does that mean our deal is off?"

He took a long, bolstering pull on his beer. "I guess it does."

She blinked in surprise. "You're serious? You're giving up that easily?"

"I know when I'm whipped."

Sinking into a chair, she stared up at him. "*Whipped* is an ominous word, Isaac."

"You don't have to worry about anything, Liz. I'm leaving, remember? And Reenie and I have decided to keep our relationship private."

"Your *relationship?*"

"Yeah."

"How private?"

"You're the only one who will know about it. But…"

She'd reached over to reorganize the napkin holder in the middle of the table, but hesitated when his words fell off. "But what?"

"I might owe you some restitution."

"Might?" She shoved the napkin holder away, knocking the salt-and-pepper shakers over in the process, but didn't bother to pick anything up. "How much restitution are we talking?"

He winced. "Anything you ask for."

She covered her mouth. "You're getting serious with her," she said between her fingers.

"Serious isn't *permanent.*"

"It's still *serious.*"

"I'm sorry." He moved closer and squeezed her shoulder. "I know you're not happy about it, but please tell me I can make it up to you." Because there wasn't anything that was going to stop him from seeing Reenie tonight.

"You mentioned restitution."

"I did. Anything."

She tapped her fingers on the table. Her cuticles were now fully healed, he noticed. She was even wearing those acrylic tips she'd worn before her world fell apart. "I haven't been able to pay the entire phone bill," she admitted.

"How much do you need?"

"Nearly five hundred."

"Five hundred dollars!"

She grinned devilishly. "Those minutes rack up."

"You must've been calling Dave every night!"

"I couldn't let the phone ring here or you might pick it up."

He dragged a thumb and finger alongside his mouth. "Are you going to continue the relationship, Liz?"

"No," she said, but seemed to struggle with herself. Finally she added, "I'm a big girl. I know women are a dime a dozen to him. I know what's best."

"That's encouraging."

"Besides, I have kids to think about. You don't."

"Okay, I'll pay the bill. No problem," he said gratefully, and walked away.

ISAAC'S CALL CAME at eleven o'clock that night. Reenie told herself she was crazy to answer the phone, to get any more involved with him. But she hadn't stopped thinking of the experience in the closet and knew she couldn't turn him away. She was already in over her head. Now all she could do was ride the rapids and hope that every once in a while she'd be able to bob up for air long enough to survive the experience.

"Hello?" she murmured.

"Are the girls asleep?"

"Yeah."

"Can I come over?"

He sounded every bit as eager as she felt. Biting her lip, she paced the length of her bedroom. *Say no. Say no and go to bed.* But that wasn't what came out of her mouth. "I'll put the house key under the geraniums on my front porch. My room's the last one down the hall on your left. Make sure you park well away from the house so no one will see your car out front. I'd come get you, but—"

"You can't leave the girls, I know. And I don't mind the walk," he said. Then he was gone.

WHEN ISAAC LET HIMSELF into Reenie's house, everything was quiet and dark. Moonlight streamed through the front windows, throwing the furniture in shadow; he could hear the clock ticking on the wall.

Feeling a heady dose of anticipation, he moved quickly and quietly to her bedroom, where he found her standing at the window, staring outside.

When the floor creaked, she turned. "Hi," she whispered.

He closed the door and locked it behind him. "Hi."

She was wearing a pair of men's-style pajama bottoms with a tiny tank top. No bra. Her hair fell down her back in a thick, wavy mass, and the light drifting in from outside lit her eyes. He could hardly look at her without immediately touching her.

Crossing the floor, he stood in front of her, but kept his hands at his side. "Where's the puppy?"

"Spike?"

"Is that his name?"

"According to Angela. She named him after the pet lizard in her class."

"We might have to make a few other suggestions."

"That's what I was thinking. Anyway, I put him in the mudroom for the night so he wouldn't make any noise."

"Good idea."

"I guess."

"What's wrong?"

"I'm a little scared," she admitted with a soft chuckle.

"Of what?"

"I'm not sure I want to be so…out of control."

"Out of control isn't all bad," he pointed out.

"That's the problem. But it's more than that. I've never had a secret affair."

He wanted to pull her into his arms, to reassure her immediately. But he waited, so he could be sure she wanted the same thing. "The secret part was your idea."

"I know. I don't see any reason to freak everyone out, especially since…since you're leaving."

He understood, which was why he hadn't argued with her. There wasn't any reason to broadcast their relationship when it could make things more difficult for her after he left.

"If I could've stayed away from you, I would have," he admitted.

She licked her lips nervously. "I don't have any birth control."

"I do." He allowed himself to raise one finger and trace the strap of her shirt. "But I'll go if that was meant as a dodge."

She shivered when his finger drew near her breast, then closed her eyes and guided his hand under her shirt. When he felt her soft flesh fill his palm, he knew there was no going back for either one of them. With a groan, he found her lips.

REENIE CLOSED HER EYES as Isaac kissed her purposefully, expertly. He smelled of clean laundry and warm skin. She brushed her lips against the pulse at his throat, and he began to peel off her clothing.

When he tossed her shirt and pajama bottoms on the floor, she stood only in the thong she'd put on just before he arrived.

He drew her into the puddle of light near the window. "You're the most beautiful woman I've ever seen," he said.

Reenie hadn't felt so attractive in years, so alive. Lowering his head, Isaac nipped at her neck and shoulder as his hands ran over her, rubbing, squeezing, admiring.

"This is far better than the supply closet," he said. "Now I can take my time."

Reenie hadn't been able to catch her breath since he'd started touching her. But she didn't care. She only knew that the dizzying sensations he was creating with his hands *had* to continue. It seemed as though her whole life had led up to the promise of his hard body joining with hers. "Don't...stop," she murmured.

"I *can't* stop," he admitted with a helpless chuckle. "I've never been so desperate for a woman in my life."

With a smile, Reenie pulled off his shirt and took in the sight of his big shoulders, the light sprinkle of hair on his muscular chest, the intensity of his expression. Goose bumps stood out on his skin as she explored him the way he'd explored her. She smiled when she heard his quick intake of breath as she touched a particularly sensitive spot.

"You like that?" she murmured.

He didn't need to answer. She could feel the tautness in his body, see the feral gleam in his eyes. Pulling her to him, he kissed her more deeply, touching her tongue to his, bending her slightly over his arm.

She tightened her grip around his neck. "I need more of you," she whispered. "I can't wait any longer. I've been waiting all day."

He swept her into his arms and carried her to the bed. But he didn't rush their lovemaking. He kissed every part of her body, used his mouth in ways she'd never experienced. She felt she was melting into the mattress, burning up from the inside out. And then, when she thought she was too sensitive to tolerate another stroke of any kind, he was finally there inside her.

"That's good," she whispered breathlessly. "That's *so* good."

"Not half as good as it's going to get," he promised.

WHEN ISAAC WOKE, it was five o'clock. A naked Reenie was still lying across his chest, sleeping. He lifted a hand to fondle her softness and felt his body stir. But he hesitated to disturb her too much. She needed the sleep. And they were running out of time.

Later, he promised himself. *Tonight.* Right now he had to leave. The girls would be getting up soon; he and Reenie had to teach.

After gently extricating himself, he sat up and rubbed a hand over his rough jaw, trying to come to full awareness. Then he gathered his clothes.

"Isaac?" Reenie murmured.

"Hmm?" He turned to see her looking up at him.

"Evidently, I've been missing out all these years," she whispered with a sexy smile.

"What do you mean by that?"

"I don't think I've ever been made love to as well as that."

He chuckled. "Don't start, or I won't get out of here before the girls wake up."

"What time is it?"

"Nearly five-thirty."

Groaning, she rolled onto her back and flung an arm over her eyes. "Already?"

He laughed at the disappointment in her voice. They'd made love three or four times last night. He'd be exhausted later, but he didn't care. Their night together had been well worth any future discomfort. "Yeah."

"I have to get up, too."

"What for?" he asked as he finished dressing.

"I have to feed the animals and milk Jersey."

She sat up and swung her bare legs over the side of the bed, but he pressed her gently back onto the mattress. "I'll do it."

"Really? You know how?"

He smoothed the hair out of her eyes. "I've picked up some skills over the past few months."

"Okay." She grinned dreamily. "See you at school."

He smiled back at her. "Will you have lunch with me?"

"I can't. Someone might see us, remember?"

"So, meet me in the supply closet."

"Who's bringing the sandwiches?"

"I'll come up with something."

"Chocolate's always good," she suggested with a yawn, and started drifting back to sleep.

"Anything you want," he said softly. Then he kissed her temple and went out to see about the animals.

WHEN REENIE ARRIVED at school, she found a vase of hand-cut roses on her desk.

"Who gave you those, Mrs. O'Connell?" Sheila, one of her

first-period students, asked in obvious admiration. Most of the other girls were gathered around the flowers, too.

There was no note, but Reenie knew it had to be Isaac. She'd found a small ivory elephant next to the flowers, which she'd slipped into the drawer of her desk. "A secret admirer, I guess," she said mysteriously.

"Who?" they breathed, pressing closer.

"I don't know. They were sitting on my desk when I arrived."

"They're beautiful!" Sheila said.

"Thank you. Now, if everyone will sit down, we'll get started. We have a lot to cover today."

There was a general shuffling as the students found their seats. Turning, Reenie wrote the day's assignment on the board. "Does anyone have any questions about last night's homework?" she asked.

Several hands shot up, but before she could call on anyone, she saw something move in her peripheral vision and glanced up to find Isaac watching her from the supply closet. His gaze felt like a physical caress, as if he could undress her from there simply by looking at her.

Several students from the front row noticed him when she hesitated. "Mr. Russell, did you see Ms. O'Connell's flowers?" Sheila asked before Reenie could continue the lesson.

Although he had his own class in the other room, he stepped out where everyone could see him, crossed his arms and leaned against the wall. "They're nice," he said, eyeing them. "Who're they from?"

He was teasing her, of course. Reenie arched an eyebrow at him. "Actually, they're probably from my *father.*"

Everyone groaned. "You said it was a secret admirer," Sheila said, her voice heavy with disappointment.

"My father admires me."

"Your father must be one heck of a guy," Isaac said, his grin hitching up on one side.

"Mr. Russell? We're finished over here," one of his own students called through the supply closet.

He shoved off the wall. "Good thing the mystery's been solved. I have to get back."

Reenie watched him go. She couldn't believe he'd risked bringing her flowers. Fortunately, she'd been able to handle the situation in such a way that their existence on her desk wouldn't mushroom into a problem. But she realized that keeping her relationship with Isaac a secret wasn't going to be nearly as easy as she'd thought.

CHAPTER TWENTY-ONE

LIZ STARED at the phone. She was nervous and self-conscious, but determined. Isaac had been seeing Reenie for a whole month. When Reenie had the girls, he slipped out late at night and returned a few hours later. On the weekends when Keith had the girls, Liz didn't see her brother from Friday night to Sunday morning. Isaac and Reenie spent every minute they could together. But at least they were being discreet. Liz had seen her brother's truck parked in a variety of places but never in front of Reenie's farm. And whenever Reenie and Isaac bumped into each other in town, they were very restrained.

Of course, anyone who was really looking couldn't miss the signs. Liz had witnessed the way their eyes devoured each other, the way they seemed to stop breathing when they met. But no one else seemed to notice. And for that, Liz was glad. Isaac had heard from Reginald Woolston just last Monday. His grant would be available in June. Since it was already mid-May, there wasn't any need to involve Chris and Mica, or Keith and Reenie's friends and family. The affair would have to end soon.

Isaac would be moving on, but Liz would remain in Dundee. Her house had already closed escrow in California. Because the balance of the mortgage was so high, she hadn't netted a lot of money out of the deal. But, as she'd expected, it would be enough to help her through the next year, when she'd no longer have Isaac's support. Keith had agreed to let her keep the whole amount, too. She was grateful for that, because he wasn't able to pay much child support right now. She was sure he'd eventually hire on with another computer company and make more than he was currently earning. He had the talent. But he'd told her he wasn't ready to start traveling again. Liz suspected he was still holding out some hope that Reenie would come back to him.

The thought of how hard he'd tried to save his first marriage stung, because he'd let go of his second so easily. But Liz was trying to get beyond all that. If Isaac liked Reenie so much—and she could tell that he did—there had to be something special about her. And if Reenie's feelings for Isaac were half as deep as Liz suspected, she was going to miss him terribly when he left. Liz wondered if he'd told her about the e-mail from Woolston. He didn't seem to be focusing much on his impending departure.

So if Liz didn't reach out to Reenie, who would? She was the only one who knew how much Reenie was about to suffer—again.

Flattening the scrap of paper she'd stuffed in a drawer the night Isaac had given it to her, she dialed before she could change her mind. Then she blinked in surprise when Reenie said, "God, I miss you. When will you be here?"

"Um…" Liz cleared her throat. "This isn't Isaac. It's Liz."

Dead silence. Liz imagined Reenie pulling her foot out of her mouth and managed to smile. "Are you still there?"

"Yes. I'm—"

"Shocked?"

"I was about to say sorry. I—I thought—"

"I know what you thought."

Another strained pause.

"If you're looking for…your brother—" Reenie's voice dropped on those two words, making Liz wonder if one of the children was around "—I'm afraid he isn't here."

No, he wouldn't be there for another four hours at least, after

the girls were asleep. Liz knew that, but she didn't say so. "Isaac'
here, mowing the lawn. I'm not looking for him. I called because
I was wondering—" she curled her nails into her palms "—i
you'd like to go to lunch with me sometime."

"You want to get together?" Reenie said, her words soundin
strangled.

"Why not?" Liz was gathering confidence as she spoke. Th
hardest part had been identifying herself. "We seem to have a lo
in common. For one, Angela and Mica have become pretty clos
friends."

"I know, but...did Isaac put you up to this?"

"He gave me your number several weeks ago."

"Why?"

"Because you were losing your dog, and he felt you could us
a friend."

"But you waited to call."

Liz took a deep breath. "Put yourself in my shoes, Reenie
It's not easy approaching the woman my husband loved mo
than me."

"I'm sorry for what Keith did, Liz. To both of us."

"I know," she said softly.

"So...where do you want to eat?"

Liz's heart beat a little faster. Could they really get beyon
what had happened? Maybe even build some type of friendshi
No one would believe it. "The restaurant out at the Running
serves a nice Sunday brunch."

"Sounds good. Do you want to go this weekend?"

"Sure. Noon okay?"

The door opened and Isaac walked into the living room. "It
getting too dark to see," he complained, stripping off the leath
gloves he'd worn while mowing. "I'll have to do the edging t
morrow."

Liz put up a hand to let him know to be quiet.

"Noon's fine," Reenie said. "Do you want me to bring t

girls? It's Keith's weekend, but he's working on Sunday, so he'll have them back by then."

Liz could hear Mica and Christopher playing Ping-Pong downstairs, shouting and laughing when one of them missed, which was often, and contemplated making it a group outing. There wasn't any need to arrange babysitting, was there? "Why not?" she said. "I'll include my kids, too."

"Great. See you there," Reenie said, and disconnected.

"Who was that?" Isaac asked.

"Reenie."

He halted mid-stride on his way to the kitchen and pivoted to face her. "You were talking to *Reenie?*"

"Yes." She smiled. "I called to invite her to have lunch with me. We're meeting for brunch on Sunday."

"Can I come, too?"

"I thought you and Reenie didn't want to be seen together."

"With you and all the kids, it should be okay. I enjoy seeing her children. Reenie doesn't let me have anything to do with her girls."

"Why not?"

"She doesn't want them to get attached."

Maybe Reenie was being careful where her kids were concerned, but she certainly wasn't looking out for herself. "If that's the case, she might not be happy if I bring you along."

"I don't think she'll mind. Brunch is harmless."

Liz considered it. Maybe Isaac's presence would make things easier, more natural. "Okay."

"WHAT DO YOU MEAN you can't come?"

Reenie barely heard her mother's voice on the phone. She was too busy staring at her computer screen, grinning at Isaac's latest Instant Message. You free tonight?

He'd been over last night, and the night before, and the night before that. If they weren't careful, they'd get caught simply because they were spending so much time together.

She was happier than she'd been in years, happier than she'd thought possible. But working all day and making love with Isaac all night was starting to take its toll. She stifled a yawn.

"Reenie, are you listening?"

"Sorry, Mom. What did you say?"

"Why can't you come over on Saturday for dinner? Your dad would like to see you before he heads back to Boise."

She wanted to see her father, too. But this weekend was Keith's turn with the girls, which meant she could relax when she was with Isaac. Those lazy days together were very precious to her.

"I'm afraid I have too much to do." It was a lame excuse, and Reenie knew it. She'd already used work and the farm half a dozen or more times to avoid get-togethers over the past month. But what else could she say? *I'll probably be naked and in bed with Liz's brother, and I can't give that up?*

Spike came trotting out of her bedroom, carrying her slipper in his mouth. "Come here," she said to him, snapping her fingers.

"What's going on, honey?" Celeste asked.

Her dog gave her a sheepish look because he knew better than to chew up any more shoes and hesitated halfway across the carpet. "Spike's ruining another pair of slippers."

"I'm not talking about that. You've become so…distracted. Even Gabe mentioned it the other day. He said he's asked you over or to go out with him and Hannah several times, but you always make excuses."

"Stop worrying about me. I'm fine," she said, ignoring the slipper issue, for the moment, and holding the phone with her shoulder so she could respond to Isaac.

Don't you need to get some sleep? she wrote.

I'll sleep with you, came Isaac's reply.

Somehow we never close our eyes for very long.

That's not my fault. <G> But I can't say that I mind.

It was true. She couldn't sleep when Isaac was around, because she didn't want to waste a single moment of their time together. She loved it when his larger body cradled hers. Loved the
way he kissed her, how he touched her, the stories he told of Africa, the sound of his laugh.

"Lucky said you rarely return her calls," her mother continued to complain.

"There just aren't enough hours in the day," she responded.
Isaac had started milking the cow and feeding the animals before he left each morning, but she still didn't have a minute to
spare. "Things will slow down once school ends, I promise."

"Keith thinks you're seeing Isaac. That's not true, is it?"

Reenie straightened so quickly Spike skittered away. "What
makes him think that?"

"The puppy, I guess."

"Oh." She let her breath go in relief.

"You're not, are you?" Celeste persisted.

Reenie couldn't lie to her mother straight out. "Not *exactly*.
Why?"

"When I asked Keith if he planned to apply for a better job,
he said he'd be sticking around for a while. He said you're infatuated with Isaac right now, but when Isaac leaves in a few
weeks, you might come to your senses."

Reenie froze. "In a few *weeks?*"

"Didn't you hear? Isaac's grant came through. He'll be going
to Africa soon."

A sudden hollowness engulfed Reenie. "Are you sure?"

"Pretty sure. It was Mica who told Keith."

Her heart began to pound so loudly it seemed to echo off the
walls. Isaac hadn't said anything to her. Not one word.

"Reenie?"

She couldn't breathe. She'd been living in a fantasy world, ig
noring the fact that it was all going to come to a crashing halt
The end hadn't seemed important. Goodbye was always going
to happen later. But three *weeks?* That made Isaac's leaving very
real. "You can tell Keith I won't change my mind," she managed
to say.

"I already tried. For his own sake, he's got to move on. But
there's no reasoning with him."

"I have to go, Mom. I'll call you tomorrow."

"Are you okay, honey?"

"Of course. Just tired."

Reenie hung up, then ducked her head between her knees to
stop her head from swimming. As usual, she'd been too impet
uous. She'd put the inevitable out of her mind, held nothing
back. And now she was head-over-heels in love with a man who
was going to walk away from her in three weeks.

When she sat up, there were several lines of text on her com
puter screen.

Are the girls asleep yet?...

Want me to bring you an Oreo shake?...

Hey, I got that movie you wanted to see...

Are you there? Where'd you go? I want to kiss you
neck, feel you against me, make you moan... I like it when
you moan. <G>

A single tear slid down her cheek as she thought of how badl
she was going to miss him. Certainly she wouldn't be very goo
company tonight.

I'll see you tomorrow, okay? she wrote.
There was a long pause. Then, What's going on?

I'm tired.

So we'll sleep...

Not tonight.

Seriously?

She told herself to say yes and sign off, to let it go at that, but she couldn't.

When were you going to tell me that your grant came through?

Several seconds passed, but finally, she got another response. told you from the beginning that it would, Reenie.
I guess you did, she said. Good night.

SLEEP SHOULD'VE COME easy. Isaac had been so involved with Reenie he'd barely closed his eyes the past five weeks. But he didn't feel as though he belonged in his own bed anymore. He missed having her head on his shoulder while they talked and laughed, missed rolling over whenever he wanted to make love, missed waking with her arm tossed possessively over his torso.
   They had so little time left. Why was she wasting it?
   The amber numerals on his alarm clock flipped from 3:43 a.m. o 3:44 a.m. He'd be exhausted in the morning.
   With a frown, he wondered if whoever had coined the phrase hank God, it's Friday, had experienced what Isaac was experiencing right now. He'd never been so grateful to know that Sat-

urday was just around the corner. Only one more day of school. Then Keith would take the girls and he and Reenie could spend the entire weekend together.

If she'd see him. At this point, he wasn't sure what she was thinking. But he knew what would've been the fastest three weeks of his life would turn into the slowest if she decided to break things off early.

Frustrated, he got up and pulled on a pair of jeans and a sweat-shirt. As June approached, the days were getting longer and warmer, but it was still chilly early in the morning.

A light wind rustled the trees as he slipped out the front door and strode to his truck. As usual, the houses around him were dark, the streets empty. He drove through town, parked at the periphery of Elzina Brown's property, which had become his favorite spot, and walked the rest of the way.

Fortunately, the key Reenie always left out for him was still under the geraniums next to the door, which made him feel slightly better. He let himself in as quietly as possible and peeked into Reenie's bedroom to see that she was sleeping soundly. Spike was there, lying at the foot of the bed. But he didn't bark. He knew Isaac. He simply lifted his head, jumped to the floor and followed as Isaac went out to do the chores.

The horse whinnied when he patted her; the chickens followed him, scratching in the dirt until he spread their feed. He was a little earlier than usual, but Jersey, the cow, merely looked back swished her tail and continued to chew as he milked her.

Once he finished at the chicken coop, he left Spike in the yard to do his business, and took the eggs he'd washed in a basin near the barn into the house. A moment later, a noise down the hall caught his attention. He expected to find Reenie there, but when he looked up, he saw that it was Isabella.

"What are you doing here?" she asked with a curious tilt of her head.

He and Reenie had slept together a lot over the past month o so. Other than that time in the supply closet, they hadn't come close to being discovered. So he found it rather ironic that Isabella would catch him at the house the one night he *hadn't* spent in her mother's bed. "Feeding the animals and milking Jersey," he said. "What are you doing up, little one?"

"I had a bad dream."

She looked flushed. He wondered if she was getting sick. "Come here."

She padded closer, staring up at him with eyes almost as lovely as Reenie's while he pressed his palm to her forehead. Sure enough, she felt warm.

"How does your tummy feel?" he asked.

"Kinda rumbly."

"Rumbly as in hungry?"

She shook her head.

"Do you think you need to throw up?"

A grimace passed over her face. "No. Will you lie down with me?" she asked, instantly brightening.

Isaac didn't know how to respond. He didn't mind helping her get back to sleep, but he was fairly certain Reenie wouldn't approve of the contact. She'd been pretty militant—too militant as far as he was concerned—about keeping him away from her daughters.

"My daddy lies down with me sometimes," she said when he didn't answer right away. "When I don't feel good."

But Isaac wasn't her daddy. He opened his mouth to tell her she'd better go get her mom, then paused. He hated to wake Reenie. "Grab your blanket and bring it out here," he said. "We'll sit in the rocking chair, okay?"

AT SIX-THIRTY in the morning, Reenie stumbled through the living room on her way to the kitchen. She had to take care of the animals, then shower so she'd be able to get the girls off to school before eight-thirty. But she was having difficulty waking up. Not only was she sleep deprived, she was mentally resisting consciousness. She didn't want to think about Isaac, and she knew, as soon as she came fully awake, he'd be the first thing on her mind.

"Life goes on," she muttered to herself, angry that after everything she'd been through, she could still be so vulnerable. But then she saw the basket of eggs on her counter, heard a movement over by the television, and realized it wasn't Spike.

Heart pounding at the unexpected intrusion, she whirled to find Isaac sitting in the rocking chair next to the fireplace. Isabella was bundled in a blanket on his lap. The noise she'd made while getting up must've awakened him because he was shifting in his seat and his eyes were open.

When their gazes engaged, Reenie felt a whole bunch of mixed-up emotions. "What are you doing here?" she whispered, pressing a hand to her heart to slow her pulse.

"I couldn't sleep."

She waved to the counter. "So you came over to gather my eggs?"

He grinned. "I figured you wouldn't mind."

She didn't. It had been wonderful having his help over the past several weeks.

She nodded toward Isabella. "What's up with my baby?"

"She came out while I was putting away the eggs. She wasn't feeling well and wanted me to lie down with her. I figured this was a better option."

"Why didn't you wake me? I would've taken care of her."

"There was no need. I was up already."

She was tempted to be angry with him for going against her wishes. She'd been very clear that she didn't want him in her children's lives. But she had to admit that was pretty much a moot point now. "I guess it's okay. Given the situation, there's not much danger anymore," she said.

"The situation?" he repeated.

"You'll be gone in three weeks. I'm sure they can't get too attached in that short a time."

When their eyes met again, Reenie had to admit that she'd gotten pretty damn attached—and in a much shorter time than she wanted to acknowledge.

"So you're backing off, Reenie?" he said softly. "Already?"

Isabella began to stir. Reenie moved close and pressed a hand to her cheek instead of answering. "She *is* warm. I'll have to get a sub for today."

"Do I have to get up, Mommy?" her daughter murmured, her little rosebud mouth stretching in a yawn.

"No, honey. You're going to stay home with me until you feel better. Isaac will put you back to bed, okay?"

"I don't want to go to bed," she said.

"Would you like something to eat?"

"No." She snuggled against Isaac's chest and closed her eyes again. "I'll just stay right here."

Reenie couldn't blame her. She wanted to be in Isaac's lap herself. She wanted to cry and beg him not to leave her. But she knew better than to give in to that impulse. If Isaac didn't know what they had, if he didn't value their relationship, nothing she could say would make any difference.

"You didn't answer my question," Isaac said.

Reenie continued to stroke her daughter's soft cheek. "What question was that?"

"Are you backing off?"

"I haven't decided yet."

The doorbell rang.

"Who could that be?" he asked.

"This early, it has to be Keith." She looked down the hall, out the back window, in the kitchen, wondering how she was going to hide Isaac.

"I'll put her to bed and slip out the back," Isaac said, making the decision for her.

Fortunately, Isabella's eyes remained closed. Either she was too comfortable to move, or she'd fallen back asleep.

As Isaac hurried down the hall, Reenie went to the door.

Surprisingly, her visitor wasn't Keith. It was a neighbor, Elzina Brown.

"Hi, Elzina," she said. "What brings you by so early?"

Elzina was young for her sixty-something years. She generally wore blue jeans and boots and Southwestern jewelry, with her long gray hair pulled back into an attractive chignon. "Sorry to bother you, Reenie," she said. "I was just hoping you could ask Isaac to move his truck."

"What?" Reenie said.

"He parked over at my place. But Jon Small and his brother are coming to cut down the dead limbs on some trees, and I'd hate for anything to fall on his vehicle."

"I see." Reenie swallowed hard. "But what makes you think he's here?"

With a wink, Elzina pulled on a pair of leather work gloves and started toward her own truck. "Where else would he be? He comes here 'most every night, doesn't he?"

Reenie wasn't sure how to respond, except to be completely honest. "Elzina, I'd rather no one else found out."

"Well, your secret's safe with me," she said sympathetically. "Just have Isaac hurry, before they show up."

"I will," she said. But Isaac was already gone when she went to find him. And she had no way to reach him until he got home.

She put the eggs in the refrigerator, hoping and praying he'd slipped away in time. But her phone rang a few minutes later. It was Elzina again. She said Isaac had jogged up after Jon arrived—five minutes too late.

CHAPTER TWENTY-TWO

REENIE PASSED THE next week and a half dodging personal questions and meaningful grins from almost everyone she saw—especially Guy, Beth, Deborah and everyone else who worked at the high school. Her own brother shook his head when he saw her on his way to football practice. Earl down at the feed store grinned knowingly when she stopped by to pick up more chicken scratch. Judy at Jerry's Diner asked how she and Isaac were getting along. Shirley at the Gas-N-Go said they made a handsome couple and wanted to know what Liz thought of the whole thing. Even Jennifer asked if Isaac was Reenie's boyfriend.

But Keith didn't call and harass her as she'd anticipated. When he came to pick up the girls for the weekend, he acted smug, as if he'd been right about her and Isaac all along. But he also seemed content to bide his time. Reenie understood why. He believed he'd have another shot at a relationship with her once Isaac left—and she didn't disabuse him of the notion. She was dealing with enough already. For the same reason, she rescheduled her brunch with Liz until the following week. Then she focused on her children and her work while waiting for the gossip to die down.

To help combat the sudden deluge of outside interest, she refused to see Isaac. Angry that she'd landed herself in another no-win situation—especially since she'd known from the start what to expect—she was determined not to let his imminent departure upset her routine or ruin her life.

When the next Sunday rolled around, Reenie still didn't feel up to seeing Liz. But it had taken courage for Liz to call, and Reenie was afraid Isaac's sister wouldn't reach out to her a second time if she postponed the meeting again.

So, taking more care with her appearance than usual—she curled her hair and tried on several different outfits before settling on a pair of black pin-striped slacks and a white blouse—she got ready to meet Isaac's sister. Then she loaded the girls in the van and drove over to the Running Y.

When he developed the resort four or five years ago, Conner Armstrong had built a beautiful, walnut-colored lodge. The inside smelled of expensive potpourri and gleamed with polish. The restaurant, located to the left of the main set of doors, next to the gift shop, branched off an expansive lobby with a rock fireplace, antler lighting fixtures and slate floors covered with Navajo rugs.

Generally, Reenie liked to come to the resort. She enjoyed the Southwestern flavor of the artwork and furniture, and the food at the restaurant was always good. Today, however, she would rather have been anywhere else. Especially when she saw Liz and her two children already seated at a table, waiting for them.

"They're here!" Angela said, and hurried right in.

Following her daughter at a much slower pace, she forced a smile when Liz raised her eyes. "Hello."

While she took the seat directly across from Liz, the children gathered around the other end of the table and began talking and laughing as though they met for brunch every week.

"Isaac wanted to come, but I told him no," Liz volunteered softly.

Reenie nodded. "I appreciate that."

Isaac's sister fiddled with her water glass. "You really don't want to see him?"

Worse than ever. But what good would it do? In another week he'd drive to Boise to catch his plane, and she'd be no better o than she'd been when Keith used to leave. "I—I…" She searched for something to say that would fend off the question so she could continue to protect the part of her that was hurting so badly. But the way Liz was watching her, as if she could read her pain in spite of all Reenie's efforts to conceal it, brought tears to Reenie's eyes. She swallowed hard, struggling against the sudden emotion, but her throat was too tight to speak.

Did she *have* to break down in front of Liz? Of all people?

She started to stand. She had to escape, go to the restroom and pull herself together, something. But then she felt Liz's hand close over hers and squeeze as though she understood.

"I love him," Reenie whispered. She couldn't hold it back any longer, couldn't hold back the hurt.

Amazingly, she saw tears filling Liz's eyes, too. "I know," she answered.

They sat in silence for several seconds and, oddly enough, Reenie found Liz's empathy comforting.

"If it makes you feel any better," Liz said at last, "I think he loves you, too. He's been going out of his mind since you started refusing his calls and e-mails. He actually shouted at me today when I told him he couldn't come."

"Why didn't you let him come?" Reenie asked.

"Because you're obviously working very hard to protect yourself against what's happening, and I didn't want to undermine you."

Reenie couldn't believe they could be talking so intimately. This was her ex-husband's "other woman." Yet Reenie felt a strange kinship. Maybe it was because they'd both been through so much. Or maybe it was because they'd both loved Keith, and now, although in different ways, Isaac.

"He won't stay," Reenie said simply.

Liz continued to grip her hand. "You want the truth, right?"

Reenie nodded.

"I don't think he will. You're the first woman who's been able to get under his skin," she said with what looked like a fond smile.

then sobered. "But I can't see him giving up his work. If he ever talks of marriage and family, it's always as if he expects it to happen in another five or ten years, and he never seems to get any closer to it."

Reenie closed her eyes and told herself to breathe deeply. "I knew that going in," she admitted.

"Don't be too hard on yourself. Sometimes we see the jagged rocks in our path, but we still can't avoid them."

"Was it that way for you, with Keith?" Reenie asked.

"Sometimes. I was working hard to overlook certain things because I didn't want there to be anything amiss. I was...happy, you know?"

Remorse for what had happened washed over Reenie again. "And now?"

"I'm embarrassed that I was ever so gullible. But I'm doing better," Liz said with a smile. "Much better."

Looking at the situation from Liz's perspective opened up a whole new vista for Reenie. Now that she was connecting with Liz on a deeper level—now that she was willing to *care* about her—she realized just how difficult it must have been for her to come to Dundee.

"Why'd you move here?" Reenie asked softly. "You had to have known it wouldn't be easy."

Liz nodded down the table at her children, who were laughing as Jennifer stuck a spoon to the end of her nose. "For them," she said. "But also for me. I needed to come to terms with goodbye. That Keith could really let me go so easily seemed too horrific to believe."

It was Reenie's turn to squeeze Liz's hand. "Those first few weeks, even months, were a nightmare."

"Yes. But, fortunately, that's all behind us, right?"

"For the most part, I hope."

"You'll get over Isaac," Liz said confidently. "With time."

Reenie nodded, hoping to heaven she was right.

ISAAC PACED in the parking lot of the Running Y. He'd driven out to the resort, planning to join his sister and Reenie for breakfast whether they liked it or not. Since Reenie would barely speak to him at school, and wouldn't respond to his calls or his messages, he'd really been looking forward to having the chance to be with her again. But Liz had uninvited him this morning, and now he didn't know how to force the issue without making more of a jerk of himself than he'd already been with his sister earlier.

Why couldn't Reenie smile and laugh and enjoy the days they had left? he wondered. Why did it have to get like this? He knew she wanted to let the gossip die down. But school was ending this week, and Reg wanted him to fly back to Chicago to meet with the people from CTFS as soon as possible. That meant Saturday. *Saturday, for Pete's sake!*

Reenie had known all along that he had to leave. What had she expected?

"Hello, Isaac."

Isaac turned to see that Deborah Wheeler and her father, Melvin Blaine, had come out of the lodge. "Hello," he said, but he knew he didn't sound very friendly.

"Is something wrong?" she asked with false sweetness.

"No."

"Food's good in the restaurant, if you're thinking of having brunch."

"Maybe I'll go in, in a minute."

He wished she'd continue walking to her car and leave him alone, but she didn't. "Word has it you'll be moving away any day now," she said.

He nodded.

"Poor Reenie. She bet on the wrong man again."

If Mr. Blaine realized that his daughter sounded rather gleeful about this, he gave no indication. He studied Isaac curiously while waiting at her elbow.

"She's inside, you know," Deborah went on. "With your sister. That's interesting, isn't it? They're eating together like old friends. I couldn't believe it when I saw them."

"Is there anything wrong with that?" he asked, pinning her with a level glare.

"No, of course not. It's just...interesting, that's all." With a laugh, she finally slipped her hand inside the crook of her father's arm, and they walked away.

Isaac raked his fingers through his hair as he watched them go. Reenie hadn't "bet" on him. They'd...gotten involved, had a relationship. A relationship wasn't anything catastrophic.

At least it wasn't until she'd quit seeing him.

The door swung open again and Isabella dashed out.

"Isaac!" she cried and ran toward him.

Lifting her into his arms, he gave her a hug but, preoccupied though he was, he knew the very instant Reenie appeared. He could feel her gaze, could remember every intimate thing they'd ever said or done together.

"Hello," he said hopefully, over Isabella's head. *Just smile at me. Give me one smile, please.*

But the smile she offered wasn't anything he'd been hoping to receive. It was polite, empty. "Hello," she said and, with a quick hug for Liz, she called her children to her and walked right past him.

"That's it?" he murmured.

She didn't answer, but Liz must've heard him because he felt a comforting hand on his arm. "If you're ever going to give in and get married, do it now," she said softly.

He turned to watch Reenie climb into her van. "You're kidding me," he said. "You didn't even want me to get involved with her."

"I was wrong," Liz admitted. "She's probably the only woman I know who's worthy of you."

Isaac couldn't marry Reenie. She belonged here in Dundee, and he belonged halfway around the globe, doing what he loved best. "I only want to say goodbye," he said. It was actually much more complicated than that. He wanted to thank Reenie for all the fun they'd had, tell her how much he'd miss her, maybe make love one more time. "Why does it have to be all or nothing?" he asked.

Reenie's van pulled out of the lot. "Because she's got three kids, and she's in love with you, Isaac," Liz said. "If you don't want to marry her, just leave her alone."

AFTER HIS TALK with Liz in the parking lot at the Running Y, Isaac had told himself he wouldn't try to contact Reenie again. For the past week, he'd stopped e-mailing her and quit angling to catch her alone at school, which wasn't too hard because they'd been so busy those last days. On some level—actually on all levels— he'd hoped she'd soften and call *him*. Surely she must've heard that he was leaving today. How could she act as if they'd never shared what they'd shared? His hands literally ached to touch her.

He checked the clock as he finished packing. He had to leave in an hour. But he couldn't do it without calling her one more time.

With a sigh, he picked up the phone and dialed.

"Hello?"

His heart skipped a beat at the sound of her voice. "Reenie?"

There was a slight hesitation. "Yes?"

"How are you?"

"Fine," she said, but she didn't elaborate, and he was willing to bet she wasn't doing any better than he was. Their month together had been like one big drunken binge, and they'd spent the past three weeks paying for it.

"What about you?" she asked.

"I'm tired of this hangover," he said.

"What?"

"Nothing. I miss you. I really do."

He wanted to hear her say it back, but she didn't. "Why are you calling, Isaac?"

He closed his eyes. "I was hoping you and the girls would drive me to the airport."

"What about Liz? Can't she take you?"

He was getting desperate. "She has to work," he lied. "I'll say goodbye to her and the kids here."

This time there was a *long* pause.

"Isaac…"

"Are you really going to let me go without saying goodbye?" he asked.

Nothing, but finally she said, "When do you want me to pick you up?"

His hand tightened eagerly on the phone. "In an hour. And I hope you don't mind taking the van," he said. "I sold my truck to Earl."

"I saw him driving through town in it yesterday."

"He needed an extra pickup to help move things around at the store."

"See you in an hour," she said, and disconnected.

REENIE LET Isaac drive. The girls chattered the whole way in the back seat, talking about everything from what they had planned this summer to what they wanted to eat once they reached Boise. But Reenie had little to say. Isaac didn't seem particularly talkative, either. Almost as soon as they got started, he reached over and took her hand, though. And she couldn't help curling her fingers through his.

When they were only fifteen minutes or so from the airport, he looked over at her as though he wanted to break the strange silence between them.

"What?" she murmured.

"I'll be back at some point. You know that, right?"

"When?"

He hesitated. "I'm not sure, exactly. That hasn't been tied down yet. But I'll come as soon as I can."

"For a visit."

He turned down the music. "It's better than nothing."

Reenie was tempted to accept what she could get. She'd thought along those lines once—that something was better than nothing. But she'd spent almost her entire marriage frustrated with Keith's absences. She couldn't take on the same old problem. She wanted a closer relationship. She wanted a man who'd be happy staying with her in Dundee.

"I'm sorry, Isaac. An occasional visit isn't enough."

His eyebrows drew together in an obvious sign of displeasure. "Can you honestly tell me that you don't want me anymore?"

She looked at him squarely. "No."

"Then, why not hang on?"

"Because I don't want to miss you, to constantly wonder if and when you'll visit, to worry about how long you might or might not stay. I'm looking for something deeper."

"But I've never…"

"What?" she prompted.

"Met anyone like you."

"You'll find someone else," she said softly. "Maybe in a few years, when you're ready."

The airport exit came up on the right and he took it. A few moments later, he angled up to the unloading dock, came around to her side of the truck and pulled her into his arms.

She clung to him, praying he'd change his mind.

"I love you," he murmured. But he didn't get back into the van. After saying goodbye to the girls, he kissed her quickly on the mouth and gathered his bags before striding purposefully through the sliding doors.

THE AIRPORT WASN'T very crowded. Isaac sat near the gate, feeling empty and strange. He considered setting up his laptop so he could return some e-mail. He needed to let certain people know he was coming home, to schedule a physical, to do a final read-through on the research he'd managed to organize in Dundee. If he could get into his old groove, he'd probably feel more like himself, right?

He rubbed his hands together eagerly, but couldn't manage enough enthusiasm to act on the thought. He kept picturing Reenie at a restaurant not far away, eating lunch with her daughters.

After several seconds, he let his eyes drift over to the window. Outside, the day was sunny and bright.

He put his computer at his feet and stood for several minutes watching the planes take off. He was doing the right thing by going back to his former life, wasn't he?

His melancholy suggested otherwise. But he'd wanted to return to Africa for a long time. His work wasn't finished there. Now that the grant money had been awarded, he could continue to fight for conservation of the rain forest, which meant a great deal to him.

He imagined the long flight to the southern hemisphere, the trek from Ouesso, the people with their interesting customs and languages. He loved the uniqueness of Africa. Every moment there, the whole ambience, stirred his blood.

So why did the trip suddenly sound less appealing than it had before?

Probably because he'd been out of circulation too long, he told himself. He'd gotten used to living at a slower pace, to paying less attention to his research, to thinking about Reenie.

Reenie again. Shoving the nagging thoughts and memories of the woman he loved from his mind, he called Reggie on the nearest pay phone. He planned to leave a message saying he was on his way, to suggest a meeting first thing Monday morning.

But his boss surprised him by answering. "Hello?"

"Reg?" Isaac said.

"Yes?"

"What are you doing at the office on a Saturday morning?"

"I'm behind, trying to catch up," he replied.

Isaac couldn't remember if he'd ever heard his boss speak of a family. He and Reg had worked together on and off for several years, but theirs had been a strictly business relationship. Unless Reg had made a comment Isaac hadn't catalogued, they'd always confined their dialogue to other topics.

"You work too hard," Isaac said.

"Goes with the territory, I'm afraid."

That "territory" was obviously very important to him. Reg's voice was brisk, as though he felt pressed even now. But was his work truly fulfilling enough to devote his whole life to it and nothing more?

"How old are you?" Isaac asked. He knew the question came out of nowhere. But he didn't care. The answer was significant to him.

"You want to know how *old* I am?" Reg repeated.

"Yeah."

"Fifty-seven. Why?"

Fifty-seven. And the most he had to look forward to on the weekend was more of what he did during the week? Crazy thing was, Reg was so busy, he didn't even seem to notice that he was missing anything.

A baby squealed. Isaac glanced over to see that a young couple with an infant had taken the seats not far from him. The mother dug through a diaper bag while the father gently jiggled the baby on his shoulder.

"Isaac?" Reg said. "Have you gone a little daft on me out there in cowboy country?"

Suddenly Isaac saw himself in thirty years. He could be Reggie, a bonafide workaholic; he was following the same course, wasn't he?

He watched the father settle the baby in the crook of his arm and give it the bottle the woman had finally located. The baby's cries immediately turned to a few whimpers, then fell to complete silence, while the father gazed dreamily at the bundle he held in his arms.

"Isaac?" Reg prompted again.

"No, I'm...I'm just wondering, that's all."

"About what?"

If I can live without Reenie's laugh and the girls and Spike and the farm...

A flight attendant walked to the podium near his gate and began to call for boarding. "I've got to go," he said.

"Is someone picking you up at the airport?"

"I was planning to take a taxi."

"Give me a call when you get in. I'll swing by if I can get away. We need to go over a few things for the trip."

"Right," Isaac said. "The trip." But watching the little family he'd noticed earlier suddenly held more allure for him than the trip.

When the flight attendant made the final call for boarding, he told himself to stride up and hand her his boarding pass. He was a field researcher and a biologist, not a high school science teacher.

But five minutes later, he was still standing at the window, watching his plane take off.

REENIE, ANGELA, JENNIFER AND Isabella were sitting down to watch a movie when she heard someone at the front door. She stood up to see who it was, tensing when a key clicked in the lock.

"Who is it?" she called. She hadn't been able to make herself remove Isaac's key from beneath the geraniums. It was too much of an admission that he wouldn't be coming back. But she regretted that now. Maybe there wasn't any crime to speak of in Dundee, but if by some remote chance she'd left her children vulnerable to harm, she'd never forgive herself.

"Reenie?"

Isaac's voice reached her ears before she could round the opening to the living room. But she recognized it instantly. The kids recognized it, too.

"Isaac!" Isabella cried, and brushed past Reenie in her hurry to reach him.

"Hi, squirt," he said, swinging her up into his arms.

"What are you doing here?" Isabella asked.

He shot Reenie a devilish grin. "I live here now."

Reenie felt her heart stop. "What?" she breathed.

Setting Isabella down, he mussed Angela's hair, grinned at Jennifer and swept Reenie into his arms. "Hi, honey," he said. "I'm home."

Laughing, Reenie let him twirl her around. He felt so solid, so warm and wonderful in her grasp. She even liked the scratch of his whiskers as he kissed her neck. But was he serious? Would she get to wake up with him for the rest of her life? She wanted that more than anything, but she hated the thought that he might regret his decision and feel deprived later on.

"Isaac," she said, breathless from the spinning and the sudden excitement.

He let her feet touch the floor. "What?"

"He loves Mommy," she heard Isabella loudly whisper to her awed sisters.

"Are you going to get married?" Jennifer asked.

Isaac's gaze was still locked with Reenie's, but he answered. "Yes."

"Goody!" Angela clapped her hands. "Does Mica know?"

"No one knows yet," he said. "I'm sill waiting for your mother to say yes."

Reenie caught his face between her hands. "What about Africa?" she asked. "You know I want you here with us, but…"

"I would've been miserable without you, Reenie. Since I met you everything's changed."

"But the forest elephant, and your work—"

He silenced her with a kiss. "Don't worry about that. I'm going to write a book incorporating my research and ideas. And when the girls are older, we'll all go there together. As a family."

"A family," one of the girls echoed, sighing, as though what she'd just witnessed was the most romantic thing in the world.

"Tell him yes, Mom," Jennifer said.

"Tell him you love him," Isabella added passionately, and Angela giggled.

"Will you marry me, Reenie? We might have to some juggling while I write and teach. We might not have much money for a while. But I'll always be faithful to you, I'll always love you and I'll be a good stepfather to your children."

Tears welled in Reenie's eyes. She couldn't remember ever being so happy. "Then how could we be any richer?" she said.

He grinned at their small observers. "That's a yes," he told them.

"That's a yes," she confirmed and felt Jennifer, Angela and Isabella crowd close as Isaac gave them all a hug.

* * * * *

Watch for Elizabeth's story,
THE OTHER WOMAN,
coming in May 2006.

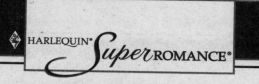

THE WINTER ROAD

**Some say life has passed Emily Moore by.
They're wrong.
She is just waiting for her moment….**

Her moment arrives when she discovers her friend
Daniel is missing and a stranger—supposedly Daniel's
nephew—is living in his house. Emily has no reason not
to believe him, but odd things are starting to occur.
There are break-ins along Creek Road and no news from
Daniel. Then there's the fact that his "nephew" seems
more interested in Emily than in the family history
he's supposed to be researching.

**Welcome to Three Creeks,
an ordinary little Prairie town where
extraordinary things are about to happen.**

In
THE WINTER ROAD
(Harlequin Superromance #1304),
Caron Todd creates evocative and compelling characters
who could be your over-the-fence neighbors.
You'll really want to get to know them.

Available October 2005.

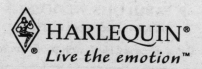

eHARLEQUIN.com

The Ultimate Destination for Women's Fiction

For **FREE online reading,** visit
www.eHarlequin.com now and enjoy:

Online Reads
Read **Daily** and **Weekly** chapters from
our Internet-exclusive stories by your
favorite authors.

Interactive Novels
Cast your vote to help decide how these
stories unfold...then stay tuned!

Quick Reads
For shorter romantic reads, try our
collection of Poems, Toasts, & More!

Online Read Library
Miss one of our online reads?
Come here to catch up!

Reading Groups
Discuss, share and rave with other
community members!

For great reading online,
visit www.eHarlequin.com today!

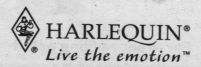

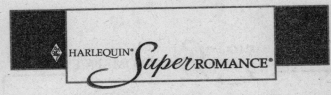

COMING NEXT MONTH